A GRAVEYARD OF STARS

SCI-FI HORROR NOVELLAS

JOSEPH SALE,
LEE MOUNTFORD,
AND DAN SOULE

BOOK 15 IN CRYSTAL LAKE'S DARK TIDE SERIES

Let the world know:
#IGotMyCLPBook!

Crystal Lake Publishing
www.CrystalLakePub.com

Join the Crystal Lake community today
on our newsletter and Patreon!
https://linktr.ee/CrystalLakePublishing

Download our latest catalog here.
https://geni.us/CLPCatalog

ISBN: 978-1-957133-94-2

Cover art:
Ben Baldwin—http://www.benbaldwin.co.uk

Layout:
Lori Michelle—www.theauthorsalley.com

Edited and proofed by:
Jodi Shatz and Carson Buckingham

Follow us on Amazon:

WELCOME

TO ANOTHER

CRYSTAL LAKE PUBLISHING

CREATION

THE TEMPLE

JOSEPH SALE

MISSION LOG
DATE: 0236 (N.I.C.)
LOCATION: THE BORDER OF EARTH-ALGOL SPACE
SHIP: "THE ROSSETTI", 14-KAR1, MIDAS CLADE
MANUFACTURED: ARTEFACT-CLASS, PRIVATEER
CREW: 3
MISSION: ARTEFACT ACQUISITION, ALGOL SPACE

"Since then, at an uncertain hour,
That agony returns:
And till my ghastly tale is told,
This heart within me burns . . . "
—*The Rime of the Ancient Mariner,*
Samuel Taylor Coleridge

CHAPTER 1

THEY SAY THAT the ghost story died as far back as the Twentieth Century, that discovering neutrons and quantum mechanics and nuclear fission dissolved the ambiguities in which real fear breeds. They are wrong. Because any real scientist or explorer soon discovers that the more you know the more there is to know. The universe doesn't shrink when we peer into its dark corners, it expands, and there are some corners we never should have shone light into.

The star system Algol being one of them.

Look, you must get a thousand pirates coming through here—let's call us what we are, I'm not proud, not anymore—and all of them have a horror story, but I guarantee you mine's different, and it's true.

You don't believe me? I've got scars I could show you—impossible scars, scars that tell the story of wounds that should not be survivable, but I did survive them, not because I'm tough, but because the Ones who gave me those wounds *wanted* me to survive, they wanted me to experience everything . . .

But I'm getting ahead of myself. I'd rather tell you my tale, if you're willing. Come on, where else are you going to go on this godforsaken rock? The waystation's one and only brothel will give you an STD that will make you wish you had radiation poisoning. And I doubt any of the other cunts in this bar have a story half as good as mine to tell. Besides, I need to tell it. I need to warn as many people as I can.

Don't fucking go out there.

It was back in the early days, back when we didn't really know what the Agoul Space was. In fact, it wasn't even called Agoul Space. We knew it then by its old name "Algol", the system of the Demon Star. But there were clues as to its true nature. The massive rivers of semi-organic debris, the asteroid fields so rich with rare metals, gravity wells, insanely high levels of radiation, gamma, and x-rays—it was pretty obvious something colossally fucked up had taken place in that area of space. Not just a natural phenomenon such as a stellar detonation, but something *intentional*, like a war. But we didn't know who had been on either side of that war. Humanity expanded our interstellar empire a hundred lightyears from Earth to the Algol system, yet we found no real life, or even evidence of civilisations that might once have existed on far distant planets. Algol, however, provided an orgy of evidence for extra-terrestrial life—for civilisations beyond our imagining.

An orgy of evidence—you like that, huh? It's from an old movie. What, you don't watch old movies? You're missing out. I don't know when my fetish for all things Twenty-First century kicked in, but I love that ancient crap. You haven't lived until you've heard what they used to call "rock 'n' roll." It makes the overproduced garbage these days sound like it was written by machines—which I suppose much of it is.

Anyway, you know most of this, I should get to the bits you don't know. First, you should get to know my crew: Johnny, our trader and middleman; Raleigh, our on-board scientist and all-round know-it-all; and Beni, our mule, whom I named after another character from an ancient Twentieth Century movie. What? Don't pretend you don't name your androids too. Beni had more of a soul than most of the scum round here.

So where was I? Me and my crew, ah yes, and my ship, the *Rossetti*. Named after a long dead poet, one who loved Jesus Christ almost as much as my mother did. You would have thought spaceships would have put an end to the Bible, but no, Noah's ark merely changes its cladding. But I shouldn't criticise too much. I've always had a weird fascination with Christ, and with the people who follow Him. Call it pride, but I always thought I could be like Him when I was young. I guess I was more like the whore of Babylon. I even have the red hair to match.

All this is to say: I told you I have a fetish for ancient things. Or maybe it's dead things? I don't know.

We'd heard a rumour. Or more specifically, *Johnny* heard a rumour while he was chatting up three of our buyers on Proxima Centauri: the aptly named Midas Clade. Those holograph-robed, gold-fingered pricks have noses for a windfall like someone spliced their DNA with a metal-detectors. But they can never be bothered to go and get the treasure themselves—they're too busy having their dicks sucked by absurdly proportioned virtual avatars—hence why they need pirate crews like us, scavengers with low morals and a lot of resourcefulness who are prepared to either go where others daren't or piss off the Interstellar World Alliance—usually both at the same time.

Johnny tells me that the three of them were up to their usual gimmicks, making fun of Johnny because he's *au naturel*. Doesn't believe in augments, even though his bones are royally fucked from so many years off-world. But looking at Johnny, you wouldn't think him decrepit. He's got the face of a male supermodel which space and low gravity has preserved. He dresses himself like a regular cowboy complete with piercing blue eyes and flaxen hair. Could have been an actor, and I often wonder why he's not considering the absurd income those bastards earn, but for whatever reason he decided on the scavenger life. And I was grateful for the fact, because Johnny could talk his way out of or *into* any situation, and what he'd managed over the years was to talk his way into the inner confidence of the Midas Clade.

For all their mockery they trusted him like no other pirate in the Sprawl—I'd tried to meet them once or twice but I always seemed to piss them off one way or another. However, they knew and liked Johnny, and they knew our crew only ever brought the genuine article. They also knew we'd never double-cross them. It was one of our house rules never to double-cross a client. To me, it was just common sense. When the Interstellar World Alliance is hounding you every step of the way, why make another dangerous enemy?

So, the Midas Clade are taking the piss out of Johnny, pointing out he's a bowlegged cowboy (though sadly, it's not from horse-riding like in the Westerns, but low-G hollowing out his bones) and saying the wrinkles are beginning to show. Johnny does what he normally does, and makes light, "Virtual girls don't care how creaky my bones are or how small my cock is."

The Midas Clade howl at this, Johnny tells me. They have an infantile kind of humour. I suppose it comes from being so rich you can have anything and everything you want whenever you want. Resistance creates strength. That's why our bones are all rotting in space. No gravity means no resistance.

"Johnny is wise beyond his years!" the youngest of the Midas Clade says. He is unoriginally called Tertius, as the third to join their group. The Clade act like a trio of brothers, but they're certainly not related. When you join their Clade—and God only knows what the entry requirements are—you forsake your own name and take on their numerical designator.

"He should be a poet!" Secundus shouts.

Primus, the most mature of the bunch, only smiles glitteringly. He is the least augmented and the sharpest mind. The augments he does have are all practical in use: a titanium-clad skeleton, ocular implants that enhance his vision beyond normal spectrums, and an artificial liver that filters out every imaginable toxin from his bloodstream. There are rumours that Primus has been around for half a millennium, that he was born before the Sprawl. I suppose it's possible, but I have my doubts. Anyway, Primus raises his hands and the others curb their enthusiasm, quietening down as though they've been given an instruction by their schoolmaster.

"Speaking of poetry," Primus murmurs. "I've heard a particularly pleasing little rhyme of late."

"Oh?" Johnny says. He knows never to interrupt when Primus is speaking—to listen with reverence. I personally couldn't stand doing that for more than five seconds, but Johnny is a social chameleon, and can do anything he sets his mind to if it will lead him to an advantage at the bargaining table

.

"A floating temple lies beyond the veil,
where mortal and immortal worlds are shorn;
across the battlefields of black Algol,
the Great One's Treasure waits to be worn"

I'm told Primus uttered the poetic stanza as though it were nothing more significant than a shopping list, but Johnny could tell it meant something, that Primus believed every word. Even artificial eyes can betray emotion. So, politely I might add, Johnny asks the provenance of this little riddle.

"An ancient tablet," Primus says. "Recovered by one of our other scavengers. It took us a while to complete the translation."

Johnny asked how the hell they were able to translate a language that no human being has ever spoken, a language that existed possibly before human beings even started to walk on two legs and think for themselves. Primus wouldn't give specifics, but Johnny thinks they've gone and captured an Agoul.

I can see from your face you don't believe it. And I'm inclined to agree with you. Don't ask me how you trap something like that. Maybe they locked it in some kind of stone chamber? That would be a spectacular irony, wouldn't it, in our technological age—even more so for the Midas Clade, who practically worship tech like it's a god. But that's one of the only ways I can think of that could stop the Agoul. Good old-fashioned stone, lots of it, at least three meters thick. God only knows how they then extracted the information. No doubt the process was . . . messy. And incomplete. But it seems like they got enough to translate Algolian, or whatever the fuck you call that dead language.

So, Johnny asks a few more clarifying questions, and then he brings the information to me. There's a temple somewhere out in the Algol star system, what we call now Agoul Space. It's so big that it drifts through space and has its own regular orbit and gravity. Inside, there's an ancient artefact, made by a race of people arrogantly calling themselves the Great Ones. And the Midas Clade, they wanted us to break into this thing and retrieve the artefact for them.

Needless to say, I asked Johnny if he'd been smoking Pink Crystal with the Clade. Sure, there are a lot of artefacts in Agoul Space, leftovers from the war. But a floating temple? Cryptic poetry? It all sounded a bit *Indiana Jones* to me, and whilst I love that ancient picture, I'm not about to treat it like a documentary.

Then there's the danger. No one ever returns from Agoul Space. I mean fucking no one. The only thing that ever made it back out of there was a broadcast from the *Palatine*. But even then, some people think that's fake. Me, Johnny, Raleigh, and Beni had made a thousand or more expeditions during our careers as pirates—if you want to call it that—but never *into* Algol. We've been to the border. Plenty of wreckage and things to loot there. But never across that invisible line.

Then Johnny tells me the price the Midas Clade are willing to offer. And the price, well, it makes me fall off my chair. You'd fall off your chair if I told you now. It was the kind of money that sets you up for life. Hell, you could probably buy a small fucking planet at the edge of the Sprawl for that. So I ask Johnny once again if he's been smoking Pink Crystal or drinking Saturnine and he tells me, "Nah. I counted the zeroes and asked them to confirm. This is legit, Karla. They really want this Treasure-thing. And you know the Midas Clade, they don't invest in anything they don't think is real."

CHAPTER 2

I THINK ABOUT it now, and I'm sure the Clade did more research than just trusting to an ancient poem. They probably knew the rough location of the so-called Temple; they'd checked it out, as far as they could without getting off their asses, and made sure there was really something there to find. Like I said, they're human metal detectors. They have some kind of long-range scanning system in that palace of theirs, able to pick up energy signatures. It wouldn't surprise me. Anyway, my point being: Johnny was right. The Midas Clade never sent us on wild goose chases. Sure, sometimes things weren't as straightforward up close and personal as they made it out to be, but there was always a prize, always something real to take back to them. And, for all their posturing, they always paid, on time and in full.

No one ever comes back from Agoul Space. But as you might have gathered, I've got a prideful streak in me. Or did. We only needed to do it once. Once, and we were set for life. I reckoned if any crew in the universe could pull it off, it'd be us.

I guess you could also say Johnny's excitement infected me. It takes a lot to get Johnny excited. He normally plays it cool. Never reveal your hand in a game of poker type of attitude. But he was like a big kid jumping up and down, getting all giddy with nerves and expectation.

We had to chance it. If there was even the slightest possibility this was real, we had to take our shot. Besides, I wasn't having Midas Clade give this gig to some other shitty pirate. The *Rossetti* and my crew are the best of the best.

So, we informed them of our decision, accepted the usual terms and non-compete clauses, and then we decided to break the news to the others. By others, I mean Raleigh.

Raleigh is an odd sort even by the standards of pirates—and by the way, he resented that term. *"We're explorers,"* he would say. Or, "*We're privateers.*" Sure thing, Raleigh, you're the one with a brain the size of Earth's moon. I mock, but Raleigh really did have a mind on him, a mind for quantum physics and black holes and the way the space-time continuum bends and breaks out here. He's the kind of person who got humanity out into space in the first place.

We found him doing the usual: destroying his colossal intellect at a bar—very unlike this one, I might add—where they mix Saturnine with alcohol to create the grey, slushy narcotic of your nightmares. I don't know how many brain cells it kills, but it's got to be in the millions. I've only ever tried Saturnine once, unmixed, and it was hell. I've never been suicidal—just got too much of a zest for life—but that's the closest I've ever come to wanting to end things. The downer was so deep, I imagine it's how a black hole feels as gravity crushes you to a pinprick. I can't see why anyone would do that to themselves. But then, a brain like Raleigh's probably thinks about a whole lot of existential questions, and maybe when he's drunk on Saturnine and alcohol it quietens the voices in his head, the relentless *thinking,* for just a moment. That's just me guessing, though. We never talked about it.

Anyway, we're in this bar—think it's called *Nessus Point*—and we soon find Raleigh in his usual place, slumped in a corner. There's a blonde with him: augmented tits and ass and a face that could cut glass. Though she's getting up to leave, because he's too in his cups to make conversation let alone do the deed. Raleigh honestly doesn't seem to care though. Sex seems to be of little interest to him.

It doesn't matter your preferences or types—when you're out in the cold vacuum, sooner or later, the biological urges surface, especially in men. But I got lucky. Johnny's not interested in women, so I don't have to put up with advances from him, although if I'm being honest, there are times I wouldn't have minded. And Raleigh doesn't seem interested in the needs of the body at all. Honestly, I doubt he'd get hard if a girl sucked him off, but talk to him about Heisenberg's Uncertainty Principle and he'll jizz in his pants.

We sat down in the booth. Plush leather seating, a steel table with a digital ordering system embedded into a plate of shiny glass, far too fancy for Raleigh, whose slouching posture and shabby overalls were at odds with *Nessus Point's* polished, billionaire-playboy aesthetic. Pink and green lights tactfully illuminate the dancefloor, bar, booths, and restrooms, never glaring or too much for the eye, finely tuned to perfect moderation. They say places like *Nessus Point* have layers of decoration visible only to those with ocular bionic augments, which is most of their clientele. I wouldn't know as, like Johnny, I've never seen the appeal of endless augments. The only one I have is necessary. Listen well and you'll find out where it is.

Raleigh roused himself at our presence, dragging his face from the steel tabletop with some difficulty. He rubbed his nose. His pupils were so wide they could have swallowed suns. His dark hair was unkempt yet thick for a guy. His domed forehead resembled an egg. He looked a little bit like a knock-off, drunk Shakespeare.

"What time is it?" Raleigh asked, blearily. Then he grinned at a private joke, no doubt about time's relativity. "Nevermind. More Saturnine."

"I think you'll want to be sober to hear what we've got to say," I said, unable to repress my excitement.

"Another job?" Raleigh sounded not only disinterested but disgusted.

"*The* job," Johnny said, emphatically. "Trust me, this isn't just a relic grab, it's far more your cup of Saturnine. There's even poetry and orbital mechanics involved."

I had to repress a laugh, because Raleigh genuinely began to sober up at this, his forehead crinkling, eyes regaining some of their lustre and focus.

"Tell me everything," Raleigh said.

Needless to say, Raleigh was on board, though for completely different reasons to me and Johnny. Raleigh didn't care about the payout; I think he just wanted a good enough reason to climb out of his cups. Something that would be a worthy adversary to grey matter. I think he just wanted the intellectual challenge.

Plotting a course towards Agoul Space is no easy feat at the best of times, not with increasingly regular I.W.A. patrols. And then, as you draw nearer the boundary, there's the threat of the Agoul themselves. Back then, we knew even less than we know now. Ships just vanished off the face of the fucking galaxy. Terrifying doesn't describe it. But like I said, I thought we were in with a chance. Maybe that's ego. After all, my mother always called me, "My little child of the void", as though all of space belonged to me.

Navigating to the border of Agoul Space was one thing. Plotting course for a planet-fragment that's established its own orbit in asteroid-riddled dead-space? Now *that's* something even Raleigh's mind needs to chew before it swallows.

We headed back to the *Rossetti,* me and Johnny practically carrying Raleigh. While his brain had thrown off the stupor of that toxic Saturnine brew, his body still remembered the obliterating power of narcosis. Jelly-legged, he stumbled and staggered while we rectified his shambling gait.

"You look like a proper pirate," I teased.

Raleigh growled in response, but couldn't refute the claim.

Proxima Centauri's docking bay is a dizzying affair, even for experienced pilots. In a lot of the old movies I watch—and you really should check them out if you make it off this shithole—characters complain about the gridlock of built-up cities. I envy those ancient fuckers, because they really didn't know what they were in for when gridlock became vertical as well as horizontal. Proxima Centauri's docking bay is like an old-fashioned airport built vertically. A thousand ships come and go every hour, landing at one of over a hundred strips built into megalithic steel and concrete towers. The timings of take-offs and landings are carefully overseen by a workforce thousands strong, from traffic controllers to refuellers to engineers, all paid for out of Midas Clade's deep pockets. The I.W.A. *wishes* it could orchestrate a system that runs so efficiently and profitably. As it stands, they content themselves with creaming tax from the Clade's generous revenue stream.

The *Rossetti* was parked at loading bay 193. We'd been parked up a while, blowing off steam after our last venture, so the ship had already been refuelled, restocked, and serviced, courtesy of Midas Clade. As we approached the door, it swung open for us, and the unconventional fourth member of our crew greeted us with a beaming digital face, almost disturbingly happy.

"Greetings, friends. I trust your stay in Proxima Centauri was a happy one?"

No matter how good the vocaliser in Beni's throat was, his words always came out with a metallic twang. I've often wondered if this was not an intentional design trait, the developers not wanting their machines to sound too human. As far back as the Twenty-First Century, engineers and software developers achieved artificial speech almost indistinguishable from the human, so it had to be a deliberate choice. A bizarre one, however, because little else about Beni was remotely human. He walked on four legs, vaguely equine in design, a slight curvaceousness to the warp of the metal, similar to the blades you see athletics competitors using to augment their speed on the track. His face was a TV monitor, set where the horse's chest would be. But for some strange reason Beni's creators had not stopped there, and had also given him a humanoid torso erupting from the top of the "horse's" body, complete with two arms ending in human hands, but no neck or head. He therefore resembled a headless centaur. Or perhaps the Headless Horsemen of ancient legend. The truth, however, was that he'd been designed with disgusting pragmatism over aesthetics. I would rather his head was positioned where a centaur's head should be, atop the humanoid component of his body, that way I could at least pretend he was a mythical creature. But Beni's architect had decided that was far too pleasing to the eye, and that his field of vision would be greater at the midpoint between "horse" and "man". In reality, Beni was neither, a gleaming chrome golem of hybrid parts.

Raleigh grunted at Beni in greeting. He didn't like the robot, perhaps because he felt an artificial intelligence, capable of scanning documentation and resources in milliseconds, was the only true rival to his own intellect. Or perhaps simply because Raleigh liked virtually no one. Johnny waved happily. Beni's primitive, digital face became an emoji of happiness. I grinned.

"You've been looking after her for us, Beni?"

"Affirmative, Captain Karla." He withdrew back into the ship's interior to make room for us. Beni's absurd design meant he blocked any doorway he stood in. He seems aware of this fact, however. In fact, his spatial awareness really surpasses that of many men I've met over the years.

"Cheer up, Raleigh," Johnny said. "Having Beni as our fourth means we only need to split the winnings three ways."

Johnny punched Raleigh on the arm. Some might have viewed this as pure male braggadocio and banter, but I knew Johnny, and it was a calculated move, a risk to bring Raleigh out of his insular shell—just inciting enough to stir action but perhaps not so aggressive as to force him deeper into his mental seclusion.

This time, the gambit paid off, and Raleigh smiled. He might not have been in it for the money, not at his core, but no one turns down the kind of figures we were looking at.

Although now, of course, I wish I had.

What's the old saying? No good crying over spilled crystal? It's easy to say it, and those who do have their cups full don't know what it's like to lose everything. That's why I have to tell you, tell everyone, what happened when we got to that Temple. Oh yeah, the Midas Clade are many things—undoubtedly crazy—but not stupid. The Temple was real. We found it. And no, I won't tell you where it is. That's the whole fucking point of this story.

By the time I'm done, you'll understand why. At least, I hope you will. If you don't, I might have to kill you. Trust me, you'd rather I put a bullet in your brain than go through what I did. You'd fucking beg me for it.

Sorry, I get angry sometimes. I'd like to say it's trauma, what I went through in the Temple, but the truth is I've always been angry. As the next part of my story will illustrate . . .

CHAPTER 3

Usually, spirits are high when we first set off on a job. Even Raleigh normally summons what little social energy he has to talk excitedly about what might lie ahead, often interspersing mine and Johnny's pure speculation with his scientifically grounded predictions. This time, however, it was as though a cloud hung over all of us.

We all knew that we were attempting something we had never attempted before, though it went unspoken between us, as though if we admitted to the insanity we'd lose our nerve. To not only go to the border of Agoul Space, but to go *into* Agoul Space, into the fucking madness we'd glimpse at the edge of what might as well have been another reality.

Maybe, too, it was the damn poetry. Only a fragment, but it suggested worlds entirely alien to the modern mind, worlds of ancient mystery and slaughter and devastating powers and wonder. A time when mortal and immortal worlds weren't split asunder, as the poem alludes. A time of gods, in other words. I see your lip curling, the suppressed sneer. You may roll your eyes and think me crazy, but what I've seen would make a believer out of anyone.

The first week was tense. And trust me, when you have a crew of only four, one of whom is a robot who doesn't read social cues all that well, you feel the tension all the more, bone deep.

We headed for the Algol system, a journey of some 90 plus lightyears. Yes, we pirates do the length and breadth of the Sprawl more often than anyone else in the damn universe, I'd wager. It's hell, to be honest: cramped, boring, desolate. The stasis pods that protect our bodies feel more and more like cages the older you get. But, I have to admit, there's also something I like about it. For me, being in those pods over those vast stretches is the only time I can think clearly. Because the ship is largely on autopilot when travelling in known space, following one of the grand pre-prepared flightpaths through the Sprawl, I have time to let my mind wander, to dream. The starkness of space gives me room to think, to interrogate my feelings. I guess I'm not good at tuning in to how I feel, which is why the anger comes on so suddenly. But in those moments, as the *Rossetti* plunges through the blackness, I get time to myself, time to check out of physical reality and go inward. I think the others also enjoyed the travel, in their own different ways, which is why we made such a good crew. Johnny buries himself in audiobooks, usually of the personal development kind. And Raleigh relishes the opportunity to lose himself in equations and calculations without being disturbed.

When we're travelling normally, rather than on the FTL paths, he makes sure we don't interrupt him by plugging into his classical music selection. I'm more of a rock 'n' roll girl, like I said, but I respect Raleigh's passion for his genre, and I see a kind of weird link between those artfully arranged symphonies and his own perfectly geometric patterns of thinking. Well, perfect in some ways, problematic in others.

There was no better example of the problematic side of Raleigh's mind than an incident which occurred nine days after we departed Proxima Centauri.

As I'm sure you know, FTL is fucking expensive, and I mean that in the energetic sense. The antimatter cores generate a hell of a bang, enough to catapult a ship practically at the speed of light across the galaxy, but pretty frequently you have to stop and let the energy cool, then start the process again. Keep pushing and you risk overload. More than a few ships have gone down by fucking with their cores too much. Luckily, Raleigh knows how to manage ours as though he's made out of antimatter himself.

We were on one of our cool-downs when Raleigh stormed into the cockpit. I was sat at the controls. We were crossing over from one flight path to another, and we'd hit a cosmic dust-cloud. I needed to be at the tiller, so to speak, ready to steer us out of the way of any larger asteroid particles. Johnny was there with me in the co-pilot chair, though doing no co-piloting whatsoever. He was instead smoking a chem-vape stick and playing digi-cards against an AI. He prefers real cigarettes, but the ash fucks with the air-recycling system. He prefers a real opponent too, but I've never been interested in card games, or games of any sort really. Raleigh might have been interested in playing, if other obsessions hadn't already established their claim on him.

Raleigh bursts in on our silent and contemplative bubble—the only sound Johnny's puffing on the pipe, which is so rhythmic it's soporific—bringing the aura of a thunderhead about to unleash a payload of lightning with him.

"Karla!" he snapped. Whenever Raleigh's hackles are up he completely disregards all notions of hierarchy or respect.

"What is it?" I tried to keep my tone level, respectful even. Raleigh was having none of it.

"You promised me!" he barked.

"What?" I was genuinely confused. Raleigh's trains of thought are hard to follow, and because his memory is eidetic, he picks up conversations or threads from weeks, months, even years ago as though you were talking about them that morning, then gets frustrated when you don't immediately see what he's on about.

"You promised this wasn't a wild goose chase," he growled. He held up a data-slate with frankly impenetrable diagrams and calculations upon it. "But I've been looking at Algol's current position in the galactic co-rotation radius, coupled with the Doppler effect . . . "

"Slow down, Robot," Johnny quipped.

Whilst Johnny is perhaps the most socially adept person I've ever known, his patience seems to wear thin with Raleigh quicker than anyone else in the universe.

"Fuck off!" Raleigh snarled. He turned back to me, perhaps believing I had at least a chance of understanding his theories. "The distances and gravity aren't right for something as small as a planet fragment to be orbiting successfully in that zone."

"Are you saying you don't think there's a Temple there?"

"Don't think? Don't *think*?" He somehow grew even angrier. "It's not about *thinking,* as though it's a matter of opinion. This is fact!" Spittle flew from his mouth. It always amazed me the juxtaposition between Raleigh's intense emotionality and his religious advocacy of data and naturalistic science.

"The Midas Clade wouldn't lie," Johnny said.

Raleigh laughed hysterically.

"Oh, wow, Jeez mister genius . . . " Raleigh patronised like no one else. "I didn't consider that . . . I'll have to redo all my calculations!"

Johnny's lip curled in disgust.

"Raleigh, calm down," I said.

He took a shuddering, ragged breath.

"You're right, you're right," he said. His eyes bored into mine. "I wouldn't expect two monkeys to understand anyway."

Then he turned and left.

Johnny audibly ground his teeth.

"I should break his nose for that. Hell, maybe a blow to the head would knock some manners into him."

"Stay here. I'll deal with him."

The truth was, I was far angrier than Johnny or even Raleigh in that moment. I can tolerate vitriol, insults, arguments, but I can't tolerate disrespect. Not on my own damn ship.

I stood up and went after Raleigh. I found him in the corridor, sulking and slinking his way back to his quarters. I grabbed him without warning, spun him round, and slammed him against the wall. Raleigh isn't your standard intellectual—he's pretty big and muscular for someone who spends all their time looking at mathematics. But unlike Raleigh, I spent thirteen years of my life training. I'm the combat operative on the ship, and I've a number of special weapons at my disposal. You might have noticed the little cannister at my belt. It's an electro-bo-staff, six feet long. Handy to have about you. I also have an AK, one of those ancient slug-throwers from the Twentieth Century. It's suicide to fire it onboard a ship, but it's saved my life more than once planet-side. The reliability of the analogue mechanism, no electrical power, means that you can operate it even during an EMP blackout. I've caught more than a few enemies by surprise with that trick. I have to make the bullets myself now, of course, because no one's manufacturing old fashioned rounds save as memorabilia, but it's worth the effort.

But I didn't use any weapons that day, I didn't need to. Raleigh never stood a chance. I pinned his throat to the wall with my forearm and applied bone-jarring pressure to the side of his knee with my own. One tweak and it would snap. It doesn't matter how big and strong you think you are. The right leverage always breaks bones.

He spluttered some feeble apology. His eyes were bugging out of his face even more than normal.

"Oh *now* you say sorry," I snarled. "Well let me tell you

something: I'm sorry I hired you. I'm sorry I hired someone who gets his knickers in a twist every time a tiny bit of data doesn't add up. I'm sorry I hired a fucking alcoholic who's constantly slowing us down with his self-pity. I'm sorry, Raleigh, that Johnny and I—hell, even Beni—has to be subjected to your whining."

Again, he choked out an apology, and this time he was trembling. I didn't let up the pressure on his knee. I could feel the joint creaking beneath the pressure. He had turned blood-red from where I cut off airflow and blood-supply to that mammoth brain of his. His eyes pleaded for release.

"This is the most important mission of our God-damn lives. We can retire after this, Raleigh. No more risking our necks unless we want to. No more putting up with the Midas Clade. That means all the Saturnine, or whatever fucked up chemical shit you want to put inside yourself, you could ever want. You hear me? I want you to get out of your fucking head and into the game."

I released him at last and he hovered there for a moment, like a mouse uncertain it had escaped death in the jaws of a cat, then I punched him as hard as I could in the gut, so hard he doubled over and vomited whatever gruel he'd eaten that morning. I felt guilty then, I won't lie. I didn't like to rule with an iron fist, but I found Raleigh's doubt intolerable. I don't know why—I have moments where I feel heartless, like I can't feel empathy as much as I want to. Normally I encourage healthy scepticism, but something about this mission felt different.

Raleigh fell to his knees, whimpering slightly.

"Get up," I snarled.

He didn't, at first. Disgustingly, he was running his hand through his own vomit, as though he was studying runes. Slowly, he clambered to his feet. There was a strange clarity in his eyes.

"I miscalculated," he whispered.

"What?"

"I miscalculated . . . " His eyes were wide as moons. "My vomit. Little bits. Friction." He shook his head, as if to reorganise his thoughts like physical objects, or perhaps seeking another answer from a magic 8-ball. "The Temple, it's a planet fragment you said . . . Therefore a planet got blown up, destroyed. That means dust, asteroids. Friction. Orbital friction. Yes, that would decay the orbit." His eyes pierced me. "Thank you!"

Then he rushed off to revise his theory.

CHAPTER 4

AS YOU KNOW, humanity's first encounters with life outside of Earth were the Agoul, though for a while no one believed the stories of the "ghosts of the Demon Star." There were legends about ships meeting Agoul out there and worse, like *The Palatine*, but the I.W.A.'s propaganda was always "Astraecy", which is understandable, because there's a lot of it about. Let me tell you, I don't fear physical decrepitude. I don't fear being flushed out of an airlock, or even dying of radiation poisoning. No, it's Astraecy I fear, losing my sense of self, losing memory, going completely insane. The things people do when they succumb finally to the madness are just unspeakable. I never want to become like that. Johnny was under strict instructions to shoot me if I ever showed signs.

So anyway, we're getting fairly close to Agoul Space now. We stop off at a waystation—this waystation in fact—and we enjoy a last supper. It's a strangely depressing affair, considering what's on offer, what's at stake. But all of us are wrapped up in our own personal fantasies of what we'll do when we're rich. At least I was. I assume Johnny was the same. Raleigh was probably thinking of more cosmological things, like humanity's place in the stars if we're a footnote to this much older species. Maybe he was also thinking about what, precisely, the Treasure was. I'd been thinking about that too. The poem implies a crown, something that can be "worn", but that's putting a lot of faith in the translation and making a lot of assumptions. What I didn't know then, but do now, is humans always interpret things in relation to themselves. We believe the universe is anthropomorphic, and to a degree it is, but there are some corners of this universe that feel like they weren't made for us . . . Anyway, I'm getting ahead of myself again.

We sat right over there, in that booth where the stag is—for sure, he's getting married tomorrow. We sip our drinks. Raleigh refrains from Saturnine or any other substance, just drinks water with a bit of clone-lemon and -lime in it, which I think speaks to the severity of the situation. We're meditating, waiting—like waiting for damn God or something.

The next day, we're out on a direct course towards Algol. No more automated flight paths. Raleigh's new calculations have revealed what he calls a "shadow", a "gravitational anomaly" that he thinks could be the Temple. Our excitement begins to mount, depression and introversion giving way to a kind of bouncing mania. I don't think any of us slept over the next few days. But our hyper-alertness proved useful, because we spent most of our time dodging I.W.A. patrols.

The *Rossetti* has two major defence mechanisms. The first, Total Dark, is very useful for dealing with I.W.A. ships. Essentially, we flip a switch in the cockpit and the ship's engines and operations all cut out save life-support, which runs on an energy-saving protocol that is so efficient not even the most advanced energy or heat scanners can detect it. Total Dark essentially means lights-out, drifting, until the patrol passes. The only problem is you have to make sure you detect the patrol *before* they detect you. Otherwise, they're going to know something's up.

But we were pretty good, and Johnny has ridiculously sharp eyes. The number of times he's eyeballed a bogey in the vast gulf of space before one of the Rossetti's sensors has picked up their signature is beyond count.

Because we're ducking all these I.W.A. patrols—which when I think back to it now should have given us a clue something was up—progress was glacial. And this only makes the build up of excitement worse, until we're all talking at a thousand miles per hour and practically bouncing off the walls like hyper-active kids. But then, finally, we get beyond the band of I.W.A. ships—because even they're too scared to get near Agoul Space—and then we're right where we want to be.

Raleigh makes some final calculations and triangulations. I triple check the antimatter core. And we set a course for this "shadowy anomaly" that I know, deep in my heart, *has* to be the Temple. Raleigh calculated its orbital path, with a margin of error he claims was egregious but seemed exact enough to me, and which we'd intercept after five days.

Little did we know that those five days would be almost as filled with terror as when we finally reached the Temple . . .

CHAPTER 5

"KARLA," JOHNNY WHISPERED.

We were at our usual posts: Johnny in the co-piloting seat, myself in the pilot's chair, and Raleigh skulking somewhere else aboard the ship. Beni had deactivated himself to save his power for landing. There isn't much he can do on-board save crunch numbers, and Raleigh is pretty much the robot's equal in that regard. I wonder if Beni dreams . . .

"Karla."

I heard the note of concern, even fear, in Johnny's voice.

"What's up?"

"Three flickers across my screen. Could be nothing. Could be interference . . . "

My eyes widened. I knew exactly what he was implying.

I pressed the intercom button, which would broadcast my commands to every room and corridor of the ship.

"Raleigh, prepare for contact. Agoul."

We knew this was coming, but in that moment, I think we realised how unprepared we were. Johnny is *laissez faire* when it comes to most things, but here he sat rigid in his seat, bolt upright, the stars illuminating beads of sweat running down his neck. His hands hovered over the button for Total Dark.

"Not yet," I said. The truth was we didn't fully know what an Agoul ship could do. We'd heard stories, read reports, even seen one or two videos that managed to capture them for a moment, but the full scope of their abilities was unknown. Maybe if we turned off all the ship's functions they'd leave us alone; or maybe that would seal our deaths.

"Can you hear that?" Johnny said. I've always been jealous of how sharp his senses are.

"What?"

"Hissing."

"Can't be a breach." If there was a breach in the ship, you wouldn't hear air escaping, because there was no atmosphere for it to escape into.

"Static?" Johnny whispered.

Now my screen was flickering too, white vertical lines appearing, cutting across information, travelling from the left side of the screen to the right and back; reminded me of a slitted eye searching for something.

Johnny was right; it *was* static. Rising. Growing. Like falling into a pit of sleeping serpents, hearing them slowly rise, angry at having been disturbed. The hissing was all around us. Johnny was bone-white, staring forward through the windshield at the intense blackness of Algol's canvas, as though searching for a light at the end of a tunnel. I gritted my teeth, wanting so badly to reach for my bo-staff, thinking it would be pointless against the Agoul. No one survives contact.

"Get ready," I said, but I don't think Johnny could have been more ready.

Then every electrical device exploded at once—with sound, with frenetic movement, with data and mathematical symbols and characters of unknown origin. The controls became rebellious and I had to apply every ounce of strength to hold them steady.

Warning systems and alarms rang. Every type of emergency light flashed at once: blue, red, green, yellow. Our eyes were dazzled by it. The static reached such a pitch my ears rang with tinnitus.

A voice gargled and crackled its way from the speakers—our ship's own voice.

"Turn . . . back . . . " The static spiked and I had to take my hands off the controls, clapping my palms to my ears. Our ship was now drifting rudderless through space. The blackness seemed greater now, yawning, the gaps between stars too wide. Even someone like me—not born on Earth—finds the constellations of Algol unnatural. Johnny reached for the Total Dark button but an electric spark, like a fist of lightning, shot from the controls and struck him in the chest. He was launched not only out of his seat but into the air, slamming against the rear wall of the cockpit, sliding down, dazed, his flesh ruddy, his white shirt burned black, a black mark over his heart.

"No . . . return . . . " It spoke using the Rossetti's in-built communications system. Even as terrified as I was, I felt rage and indignation that it would abuse my ship so.

The console sparked and fizzed. The *Rossetti,* which had served us so faithfully for so many years, went haywire. Afraid of catching a bolt like Johnny, I threw myself out of the chair and crawled away from the electrified panels. The ship began to list, the artificial gravity system compensating for the ship's rotation. This created a bizarre contradiction—my eyes told me I was upside down, but I still felt like I was upright. I searched the cockpit for something, anything, that might help us, but the only thing I could think of was the Total Dark protocol, which was now shielded by jagged electrical arcs. The damn Agoul had booby-trapped my own ship against me.

But one thing remained certain: I would not turn back.

A shape began to coalesce, like iron filings drawn across a flat surface towards a magnet head. But that flat surface was nothing but air itself. The shape was near enough that of a man. Or an impression of one, shifting, as though the forces that held it together were temperamental; the shape at one moment seemed a solid grey sculpture, a human form hewn from concrete, and at other times a mist in the semblance of a shadow.

"Turn . . . back . . . !" the figure said with no mouth. It sounded desperate, as though its own life depended on our failure.

"I can't!" I yelled, not sure if it could hear or understand me. To my surprise, it did, for the frothing sculpture of atoms, continuously remaking itself, cocked its faceless head.

"You *must!*" A swarm of grey particles fled from the figure and attached themselves to the ship's many screens and controls. I did not try to stop it—it would have been like trying to catch a swarm of flies. The screens, which previously had flickered and flashed with electrical interference and reams of alien data, now began to show a single hieroglyphic, etched in pixels so white they hurt to look at. The hieroglyph grew whiter and whiter until I was forced to shield my eyes, the afterimage burned into my retinas, visible even when I closed my eyes. I can still see it now, that sigil. A curse upon it!

"Fear . . . *Gha'agshebla!*" the Agoul thundered.

I didn't know, at the time, what he meant by those nonsense syllables. But now I think I've figured it out . . . That was what the Temple was called.

The Agoul knew exactly where we were headed, perhaps had been listening in on our conversations. I don't know the full extent of an Agoul's capabilities—we still don't. But I got the feeling this was a warning. A last chance to turn around kind of deal. Rough us up and scare the crap out of us, sure. But not kill us. I know it sounds crazy. An old spacedog's tall tale. I know what you're thinking: no one comes back from the Demon Star. But I swear on my captain's licence it wanted to warn us: that the Temple meant madness, meant death, though perhaps not the literal kind.

The word, Gha'agshebla, so magical, so alien, brought me up short. I found there was nothing I could do. I'm not sure anything could have compelled me to turn around, but I think I might have given up at that moment, allowed the Agoul to steer our ship into whatever oblivion it wished. But then something unexpected happened.

Raleigh.

He came charging into the cockpit with bristling rage—and perhaps a little manic delight too. He was finally face-to-face with something beyond even his colossal brain's reach. Face-to-face with a force of technology so potent that the original explorers had deemed it supernatural. He paused only for a moment upon seeing the grey, inchoate form standing over me. His eyes widened as he took in its swarming body, a body ceaselessly in motion, every cell adjusting and perfecting. He squinted as he turned to take in the light of the hieroglyph, but then wrenched his eyes away, focusing again on the Agoul.

"Hold on to something, Karla!" Raleigh barked, as ever throwing hierarchy and chain of command to the wind. I didn't care at that moment; I launched myself from the floor of the cockpit to a nearby wall, where there were railings for turbulent landing procedures. I gripped one as tightly as I could.

Raleigh raised the ancient artefact he had obtained from the ship's storage—my AK-47, a slug-thrower over five hundred years old, still with the original wooden panelling. For a moment, I thought Raleigh had lost his mind. I doubted he could hit this thing with a laser beam let alone a bullet. But he wasn't aiming at the Agoul, he was aiming at the windshield.

"Oh fuck!" I managed to scream, before Raleigh pulled the trigger.

Sound warped, not entirely cutting out, but fuzzing at the

edges, as though we had been plunged underwater. The roar of the machine-gun sounded far-off, quaint even. The windshield glass was designed to withstand asteroids; therefore it wouldn't shatter like it does in those old movies I love. It did, however, receive a puncture hole, no bigger than a finger's width. The suction was almighty, even small though the hole was. Johnny, still unconscious, began to slide across the floor towards the hole. Raleigh gripped him. I don't know if Johnny's limp body would have been squeezed through the breach. I doubt it. I think Raleigh had calculated his manoeuvre exactly; he always does. We were too large to be sucked out into space, but the Agoul . . . I gripped the railing and watched in awe as those grey particles were pulled by the ferocity of the vacuum out into the darkness. One moment, a shadow had stood in the cockpit. The next, it had been sucked through the hole like a genie returning to its magical bottle.

But it wasn't over. Given time, even that tiny breach would suck all the air out of the ship. Raleigh leapt forward. He pulled a slab of metal from his pocket and a can of liquid sealant. The sealant looks like nothing more than a spray can, though if you were to mistake it for deodorant you'd coat your flesh in chrome that instantly bonds to the skin, only removable via surgery. Raleigh placed the metal cut-out over the hole in the windshield; it buckled, a dent appearing in the middle, but didn't break. He sealed the edges with four long sprays of the sealant, the windshield now sporting a crude patch. Sound was restored—the flighty, hollow noises of the cockpit and muted machinery; faint, as though reality was uncertain of itself, and our senses even more uncertain of reality.

Raleigh slammed his fist down on the Total Dark button.

"Raleigh . . . "

I felt gravity die, floating upward. Raleigh and Johnny likewise left their moorings, Johnny awakening as he floated, startled and delirious, looking around for danger, thinking he was falling.

"Quiet!" Raleigh hissed.

We waited. He was looking out of the windshield, searching the darkness. We drifted, even more rudderless than before. The ship was plunged in blue-black broken only by starlight. The screens and controls, which had been going haywire moments before, dead as a necropolis. It's amazing how much comfort we find in machines, how they deceive us into thinking we're not alone.

After a while, the air started to taste stale, the life-support running the bare minimum cleaning to keep the power at imperceptible levels. At times, I thought I could see the Agoul outside our ship, but I honestly think that was my imagination playing tricks. We felt as though it was looking for us. The vacuum didn't kill it. But now, disorientated, it could not find us.

We must have waited hours, none of us speaking, the ship coasting in dark silence. Then, at last, Raleigh nodded. Wordlessly, he turned to go.

"Raleigh . . . " I stopped him. He looked at me, a strange light behind his eyes.

"I thought they were ghosts . . . Why did it get sucked out? What are they?"

"You always were superstitious."

Ignoring his insult, I asked again.

"What are they, Raleigh?"

He paused. "Nanobots, I think," he said. And then pulled himself weightlessly out of the cockpit, carrying the AK-47 with him.

CHAPTER 6

WE WERE SHAKY after our encounter with the Agoul. I slept only at the absolute edge of exhaustion, when I'd reached my physical limits, which—not to brag—is a rare occurrence. I think the encounter left me more spooked than I dared admit to myself. When I did sleep, I kept dreaming.

In the dream, I stood upon a black planet without atmosphere, two titanic columns ahead. I'm not going to lie to you: they were phallic. Whatever black rock they'd been sculpted from was porous, fleshy . . . They rose so high I lost where they met the black canvas of space. Between these two columns was a man. I knew the man—though I couldn't understand why he was appearing to me like this, why he'd turn up in a dream so eerie and strange.

It was my father.

He was exactly as I remembered him. Well, to say "remember" is perhaps an overstatement. He died only a year after I was born. Severe asthma attack. He was another *au naturel,* didn't believe in augments.

He stands there in my dreams just like in his photos—ridiculously tall, perhaps a fraction overweight. A black goatee made him look like a wannabe wizard, or perhaps a Renaissance man out of his time. Jet black hair on his head, wavy as an ocean. He had a silver gleam to his eyes, a black radiance behind the shine.

I've always thought, looking at pictures of my father, that he held some secret, some knowledge he wanted to impart to me—but he never got the chance. My mother wouldn't speak to me about my father, said he was a madman, always in his study, writing books—by hand if you can believe it—that never should have been written. Everything I've ever learned about my father, which isn't much I grant you, indicates he was born a thousand years too late. I don't know if I truly believe in destiny. I've seen a lot of fucked up shit that inclines me to believe there's *something* beyond just physics and happy accidents in the universe. But my father, I get the sense he was a soul who got on the wrong train into existence, *missed* his fate, in a way. And it haunted him, being in the wrong time like that. But this is all conjecture. It's weird, isn't it, how you can feel closer to someone you've never met than the person who raised you? My mother taught me how to fight, how to be physically strong, and that's about it.

In this dream I kept having—still have sometimes—my father stands between these two pillars and stretches out his hand to me. He opens his mouth and whispers the word, *Gha'agshebla*. I yearn, in the deepest pit of my being, to take his hand and go with him. But I always end up turning away. I wake up sweating, and yes, I'll admit, crying too. I'm not one for emotion, but I think my fucked up sleep cycle was wrecking me. Johnny and Raleigh were similar. None of us could sleep. And it wasn't anything to do with the ship or our routine. We knew it was the mission, the Temple.

Johnny recovered fairly well from his injuries. We booted up Beni and asked the robot to check Johnny over, but there was no lasting damage, just some burns on his chest and a fat lump on the back of his head. Before long, Johnny was back to his wisecracks, and smoking like a charnel house.

By this point, we were deeper into the Algol System. Space there isn't black, it's a blue that makes you think of cleaning fluid or bleach, like some technologically advanced civilisation tried to scrub the whole dark stain out of the cosmos. This is because the main star, Beta Persei Aa1, shines with bright azure radiance. There are three stars operating in the system, and they all orbit around each other, what Raleigh calls an "eclipsing binary star system." The largest star, Aa1, is three times the size of Earth's sun; I give it distance, because I don't want the *Rossetti* to be crushed like a tin-can by its gravity.

Drifting through that blue-hazed space was eerie. Since the very earliest days of space exploration, comparisons have been made between the early nautical explorers and our ships, capable of lightspeed travel across the Sprawl. I've always thought it was a false comparison. We have far more in common with early aircraft pilots than mariners or sailors. But, searching through that eerie blue haze, I could see the comparison was a little more apt than I'd given it credit for. The Algol System was a dark ocean, and we were searching for an island in its midst, a moving island, with a name older than human voices.

Agoul Space has more than one secret, and on that journey, it revealed a few of them to us.

We found the shattered hulks of ships almost as large as moons. Their exposed scaffolding gave the impression of ribs, skeletons. Shreds of insulating matter clung to those bones, like flesh. Their vast hollow interiors glimmered with technologies that looked thoroughly alien, more like the matrix of a nervous system than wiring or computing. Had we been on any other mission, we might have taken the risk to stop and investigate these hulks. But we had a greater prize at journey's end, so we pressed on.

There were asteroids rigged together by colossal chains—the scale of it dwarfed my intellect. Some of these columns of linked asteroids had fourteen objects in their train. Each one looked like it had been tampered with, some kind of hole drilled into them, massive metal devices inserted into the breach.

"They're bombs," Raleigh said.

"What?"

"They're bombs. We're flying through a fucking minefield."

We gave them a wide berth after that.

The last and most horrifying thing we saw—or rather, Johnny claimed to see—was a spider. Yes, I find it hard to believe too, I admit. But Johnny's never lied to me. He bends the truth across the negotiating table, but never breaks it. I was distracted, probably dozing off due to the long hours and near-sleepless nights. Suddenly, Johnny let out a shriek.

I bolted upright, startled awake. My blood felt like it'd been whipped into activity. Everything seemed hyper-real, the adrenaline rendering my senses preternatural for those brief moments of panic. Johnny stared out of the windshield whiter than a fucking ghost. He was trembling head to toe. He honestly looked like he was about to lose his mind, teetering on the cliff-edge of sanity, his eyes so wide they were going to pop out of his sockets. A moan escaped his lips; the sound of a helpless, dying animal.

"Johnny? Johnny, what's wrong?"

He lifted a finger and pointed, but there was nothing to see but blackness.

"Sp-spider . . . " he choked. "Black spider."

He wouldn't speak about it again, even after he calmed down, but later I found him in his room sketching . . . Johnny had never been artistically inclined. He'd stolen some of Raleigh's tools to do the deed; they were ill-suited for illustration, being designed for geometric drawings and mathematical calculations. What Johnny produced, before he hastily hid it from my eyes, looked like a child's scrawl. But the image will never leave me. A mangled arachnid, its limbs sprawling out with too many joints. In some ways it looked more like a plant, a rotten bulb sprouting countless tendril-like roots, spearing into the far corners of the universe. A hateful thing.

I was glad that Johnny destroyed the drawing, even though it meant he was hiding something from me.

CHAPTER 7

A FEW DAYS after the spider, Johnny alerted me to a pingback on the scanner. There was another human ship with us. It's rare to meet another ship in this vast and derelict area of space, but not impossible, because after all we're not the only ones seeking riches.

"Keep an eye on them," I said to Johnny. He nodded. I couldn't help but think I needed to keep an eye on him, too. He seemed, on the surface, to be back to his cheery self, but there was something haunted in his eyes, something beyond simple lack of sleep.

"They're getting closer," Johnny said, frowning. "Judging by the ship's specs I'd say they're pirates like us."

"Don't let Raleigh hear you say that," I replied, trying to inject some levity into the conversation. Lately it felt forced.

Johnny smiled weakly.

There was a field of minor asteroids between us and them, and in the centre of this field drifted the hulking wreck of an ancient ship, a ship belonging to a race that had existed before us, that had conquered the stars and then been conquered. That left the question of "by whom?" Perhaps the annihilation had been mutual. The ancient race with the organic ships and whomever they had fought against had destroyed each other in the cataclysmic potency of their war. Only the Agoul remained, and what were they to these husks of titans?

I assumed that the other ship was heading towards this space-hulk for plunder, but then Johnny said, "They're skirting the edge of the field. I think they're still headed toward us."

"Hail them."

Johnny set up the long-range transmitter. He clicked a button and static crackled into life.

"This is the *Rossetti* hailing . . . " Johnny scanned a read-out on his screen showing all the data the *Rossetti* was collecting from their ship's network. They weren't flying dark, which itself seemed odd, as pirates generally kept a low profile even when dealing with their own kind. Had we been double crossed by the Midas Clade? Had they sent another ship to check up on us? "The *Theseus* . . . " Johnny took his finger off the broadcast button. "Bit grandiose," he quipped to me. I smiled. He continued broadcasting. "This is the *Rossetti* hailing the *Theseus,* please respond."

Silence answered us.

"What, not even an insult?" Johnny joked.

I laughed. But Johnny had a point. Few pirates missed the opportunity for a shit-slinging match. Partly it's to do with ego and status. Partly it's the sheer loneliness of the void.

Unease settled upon me like a sudden chill. Raleigh says I'm the superstitious type, and I suppose maybe I do believe in things beyond our understanding . . . Some things are beyond the world of men, they are secrets that should never be glimpsed, and we were plunging right into the heart of those secrets with reckless intent.

I swapped seats with Johnny and hailed them again.

"*Theseus,* answer us, or are you too drunk?" I snapped.

No reply.

"They're still coming towards us, Karla. They've gotten around the asteroid field. They don't give a shit about the hulk."

I glanced at Johnny. He looked scared, and I probably did too.

"Turn the ship."

"Excuse me?"

"Turn the ship!" I barked. "I want to see them with the naked eye."

Johnny did as instructed. He grabbed the controls, tweaked the engine-thrust, and put the *Rossetti* into an elegant turn, firing the side-thrusters to stabilise and slow the rotation. You may be thinking that using so much energy this deep in Agoul Space would be madness. Surely, we were going to draw the Agoul? But we hadn't encountered another Agoul since the first, and I was beginning to think they were avoiding us—or rather, leaving us to our fate. Why, I didn't know. Still don't, in truth. But I suspect it has to do with the Temple's master . . .

We were still moving, of course. Almost nothing in space is ever still. But we were now facing the oncoming ship.

My heart felt like rotten fingers had closed around it. My throat tightened to the point it hurt.

"Fuck!"

There was something wrong with the *Theseus*. Profoundly wrong.

The ship was large, much larger than the *Rossetti,* built to house perhaps twenty or thirty crew-members. It drove like a spear through the gulf of space, its metal glowing eerily in the light of Algol's aberrant stars.

You know we pirates like to customise our ships, adorning them contrary to I.W.A. guidelines, an act of rebellion and personality. But the *Theseus* had been customised to an absurd—and terrifying—degree.

None of the ship's portholes were visible because of the profusion of crude, welded spikes protruding from every inch of its hull. Impaled on these spikes were frozen corpses, atoms of flesh and blood hardened into pearls resembling the way a nautical ship cuts through the seafoam. Some of the bodies were in diverse clothing, which meant they were likely pirates like us, but some were in I.W.A uniform. Now I understood why the I.W.A. patrols were so frequent. They were looking for the *Theseus*. Trying to stop it.

At the rear of the ship, long chains floated, capped by human skulls. The vacuum had frosted the bone, making them glittering diamonds trailing behind the hulking monstrosity through the deep. The name of the ship, once boldly emblazoned on the ship's flanks in proud white lettering, had been blackened, perhaps with paint, perhaps with blood. In its place were symbols—no language I or anyone else in the land of the sane could recognise. The sigils of madness. Of minds lost to space dementia. Those were the words I shouted to bring us out of our stunned reverie.

"Astraecy!" Then a shriek of command tore from me as I pressed the intercom. "Beni, defence mode, now! Raleigh, Johnny, get your pistols."

"The *Rossetti* can't take another—" Johnny began.

"I didn't fucking ask!" I cut across him.

Astraecy is nothing to be laughed at. I'd encountered those who were taken by the madness of the vast infinite before, and they are less than human, less even than animals. They will do things beyond morality, beyond reason, beyond understanding.

The *Theseus,* which had been so monomaniacally spearing towards us, began to turn in the deep, revealing its broadside.

"They don't have guns," Johnny said, frowning. "What are they doing?"

"Escape pods . . . " I whispered, noticing the jewel-like pods shining on the ship's underbelly. They looked like spider-eggs. "They're going to try and board us."

"They can't." Johnny was shaking his head like a petulant child. "That's madness."

"They *are* mad, Johnny. Worse than mad. Get us the fuck out of range."

Johnny grabbed the controls, panic driving him with manic intensity. He began to steer the *Rossetti* away from the *Theseus*. The black-horned ship came on with soundless menace. It would be a chase. Their engines were bigger. But perhaps we could use the asteroids to our advantage.

The *Rossetti* vibrated from stern to bow, the antimatter core activating in response to Johnny's keyed inputs, colliding matter and antimatter in an alchemical explosion. We rocketed forward through the gulf, so fast the distant stars began to streak.

But the *Theseus* had already been building up speed, and its thrusters were bigger than ours. As it turned broadside, it continued to fire both side and rear thrusters bringing it in a dangerous careen towards us. I doubted the crew of that infernal ship would care whether they crashed into us. They cared for nothing except what their delirious personal gods told them to do.

"Port side!" I screamed.

Johnny practically pulled the controls out of their panels in his effort to steer us away. The *Rossetti* banked, just narrowly escaping one of the brutal metal spikes adorning the *Theseus*.

Then the escape pods fired.

CHAPTER 8

ONLY, THEY WEREN'T escape pods. They were *boarding* pods. Fifteen or so fired. Five were spunked into the void, spinning away into darkness with perhaps a billion-to-one chance of ever being recovered—even if every ship in the galaxy were to search for them. Another two were intercepted by rogue asteroids and reduced to bright smithereens. Another three simply exploded upon launch due to some unreliable mechanism. That left five. If *one* of those had hit the *Rossetti's* antimatter core, both our ships would have gone up in a supernova explosion that would have been visible from Proxima Centauri. But we got lucky. Or unlucky, depending on how you view the rest of this tale. The pods hammered into the *Rossetti's* hull and breached, landing in various parts of the ship: three in the rec-room, one in storage, and one in the stasis room. It was a miracle the *Rossetti* did not come apart instantly with so many holes in her hull, but the gaps were partially plugged by the ungainly pods.

I keyed in the sealing sequences into the co-pilot control panel, and heard the grinding sound of blast doors sealing off the compromised parts of the ship, stopping the atmosphere from bleeding away and slowing down our enemies.

I pressed the intercom.

"Raleigh, get to the cockpit, now!"

"Roger." Usually Raleigh made no reply, but the situation was so dire even he was stepping into line.

"Beni!"

Beni's voice crackled over the intercom, likely because he was linked in with the ship's communicative infrastructure, and therefore was a walking intercom himself.

"*Affirmative. Approaching stasis room. Defence mode activated.*"

I heard a sound through Beni's transmitter that reminded me of steel on a whetstone. They were trying to cut through the bulkheads.

"Kill whatever comes through," I said.

"*Affirmative,*" Beni said, happily.

I turned back to Johnny. "Where's your pistol?"

He sat white-faced at the controls, staring out at the dark. The *Theseus* was no longer moving to intercept us. It cruised in an almost causal pursuit, a Komodo dragon chasing down its poisoned prey. He couldn't believe what had happened.

"Johnny!"

He turned and looked at me, swallowing.

"I left it . . . in my room."

I cursed.

"Steer the ship. Make sure you get away from the *Theseus.* Risk a little FTL if you have to."

"But asteroids—"

"Better than what they'll do."

Finally he seemed to comprehend, swallowing again, nodding once.

"Good luck," he whispered.

I nodded.

In the hallway beyond the cockpit, I took the cylinder off my hip and thumbed the on-switch. The bo-staff extended to its full length, humming with lethal energies. I sprinted down the corridor. I, too, had left my ranged weapon in storage. Raleigh had likely gone to retrieve it. He seemed to covet my AK of late. Although in truth it would be unwise to fire it inside the ship. Lasers could be attuned to short-range blasts. Bullets just kept going.

The ship is designed like an antique key. The rear is bulbous to accommodate the antimatter core, which has a ring-shaped collider at its heart. The main body of the ship extends like a narrow blade from that ring. A hall runs through that blade, and branching off are five doors. One to crew quarters. One to the stasis rooms. One to the rec-room. One to storage. And finally one to the rear of the ship and the core.

Beni was locking down the stasis room, but three pods had ripped their way into the rec-room. I didn't know where Raleigh was, but I had to deal with the biggest threat first. Before I could do that, I needed an atmos-suit. Johnny could seal himself into the cockpit if things got hairy and more breaches appeared in the *Rossetti*. But I would be exposed to the void if I wasn't careful.

Midway down the hallway, I depressed a button. The *Rossetti* took a moment to think about my fingerprints and then a panel slid to the side, revealing four atmos-suits. I like to think of the fourth as belonging to Beni, though he doesn't need it, but the truth is it's always good to have a spare.

The suits looked like the discarded flesh of cyclopses. I grabbed the red one, and leaning my bo-staff against the wall, I clambered into the suit. The feeling of the dacron insulation against the skin is frankly repellent. The air on board the ship is stale at the best of times, but hardly any air circulates in that suit. I imagine if you wore it for too long you'd start to decay, all the grime and sweat trapped against your pores finally causing the flesh to revolt. But still, needs must.

When I was sealed in, checking the closures three times to ensure there was no breach, I breathed a sigh that crackled as the voice amplifier kicked into gear. I checked my oxygen levels and then proceeded down the hall towards the rec-room door.

Another reason I hate those suits is that the helmet narrows your field of vision. Even though it's only a minor adjustment, it's enough to make me paranoid, like you are always missing something out of the corner of your eye.

At the rec-room door, I keyed in a special code. It slid open, and beyond I saw a long hallway that ended in a blast door, the very blast door I'd activated moments before from the bridge. Shrieking came from the other side, as though the metal itself was crying out in agony. There was an orange glow at the centre of the door, like lava surfacing under volcanic earth. I knew what that meant. They had a magma-drill. They'd be through the door in another few seconds. Heart thundering, breathing shallow, I fought for control, not to waste my oxygen.

I sealed the door behind me. It might seem like a suicidal move, but if the rec-room was compromised to the void, then the entire ship could turn itself inside out once that bulkhead was breached.

The shrieking grew louder, the howling of a damned soul having its teeth drilled. The molten glow intensified, alternately red then white. I imagined some monster on the other side, burrowing. In a way, it wasn't far from the truth. If the crew of the *Theseus* had truly succumbed to Astraecy, there was nothing to be done for them except put them out of their misery.

The surface of the metal door began to bubble and shimmer with the heat, its brightness almost too much to look at. Metal sloughed in liquid runnels from the door and flowed along the floor like silver serpents. The door bulged, shrank, bulged, shrank, an artificial heart.

Then in an explosion of molten pus the door burst apart. Large metal plates were blown aside. Slabs of panelling disintegrated into liquid metal. Worse than that was the sound of the void. They say it's silent, that no one can hear you scream in space, but that's not true. The void howls. Admittedly, it howls beyond the spectrum of an ordinary human being's hearing, but it still howls.

As the bulkhead was breached, the void screamed into that narrow corridor. I mag-locked my boots to the metal flooring, the magnetism only just strong enough to stop me from being plucked where I stood and swallowed by the endless maw of Agoul Space.

And out of that mouth, *they* came.

For a moment, all my training fled me. If the *Theseus* had been a nightmare vision, the crew were its equal.

There were three. Each wore an atmospheric suit, which darkly implied a small degree of sanity left to them. But unlike my suit, which was designed to be light and sleek—predominantly used for maintenance work on the exterior of the ship—theirs were armour plated combat models. As such, they did not look like men. They towered, clad in bulky armour plating designed to turn aside low-power laser blasts. Their helmets had darkened visors, cowling their faces. Steel pneumatics augmented their joints, lending them extra power, speed, and strength. This was on top of whatever personal augments they had.

Like the *Theseus,* they had customised their armour with trophies of their madness. Serrated spikes jutted from their shoulders and elbows. Necklaces of fingers hung from their necks. One had painted his visor with an emblem that looked like a star with fourteen points, or perhaps a spider . . . Each was a hulking terror. Their weapons were the implements of sadists: one carried a meat-cleaver so huge that it had to be wielded in two hands; another brandished a diamond-toothed chainsaw; the third levelled a kind of harpoon gun.

"Fuck!"

The harpoon-wielder raised his weapon and fired. I dodged. Combat in the void is always clunky. Mag-locking makes every footstep twice as cumbersome. But thanks to the sleek atmos-suit I wore, I was still lighter on my feet than they.

Though my mind was reeling, my muscles remembered their roles sure enough. A bloodied spear sped past me and slammed into the door behind. A black chain connected the harpoon gun and its deadly bolt.

The other two came at me, one revving his chainsaw and swinging it so wildly I thought he might kill his own ally.

I spun my bo-staff and brought it sharply into contact with the lead assailant, the one with the meat-cleaver. He didn't even try to deflect or dodge, and that unsettled me. In my training, I was always pitted against skilful foes, able to match offence with defence, but these berserkers cared nothing for personal safety. The bo-staff struck his chest and discharged its payload of electrical current; Meat Cleaver staggered back. I grinned with satisfaction as his mouth made the shape of someone howling in pain, though I heard nothing beneath the blanket of the void. Lightning bolts surged across his atmos-suit, the pneumatics momentarily gone haywire. But I didn't have time to gloat, because the second was upon me.

He swung his chainsaw with such fury that I'm sure the blow would have taken my head clean from my shoulders. I barely dodged, ducking underneath. The diamond saw smashed into the floor, burying half a foot deep in a shower of sparks, exposing the *Rossetti's* cabling—what I always think of as her veins and arteries.

I struck out with my staff, slamming the butt into the back of Chainsaw's leg. He roared from the pain of impact, and lunged clumsily as the leg's pneumatics were broken and frazzled. I dodged his grasping hand and slammed the other end of the staff into his visor. The force was such that the glass shattered.

A face of deranged animosity glared back at me. He'd shaved his head, tattooed sigils onto his cheeks, and worse of all: cut off his own eyelids. The blood red eyes that stared at me, rheumy, cocaine-wide, unresting, will stay with me for the rest of my life, even after what I witnessed in the Temple itself . . .

If I'd been fighting I.W.A. personnel or ordinary mercenaries, that would have been the end of Chainsaw. But they call it Astraecy for a reason. Why would the void kill what now belongs to her? Without oxygen, eyes bugging out of skull as internal pressures catastrophically altered, Chainsaw struggled to rise.

I could have finished him then, slammed my staff through his eye-socket, had not Meat Cleaver recovered and set upon me screaming. Harpoon was not far behind, having finally dragged his chain-spear from its mooring in the door, reloading his brutal but impractical weapon. I seem to remember that harpoon guns like that were used by miners to catch floating asteroids and drag them toward the ship. Maybe that's what these men had been before they succumbed to the call of the void? I doubt any of them could remember who they once were. There were only the urges now, and the means to obey them.

Meat Cleaver swung vertically downwards. The cleaver could have cut my skull perfectly in two. The weight of that industrial blade was terrifying, beyond the strength of any ordinary man. But these were not ordinary men. Madness had made them Herculean. You can inject as much adrenaline as you like into a human being and they still won't be as freakishly strong as those fully coked on Astraecy.

I had no time to dodge, so I raised my staff horizontally to block the descending blow. The impact of the downward stroke nearly dislocated my shoulders. I couldn't suppress a scream. But the titanium helix of my staff held for those precious milliseconds.

Though my periphery was compromised, I sensed movement on my right. Scientists have long theorised we have a sixth sense, a spatial awareness that borders on the telekinetic. I've only ever experienced it in the heat of a fight. That's what I felt then, and I instinctively threw myself backwards.

The swinging chainsaw blade buzzed like a black hornet as it cut through the air, inches from my visor. Such was the momentum that it overswung and lodged itself in Meat Cleaver's stomach.

Chainsaw—his void-ravaged face exposed, a mask of psychotic fury—howled with frustration.

Meat Cleaver screamed in silence, gargling blood. The chainsaw was lodged underneath his ribs, the teeth chewing through dacron, flesh, and musculature like they were paper. Chainsaw kicked his companion down to the ground and drove the saw deeper; blood sprayed the walls and painted Chainsaw's armour a crimson of thirsting gods.

A black dart shot out at me, and then I was screaming.

The spear passed clean through my thigh. I dropped to one knee.

Though I heard nothing, I saw frothing joy behind Harpoon's visor. He depressed a button on the side of his gun and I felt the spear tugged on its chain. I collapsed onto my back, howling in pain. The madman began to drag me towards him. The expressions of his excitement were repulsive, atavistic, *insect*.

Chainsaw ignored everyone and everything else, satisfied he had killed *something* even though it was one of his own; he straddled Meat Cleaver, performing some kind of surgery upon him with his saw, his methodology and reasoning known only to the void.

The pain was excruciating, although nothing compared to what happened in the Temple. It occupied my entire leg, and even travelled up through my spine. I am amazed I did not pass out. Harpoon dragged me to his feet, staring down at me, only madness visible behind his black visor—I could still feel his hunger. Either he'd rape me then kill me, or kill me then rape me. And that was if I was lucky.

He produced a filleting knife from his belt, a cruel curved thing.

"Pretty . . . " Harpoon mouthed. " . . . face."

I raised my staff, which I had just managed to hold on to, but he stamped down on my wrist. I screamed.

"Me . . . want!" Harpoon mouthed, lowering the knife to my visor.

It all would have been over for me, except that the door to the main corridor opened, and Beni stepped through. Harpoon just had time to look up and see the headless, chrome-plated centaur raising a laser cannon before he disappeared in a smudge of red, eviscerated by a fully charged blast.

Chainsaw raised his gore-choked weapon and charged, but Beni turned his gun and a second eye-searing blast of red filled the chamber, leaving a blackened burn mark on the wall, cutting Chainsaw clean in two. His charred body parts slid to the ground and twitched.

I let out a sigh. The pain was still overwhelming, but I sensed it was over. Beni approached me slowly, crouching on his haunches like a dog might, though of course his human torso still reared up awkwardly. His screen showed a concerned emoji—cute, despite the fact he had just obliterated two people.

"Captain Karla, you are hurt," Beni patched his voice directly into my suit's internal speakers.

I looked down at the spear lodged in my thigh. The damn thing was nearly as thick as a soda can. It was bleeding, but the blood flow had been partially stemmed by the weapon still being lodged in the wound. Needless to say, the atmos-suit was ruined.

"Get me out of here, Beni. We'll seal this corridor."

"Affirmative."

The centaur rose, grabbing me by my injured wrist—which hurt like a bitch —and hauling me to my feet. I threw an arm over his equine flanks and staggered towards the door, Beni walking slowly to accommodate my limping pace. Progress was especially hard as I was still dragging the chain behind me.

"Beni, could you . . . "

"Affirmative."

He discharged a laser blast from his cannon and severed the chain connecting the spear to the harpoon gun.

I made it the rest of the way to the door. I took one last look back through the hallway and bulkhead doors before we sealed it off. I saw the rec-room in ruins, cone-shaped drop-pods—their shining black interiors exposed—had breached the *Rossetti's* hull, and were now lodged in the walls, peering in like dragon heads. The magma drill lay discarded on the floor behind the melted bulkhead. In the narrow slivers between the ship's walls and the escape pods, where the hull had been torn wide, I saw blackness and starlight.

"Children of the void," I muttered, remembering my mother's words.

We sealed the corridor off.

CHAPTER 9

IT TOOK US weeks to get the *Rossetti* functional again. All the while we feared another attack, but the Astraecy freaks, the Children of the Void as I had termed them, didn't seem to hunt in packs, which I suppose made sense. We also feared another Agoul. But it seemed even they did not like to penetrate so deep into the Algol System.

The five boarders had all been killed. Raleigh shot one in storage—he was even bigger than the ones that attacked me, and dragging his ass to the rear airlock was hard work. Beni killed one in the stasis room in addition to the two he killed near the rec-room. No casualties sustained on our side, though my leg was fucked, and now I'd have a limp for the rest of my life unless I got an expensive augment. Good thing we had the biggest payout of our lives coming down the pipeline, or so I told myself.

Our ship had sustained significant damage. The *Theseus's* "escape pods" had breached three areas, ripping through the hull. We had to completely shut down the *Rossetti* and work on repairing the breaches from the outside.

I've worked in the void before in an atmos-suit, but never in Agoul Space, and let me tell you, it's another experience entirely. As we welded new plates into place over the cavernous tears in the hull (every pirate ship carries an ample supply for quick repairs), all of us saw and heard things that we didn't want to talk about afterwards.

Sometimes, it's the little things that get you. I didn't see a black spider, like Johnny did. Rather, all I saw was a little ice-crystal forming on the ship's hull. Rare, but not impossible. There must have been a bit of moisture on the outside of the ship. But what freaked me out was that it had fourteen rays. The sign emblazoned on Meat Cleaver's helmet had been a fourteen pointed star . . . And the *Theseus,* which was now drifting without pilot into the darkest depths of the void, also had a similar emblem painted on its demented hull. Was I paranoid? Was there a pattern? Did the madness of Astraecy actually originate from somewhere, not just isolation and the fragile human mind?

When I do menial work, my mind wanders—most often to the past. It occurred to me the ancient word for ice was "rime", like that old poem, *The Rime of the Ancient Mariner.* It's funny how the word "rime" makes you think of the word "rhyme". In a flash, the poem given to us by the Midas Clade came back to me:

"A floating temple lies beyond the veil,
where mortal and immortal worlds are shorn;
across the battlefields of black Algol,
the Great One's Treasure waits to be worn"

I seriously considered ordering us all to turn around at that moment. We were like the Ancient Mariner, too deep in the rime, too deep in the ice, and the only way out was through hell.

Agoul Space was getting to me. I'd heard the stories, of course, but a part of you always dismisses them as fictitious. Now, I was seeing it first-hand.

When I worked a gruelling repair gig as a younger woman, there was always a planet in sight, even if you were working in the void. But in Algol, there are no planets in sight, just stars, blackness, and a graveyard of ships that don't make sense. Occasionally, horrible lights flash across the System, interrupting the blue, underwater pall. There's never an explanation or a source for where this light comes from, but it reminds me of a lighthouse beam passing over lost ships out at sea.

By this point, our rations were running pretty low. We'd foreseen delays, but nothing on this scale. We had barely enough to get to the Temple and back to the nearest waystation if we were careful and gunned it to the nearest flight path, rather than moving as cautiously as we had on the way in.

Johnny seemed to know what I was thinking, because he came to see me after we'd completed the final bit of work. He stood in my bedroom, saying nothing, leaning against the doorframe, half-in, half-out. He looked haunted.

"We don't have to do this," he said.

I nodded.

"Let me sleep on it. I can't think."

I closed my eyes and slept almost immediately. I dreamed of my father, beckoning.

When I woke, I rallied the crew and told them in no uncertain terms we were going to push on. Johnny bowed his head in acknowledgement, though he rubbed his eyes with his forefinger and thumb, as if there was a pain there. Raleigh accepted it without moving a single muscle or saying a word. They both understood, even if they cursed me for it.

CHAPTER 10

We set off with the *Rossetti* patched up as best we could. The rec-room was out of order. Storage had just about been saved, although we lost some of the minor trinkets too insignificant for the concern of the Midas Clade, but of interest to other pirate crews and traders. The stasis rooms were the least damaged, which is lucky, because without them we wouldn't be able to travel along the FTL flight paths. I saw a picture once of a guy who failed to reach the security of the stasis pod when his ship went to lightspeed. There was not much to see. He was a puddle.

Now, the graveyard began to thin. The asteroid mines, the hulking ships, all of it seemed to have dispersed, perhaps by a colossal explosion, and instead cosmic dust battered our ship. I dread to think how much radiation passed through us on that final leg of the journey. Our slapdash repairs could have exposed us to a fatal dose, but by now we were waded in too deep. There was no turning back.

For hours upon hours the three of us were gathered in the cockpit, straining with all our will to discover the secret end to our journey. Raleigh rarely joins us in the cockpit, but the moment was so significant even he was drawn from his Gordian equations. He wanted to be there, to be the first to spot the Temple, to be vindicated. All his calculations had helped us reach this point. In a sense, there was nothing more he *could* do. I felt the same, though my hands were on the steering controls. My body was nothing. There was only my mind, awareness, peering out into the blackness, hoping to see some glimmer of what we sought.

Shadows and dust. For countless miles. And then, as suddenly as a trap closing, we were there. Yes, somehow, out of nothingness, out of the gulf, its blackness suddenly upreared: monolithic, stupefying, immense. Made of endless shadow, made of pure darkness, a great floating island crowned by a black castle, all of it sculpted by some insane artificer out of the bleakest obsidian. The only break in its atramentous image was rime, great pale, curling serpents of rime winding their way around the spires, crenulations, and pyramids blotting out the stars. The ice glittered like a forbidden pearl.

The Temple's dimensions boggled the mind. Johnny looked brain-dead, practically drooling. Words are insufficient to describe it. The largest Destroyer-class ship in the I.W.A.'s fleet wouldn't hold a candle to it. The Temple would dwarf some moons, and yet the base of the island on which the Temple sat was hung with jagged stalactites, proving this monstrous structure had once belonged to a planet, and in some ancient epoch had been wrenched into the void.

"*Gha'agshebla*," I whispered.

The name came unbidden to my lips, dragged from me, as though by gravity. Indeed, so large was the structure, that I began to feel the tug of gravity upon the *Rossetti*. Easy as I could, given the damage she had sustained, I took her down towards the Temple. It seemed to expand infinitely, and at one point I thought perhaps we had all collectively gone mad, that the Temple was simply a mirage we could never touch.

Endless pillars, stairwells, and spires jutted out into nothingness. Bridges spanned gulfs seemingly without destination. Arches and doorways stared out from the walls like insectoid eyes. The thing's architecture was monstrous and insane, the kind of clusterfuck of assembled components a corrupted AI art-generator might produce. The closer one looked, the more uncanny its topography became: staircases wound on the outside of towers and ended in nothingness, as though ancient astrologers had believed they might climb into the stars; doorways opened over precipitous drops into the void; buildings seemingly lay on their side, their entrances accessible only by something equipped with an insect's scopulae.

At the last second, before I immolated us all, I pulled the *Rossetti* out of her descent, initiating the landing sequence, the small thrusters on her underbelly firing, stabilising us. We landed at the bottom of a colossal stairway leading up to what we guessed must be the main entrance, though in truth we had no clue. With a gentle thud, a slight judder and rocking, we set down.

None of us could believe it. We exchanged glances, awe mixed with terror. Raleigh looked more vulnerable and uncertain than I had ever seen him, like a curious toddler, unsure whether or not he should poke a hornet's nest.

"Gravity is reading at roughly the same level as Earth's moon," Johnny said, speaking like someone rehearsing a script.

I nodded.

"Atmos-suits, then?"

The other two nodded.

"Are we ready?"

The question was largely rhetorical, for there was no going back now. There were an infinite number of moments we could have turned back, especially after the attack from the Void-Children, but not now, not when we had landed, not when we had touched the Temple, determined it was real, tangible . . .

We each suited up. I had to use the spare, because our encounter with the *Theseus* had damaged my red suit, and I didn't have the energy to repair it. As well as suits, we took weapons. I had my bo-staff, Raleigh had a laser cannon, and Johnny his laser pistol. The AK wouldn't work in the void, the ice would clog its mechanisms, so it had to stay behind for this one.

We opened the door and descended the ramp, careful to keep our footfalls light to compensate for the moony gravity. Beni trotted along happily beside us. If he was intimidated by the environment, he gave no sign. I think without Beni beside us, our nerves might have failed.

Standing now at the base of the stairs, the Temple loomed so high that even craning my neck I could not see its tallest spires. The stars were utterly eclipsed by it. I felt dizzy, could almost picture myself falling backward and off the edge of the island, into the abyss. When I emerged from my reverie, Raleigh and Johnny were both looking at me, awaiting my command.

"Let's go."

The stairs would have been nearly impossible on a large planet. With our meagre rations and state of exhaustion, they would have defeated us. But in the lower gravity, we were able to bounce up them with less effort.

After a while, Raleigh spoke. He sounded uncertain—which is unusual—and even more worryingly, *humbled*.

"The geometry is non-Euclidean," he said, quietly over the intercom.

"What's that?"

We kept leaping lightly up the steps. The summit seemed an eternity away. I began to feel like I was in a dream.

He raised a hand and pointed.

"Follow that stone crossbeam with your eyes. What do you notice?"

I did as he instructed.

"It's a straight line."

Raleigh shook his head.

"No. Look again."

Again I tried to follow the line, and to my horror I found that the line was no line but a spiral, a spiral so large that we and the Temple were *inside* the spiral, everything was inside the spiral. God, the stars were bending, the shadows moving, everything drawn into the vortex of a new Becoming . . . I let out a shriek and tripped, my mind overwhelmed, nearly face-planting on the stairs. Only Johnny saved me from cracking open my visor and dying right then and there. He grabbed me and hauled me upright. It took him hardly any strength because of the low gravity.

"Easy!" he said. Then, "Don't listen to Raleigh. Don't look at the architecture." He spoke like a madman, but I drank in every word. I think Johnny's response to peril and fear was detachment. He had unhooked his brain from what his senses were telling him. "In and out. We get the Treasure and scram. Indiana Jones style."

I smiled at that and clapped him on the shoulder. Johnny was the grounding I needed.

"Indiana Jones," I said.

He gave a weak smile.

"Don't look at anything for too long."

We trudged on. Raleigh fell silent, no doubt lost in his own insane calculations, trying to solve the enigma of the Temple then and there. I was with Johnny, the less attention we paid to it, the better. I didn't want to know who had built it. One would think that my human curiosity was piqued. But no, I didn't care if it was Agoul or Gods that had made it, all I wanted was to get the Treasure and run.

"I'm detecting heat signatures within the structure," Beni said, mildly. He had perfectly adjusted his movements to the lower gravity, springing like an antelope, using the enhanced buoyancy to bound several steps at a time. It was a strangely beautiful sight, his chrome body dancing through the void, but I couldn't feel anything other than dread at that moment.

"Lifeforms?" I dared ask the question.

"Difficult to tell, Captain Karla."

"Proceed with caution," I said.

Johnny charged his pistol. Raleigh didn't give any indication he'd heard my order. I think perhaps he had come to the same conclusion I had: that if there was something here to fight, it wasn't likely our weapons would do much against it.

Now we come to the strangest part of my tale. Truly, it's even more strange than what happened after. I'll never forget the image so long as I live.

At the top of the stairs we saw a vast, brooding entryway. Imagine walking into the Parthenon, only the pillars holding up the ceiling are thousands of feet tall—or at least, they feel this way. Imagine, if you can, the black radiance shining off the stone. The wondrous formations of ice crystals snaking up the pillars and along the walls. Imagine the whole shadowy enormity of the thing, like a beast about to swallow you. Imagine the feeling of the void around you, that one crack in your visor or suit means death. Death is all around you, and this is *his* Temple, made out of the abysses between stars.

Then imagine that of all the things we could find in the entrance, waiting for us, what walks out is a man—a tall man with black hair, a goatee, glasses, and a mischievous smile. He's wearing black robes, and no spacesuit. His pale skin is exposed to the void, as though it's of no consequence to him.

And you know this man. I know this man.

It's my father.

CHAPTER 11

"CAN YOU SEE HIM?" I whispered to the others.

"Yes," Johnny replied, perhaps confused why I would ask, but I wanted to make sure I wasn't hallucinating, that Astraecy hadn't taken me.

There he stood, as I had seen him in my dream, between two colossal pillars. I half expected him to make the same beckoning gesture, to smile a smile that said, "Oh, dear daughter, where hast thou been?" If he had, I might have followed him into whatever oblivion he chose. But instead he came forward and bowed.

"Welcome to *Gha'agshebla*."

His voice carried in a world without atmosphere, sounded in a silence that was supposedly absolute. Every hair on my arms and neck raised to attention. My mouth was dry. My heart pounded. This was magic, had to be magic, or else it was a technology beyond comprehension. *A hologram, surely,* my rational brain asserted. But it did not seem like one. It felt like the realest experience of my life.

"Dad?" I hated how childish, how like a little girl, I sounded in that moment, but I was exhausted, overawed, confused, my psyche battered by impossible possibilities, by insane thoughts and feelings.

He turned his bespectacled eyes on me, a look on his face that was curiously warm, despite his Machiavellian stylings.

"Dear daughter," he said, as though he had ciphered my earlier imaginings. "I always knew you would find me. I was not able to leave as many breadcrumbs as I would have liked, but you still found the road, out into the stars!" His voice was breathless with wonder. "When the gods call, we must answer. You have come seeking the Treasure belonging to the Great Ones. In time, you will be granted it, but first you must show you are worthy to receive it."

"How about I blow you to fucking smithereens and we take the Treasure?" Raleigh growled.

"You'd die!" I snarled, raising the bo-staff, thumb hovering over the activation button. I had not travelled to the edge of mapped space, to meet a man I'd thought dead, only to have Raleigh fuck it all up.

My father, however, was not threatened by Raleigh's outburst.

"Come now, Raleigh, be reasonable. You are a man of science, of intellect and logic. A fine mind, you have, one that rises above the ophidian urges for violence and gratification. For too long your body and mind have been at war. I can help you make the two one."

"Psycho-babble," Raleigh growled, his finger still itching on the laser cannon's trigger. "Mystical gibberish. It's all rubbish, a lie."

My father only smiled, and though the pleasant facade remained, I could see a darkness in his eyes, a terrible potentiality, of things done and things possible to do, things beyond our imagining.

"You have seen the size of the Temple, Raleigh. It seems to me that without my help you will be wandering a lifetime within its maze, searching for your prize— unless you accept my help. How much oxygen is left in those suits, I wonder? How long do you think it will take? I may show you the quick—though narrow—way of initiation. You will cut right to the heart, where the Treasure lies."

Raleigh seemed to see sense in this, finally lowering his gun.

My father's smile at once became benign.

"Excellent. And Johnny, are you, too, ready to face the trials of the Temple?"

Johnny nodded. It was then I realised just how much the journey had changed Johnny. Once so voluble, now he hardly talked. Once so charming, now he only glowered darkly. It seemed to me, strange though this might sound, that my father had taken, from each of us, the characteristic that most defined us. He was charming and sociable, as Johnny used to be. His intellect shone fiercely in the way he articulated the absurdities of this place—like Raleigh's. And like me, he harboured an inner darkness, a heartlessness, one he constantly had to hold in check. Even Beni, it seemed, had loaned my father one of his characteristics: like the robot, my father didn't need a suit to survive the void.

"Come," my father said. "This way."

He turned and disappeared through the black entryway of the Temple.

One by one, we followed.

CHAPTER 12

THE CHTHONIC ENORMITY of that place rendered the senses helpless. Its proportions were perhaps designed to reflect the immensity of the universe itself. One could easily forget that beyond the black walls there was another void. The Temple's shadowy recesses formed a cosmic horizon; the vault of the colossal chamber shone like the wheeling stars of alien constellations.

The gravity was still subnormal, and so though we tried to walk reverently, our gait was loping and uneasy—especially mine with my wounded leg. My father walked naturally as though the gravity were the same as Earth's.

Eventually, we found the other side of the main hall. There were countless doors. Through their shimmering darknesses, we beheld visions of spaces that should not—could not—exist. Yet there they were, taunting any eye that tried to cut through the veil to truth and reason. After a short time, a headache began to bloom ripely at the back of my corneas.

"This one," my father said simply.

We followed him through an archway, half-expecting to arrive on the shores of another world, but it merely led to a long hallway. Sconces set into the walls revealed the graven images of fourteen deities, each one sculpted with detail so meticulous it was revolting, somehow obscene. The proportions were appropriately gigantic for the scale of the Temple. I cannot remember all of the statues now, but several still haunt my mind.

There was an image unmistakably like that of a child. It lay on its side, one arm folded under its chin. Its feet were stumpy, fat, and three-toed. The head was disproportionately large, a third the size of the entire body, all its facial features sloughed, as though the sculpture had melted under intense heat. But I knew this was intentional, that the sculptor was no amateur and had captured their intended subject with an accuracy that overspilled into reverence. In the crown of the head there was a craterous depression, as though made by a blunt object. Most revolting of all was the deity's mouth: a toothy anus—puckered as though searching for a nipple to bite and suckle.

I must have stopped in the hallway to gawk at this horrifying idol, for my father lightly took my hand. It occurred to me for the first time, with terrifying clarity, that this meant he could not be a hologram, that he was *real*. A shiver ran through me, crown to toe.

"The Infant," he said, as though that explained all.

We continued down the corridor. There were many other gods there rendered in stone—if gods is indeed the right term. One resembled a cunt—there's no other way to say it. From its vulva, serpents spewed, birthed in some vile subversion of natural order and biology. The stonework was so exquisite and vivid that the serpents, and the orifice from which they emerged, seemed wet, glistening with excreted fluid. I would have vomited, had not my stomach been painfully empty. Instead, I retched and moved swiftly on.

I wonder now if Johnny and Raleigh wanted to turn back, whether we were all thinking we should get out, but none of us had the courage to speak. I suppose in truth I would not have turned back, even seeing those idols. The curiosity surrounding my father was too great. And he was real—I swear to you I felt his hand on me. But there is no point in wondering, I suppose. None of us said anything. We accepted the awfulness of that place in silent horror and wonder.

Eventually, the hallway ended, and we passed through another doorway. We were now in a medium-sized room, perhaps the first humanly proportioned room we had encountered in the Temple's vast complexity. By contrast, it seemed suffocatingly small.

The floor of the room was graven with a double-ouroboros, two circles touching, edge to edge, but without any overlap. This meant it would be possible to trace the design in a figure-8. From where Raleigh stood, he probably saw the infinity-sign. It occurs to me now that this was perhaps a key to its true meaning.

My father turned to the four of us.

"You have come a long way through the dark to obtain the Treasure of the Great Ones. But the Treasure is not bestowed lightly. Firstly, you three must pass the test."

Beni made a sad face, but stood to one side.

"Let's get it over with," Raleigh said. He looked half-mad, his finger still on the trigger of his gun, shifting his weight from foot to foot, which was not easy in low-g. Several times he unbalanced, which only added to his frustration.

"What is the Treasure?" Johnny said.

"None may perceive the image of the Truth, for there is nothing to behold and no eye that is not itself beheld," my father replied, seeming to enjoy the theatricality. "Now, let me explain the task to you. It is relatively simple. You must position yourself upon the double-ouroboros. Any place will do. Then, walk about the figure, tracing a complete circuit, until you return to your point of origin. Do not stray from the path. Once you have returned to where you started, then simply step off the circle. Do you understand?"

Raleigh's brow was furrowed, his face a mask of disgust.

"So we just have to walk around the eight?" Johnny said.

"Yes, in so many words. Return to where you started, and then leave the circle." My father smiled. I felt my guts churning.

"Fine!" Raleigh snapped. "I'll play your silly game."

He stepped onto the double-ouroboros. I half expected him to erupt in flames, to vanish into some pocket dimension, but nothing ill occurred. However, a look of surprise crossed his face. Johnny was next. I stepped on the sigil last. Immediately, I realised why Raleigh had looked so shocked: on the sigil, gravity was normal. I could walk as though I were on board the *Rossetti* or our requited home-world. It made my game-leg hurt like a bitch.

The sigil was raised up about four inches from the ground, fashioned from a pale stone that stood out against the otherwise green-black walls and floor of the Temple. The double-ouroboros appeared to have been hewn in one piece from its original source, for I could see no gaps in brickwork or evidence of it having been fitted together.

"Begin," my father said.

I began to walk forward. The stone walkway formed by the double-ouroboros was a little narrow, so I had to place one foot in front of the other, almost like I was a gymnast carefully striding along a bar. Still, keeping my balance was easy, and if I did slip, the fall would be only a few inches—if I was unlucky I'd sprain an ankle, and that was it.

Each of us moved in silence, looking down at our feet, tracing the shape. Eventually, I reached the place where the two circles intersected and began my path upon the second circle. There was something oddly satisfying about following the shape, a sense of completion and yet endless continuance. My mind began to wander to wild places. I saw myself as the Earth, orbiting the sun, completing my revolutions through the deep black of space. Then I was the moon, orbiting the Earth, but only ever showing one face toward it.

I suddenly realised that I had completed my circuit of the second circle and passed once again into the first, accidentally missing the place where I had stepped onto the ouroboros.

"You cannot go backwards," my father intoned.

I nodded. That made sense. Time didn't move backward, after all. Therefore, I would simply go around the circuit again, and re-arrive at the same point of my birth.

Birth? Where the fuck did that come from?

Shaking my head, as if to dislodge the esoteric ideas and wild images now frothing away in my subconscious, I began the circle again. I noticed, though only dimly, that both Raleigh and Johnny had also missed their destinations and were going around again.

This time I tried to concentrate, though it soon began to feel ridiculous. Did I really need to devote all my brainpower to remembering where I had stepped onto the sigil? I could easily recall the place and was not likely to miss it twice. I walked slightly faster, still making sure to place my footing precisely, but trying to gain ground. I now saw, in my mind's eye, a totem spinning on a table, a merry-go-round at a carnival, images echoing out of a distant epoch long dead. There were no carnivals now save the virtual kind. There were no clowns in space. Or were there? I began to see, in the double-ouroboros, a kind of image of the clown's overly exaggerated mouth. A dark grin clad in rough makeup.

I had missed my point once again. *Fuck. Stop letting your mind wander. Focus.*

I turned and saw Johnny and Raleigh also had missed their stations a second time. Each of them was gritting their teeth, sweat shining on their brows, visible even through their visors. They were exerting immense effort, but they could not break through, just as I could not. There was something about that sigil, something wrong with it. We were trapped in a labyrinth, caught on the spinning-wheel of time. I caught my reflection in the visor of my helmet and saw, with horror, that a streak of grey had appeared in one of my blood-red locks.

"No," I whispered.

I looked again at the place where I was able to step off from the sigil. Just one step backward and I could alight.

"You *must not* alight from anywhere other than the place of your beginning," my father said. He was grinning now, a terrifying gleam in his eye, his teeth resembling the clown's grimace I had moments ago been picturing.

I raced on, though it pained my leg greatly. Both Johnny and Raleigh were moving faster too, tracing the path quicker. I reached the midpoint and re-affirmed my intention. *Focus. Karla. There is the point. There, coming now. Step off. Step off!* But I could not step off. My feet took me past the point, onwards on the cyclical journey. I let out a throttled scream. Now I saw before me my mother's face, rotting and gangrenous, how she had looked on her last day alive. She had been so strong, so physically powerful. Even in her sixties she could have beaten strong men bloody. But now, Time had had its way with her. In her rheumy eyes, eyes that beheld nothing but smudges upon the canvas of existence, I saw again the double-ouroboros, the gears of Time grinding on with inexorable cruelty.

A fourth time, I passed the point.

Now I was running around the path of the double-ouroboros, tears scalding my face. I saw stars wink out. Planets collapse. Black holes turn.

Fifth. Sixth. Seventh.

I was losing Time, yet running faster and faster to make it up, my leg ablaze with pain. Johnny and Raleigh were the same. I could hear the low, monotone whine of their strangled shrieks. My heart thundered in my chest and I was sure, then, it could well burst, that we would each dash ourselves upon the double-ouroboros, broken upon the cliff-edge of unyielding Time. It could not be outrun; it could not be fought. My every effort of will was defeated by the loop.

Eighth. Ninth. Sprinting now. Out of breath. The oxygen in my suit was dropping rapidly towards the red. I could feel tears digging paths across my cheeks, spit drooling from my animal lips, raggedly sucking in breath after breath. And the pain in my leg grew to a tearing agony, drawing more tears to mix with my sweat.

Stuck. Stuck. Stuck in the monotonously cyclical progression of Time. What could possibly break this?

I passed the tenth loop, onto the eleventh. I sobbed uncontrollably where I could draw breath. My footsteps were stumbling now. Soon I would trip, fall face-first. I welcomed it. I hoped my visor would smash and the air be sucked from my lungs and my life end. Better than that endless circuit, and the visions I saw within it, the true terror and horror of a universe subject to Time's vicissitudes.

The point was coming. I could see it as I lurched down the final curve of the strange symbol, the self-enclosed loop of infinity. I saw it there. *The place of my birth. The place of my beginning.* The strange thoughts couldn't be dismissed. They rose unbidden from some deep place. I no longer had the strength to fight them or call them nonsense. Besides, I began to detect a dark truth in them.

I must step off. I must. I must.

But how? How to summon the strength? How to stop the relentless momentum?

I saw a flurry of images, but one returning more frequently than all the others: my mother's eyes.

The eyes!

It was the only way—a way of madness. Otherwise I would remain forever ensorcelled, entrapped. I had to cut off the conventional way of knowing in order to know more deeply. I had to look without looking. I had to abandon hope.

I closed my eyes.

I ran. I ran as fast as I could. Every step I feared my foot would come crashing down on the edge of the stone and I would fall, my ankle wrenched out of shape, but every time my sole found solid footing.

And then suddenly I was flying, leaping.

I opened my eyes and found myself falling slowly upon the deranged gravity of the Temple. I came to land with a soft thud, enough to knock the wind out of me, but my visor and suit remained intact. I sobbed with relief, with release.

I did not waste further time, however. I had to help Johnny and Raleigh. I rose, but to my surprise, each of them stood still, blinking furiously. The spell of the sigil had been lifted by one of us breaking its hold. My father was smiling warmly.

"Well done. You have collectively passed the test, passing

through the ouroboros into the Time of the Great Ones and the beginning. You are ready, therefore, to receive their Treasure. Come with me into the audience chamber. There, you will experience the Treasure."

I frowned. "Experience" the Treasure? That seemed an odd wording. But my mind did not have the strength to dwell on it. Johnny, Raleigh, and I actually embraced, perhaps for the first time in all our years of space-faring. We remained in that familial posture for a long time, before finally we started off after my father, who had passed through another doorway into a vaster room beyond.

"I won't do another trial," Johnny said. "I can't."

"We kill him if he tries to make us do another," Raleigh said, grimly. "Right, Karla?"

I nodded, earning my heartless epithet. I wanted so very badly to have some kind of relationship with my father, but how could I? He was clearly in service to powers we did not understand, barely human. He had almost killed me, and actively tortured me, in that trial. We had delayed enough in achieving our aim. The Treasure was ours. Either he would provide it, or we'd kill him and take it.

Little did I know my father was going to give us the Treasure all-too willingly.

And we would come to wish he never had.

CHAPTER 13

THE ANTECHAMBER WAS SQUARE—and empty. This surprised all of us. We had expected, perhaps, a living version of one of those fourteen effigies: some monstrous being beyond our comprehension. That or a glowing orb of cosmic power. But the chamber was devoid of entity or ornamentation.

Including my father, who had vanished without a trace.

"Where's the Treasure?" Raleigh growled.

"Dad?"

No answer came.

We searched the room, but it was bare. Was this a cruel joke? Or was something about to manifest in the void?

"Karla, what . . . " Johnny began, but his words failed as he looked down at his hands.

"Johnny?"

He was stooping, as though a tremendous weight had suddenly fallen upon his head. It looked like he could hardly lift his skull above shoulder height. Down, down, he drooped, seemingly unable to control it.

"Karla!"

A voice reverberated around the empty chamber.

The greatest gift of those who never die:

experience, unending, your eternal bliss!

Johnny screamed now as he dropped to his knees, his head bent downward at a sickening angle, beginning to curl in on itself, beginning to curl between his legs. They were bending him into a pretzel. How, I didn't know. I ran toward Johnny and grabbed him, tried to wrench him back into shape, not thinking that would be just as likely to kill him as allowing this inhuman process to continue.

His face was a mask of terror, tears streaming down his cheeks.

He looked in agony, and closer to him, I could hear the bones in his spine popping as his head continued to travel farther and farther. Now he was fully folded over himself, his head coming back around towards his own anus. Despite all I felt for Johnny, how much I wanted to help him, how much I was horrified by this unjust punishment, the dark irony did not escape me. He had spent his life kissing arse. Now, he was being forced to kiss his own. Perhaps the gods, or whatever they were, interpreted this as what he really wanted.

"Johnny!" I cried, reaching out, gripping his hand.

"K—" Words failed as Johnny's head was brought fully round with a sickening crunch, his visored face pushed into the folds of his own perineum. I heard glass crack, the force acting upon him far stronger than the plexiglass helm. The noise that left his lips, even muffled, will stay with me for the rest of my life, a groan of dire agony as glass pushed its way into his face and genitals, but also a sickening pleasure, as though he had at last arrived at a destination he'd long sought. It might have been funny if not for the disgusting way his spine was bent, the bones jutting aberrantly out through the flesh.

I leapt back as Johnny began to crawl. His legs were now uselessly cocked backward. All he could do was drag himself along the floor, blindly, with his hands. It's one of the most twisted things I've ever seen. He left smears of blood where he went.

"What the fuck are you doing?" I screamed to the vaulted ceiling, hoping some god—or maybe my father—would hear me.

The answer that came was a dark litany, *Enter the backward abysm of dreaming . . . Come forth into the extasis beyond the ouroboros . . . Drink of the Cup that hath no bottom . . . Impale thyself upon the Sword that hath no point . . . Enter . . . Enter . . . Enter . . .*

When I turned around I saw Raleigh. He, too, was undergoing changes.

"No . . ."

Raleigh's head had left his body—though he was still alive. It floated maybe seven feet from his twitching, puppet-like trunk. The head was still connected to the gushing stump of his neck by a horribly stretched thread of tissue and nerves. When all is said and done, we really do resemble machines. His elongated nervous system looked like the *Rossetti's* inner cabling. Raleigh's helmet had fallen to one side, and he spluttered blood from quivering lips; the blood drifted slowly from his mouth, touching the ground with the delicacy of a slow, autumnal leaf.

He twitched and spasmed, repeating two words over and over again.

"I know . . . I know . . . I know . . . "

Every repetition brought gouts of blood from his mouth.

Become the enfolding chiral of self-knowledge . . . Follow the path within the point . . . Cross the interstice and become extasis . . .

Raleigh's body fell to its knees, perhaps finally discarded. The motion stretched the nerves connecting his floating head even more, like the taut strings of a marionette. His eyes rolled into the back of his head as the secrets he had long desired poured into him, froth and phlegm spilling from his mouth, moon-white, lunatic.

"Raleigh . . . " That was all I could whisper, tears falling down my cheeks. I felt helpless, powerless. And indeed I was.

Then, it was my turn.

Beni stared at the proceedings blankly. Perhaps he'd had a power failure. Perhaps he too, in his own robotic way, was experiencing something that his sensory apparatus could not make sense of—and hence was frozen like a deer in headlights, or so the ancient saying goes.

Me. I felt their attention on me. I sensed their glee, too, like they'd saved the best for last. I knew I could not prepare myself for what was coming. I knew I could not possibly stand against the tsunami.

Becometh thy pride!

And then suddenly I was lifted up. No longer was I in that dark room. I was naked, nailed to a cross, in the midst of a bleak ocean. The waves rose and struck me, scouring my skin with their saltiness. I only had moments to take a breath before the next wave would come and batter me. Gasping, drowning. The pain in my hands and feet, exquisite.

Dark birds wheeled overhead. Then they descended. Horrid things they were. Neither crow nor vulture, black and filthy and cruel-beaked. They began to peck at my flesh, taking chunks out of my arms. I screamed in pain but then the waves came and I swallowed down water so sharp it cut my insides. I choked and spluttered. I coughed up a great deluge. The birds had taken flight moments before the wave came. Now they settled again, this time nibbling at my cheeks and breasts. Blood flowed from my nipples. It was excruciating.

It was bliss.

Please do not think me a psychopath, or cast judgement upon me, when I say this. But the experience was, in some fucked up way, exactly what I desired. I had been exalted to the same level as Christ. I had been elevated to a god, to suffer purposefully upon the cross, to rise above other mortals. The ocean, I knew, was a metaphor for the depths of space I had crossed time and time again. I was the Goddess of the Great Black Sea that we are all beholden to, we pirates and merchants and scavengers. So, it was glorious even as I suffered. And I began to welcome the bites of the crow-things. I began to welcome the asphyxiating battering of the merciless waves. The sting of salt in my wounds. The slow sandpaper scouring of my flesh. I looked forward to the time only my bones remained nailed to the cross, my consciousness peering blindly out from empty sockets, my skull-face grinning obscenely at the harshness of this new, divine reality. I hoped they took my eyes next, so I could more fully embrace the sensations of pain.

But the birds had other ideas. They alighted on my chest. They began to take pieces out of my sternum. The work was slow, for the waves kept up their relentless assault, and the birds had to scatter every time. But slowly but surely, piece by piece, they removed flesh, muscle, cartilage. They were diligent workers, peeling the pink and red tissue out of the wound. My screams were orgasmic. The washes of salt-water in the wound took the pain to a transcendental level. In the euphoria of my embodied arrogance, I thought: *Not even Christ suffered like this!*

Yes, I was mad, of that I have no doubt. But we are all mad. The Great Ones simply exposed our madness, and made it flesh.

I knew what the birds were digging for in my chest. They wanted to reach my heart. But what they found instead was a metal wall. *Tink, tink* went their beaks upon the cardiovascular augmentation, one I had carried ever since I was a little girl.

The doctors had never been able to explain why my heart failed when I was just a child. My mother told me it was a broken heart, because I couldn't let go of having never known my father. People used to believe that maladies of mind manifested in the body. I used to think that was nonsense, but now I'm not so sure. I think maybe my mother was right, after all. Wiser than I gave her credit for.

The birds wanted my heart, but I had no heart. My heart had been broken and destroyed long ago by a man I never met. In its place was an ugly metal thing. And as they tapped upon it, it was like a piece of me still existed in another reality. I could feel myself, in the dark room of the Temple. I could feel that material, physical body, with all its flaws. I was not naked, but still in my atmos-suit. I had been digging at the chest of the suit with a small, sharp stone. I could feel the stone in my hand now, roughly the size of a beak. My oxygen levels were flashing as low. I had wounds in my hands and feet. The suit was nearly compromised.

I stood upon a threshold then, one foot in the reality of my suffering godhood, and one in the real world—although I sometimes wonder how real this world can possibly be if it can be so easily cheated. I faced a choice: to follow the tapping of my metal heart back to limited reality, or to embrace ecstatic union, to let the waves drown me, the crows pick the flesh from my bones, to become a living effigy of my pride.

The latter was sorely tempting. What, in real terms, did I have to leave behind? Johnny and Raleigh were both taken by the Mystery. I had no family left. No real friends.

But then I heard a voice, not like the dark, sonorous whispers of what I presumed to be the Great Ones themselves, but a more human voice—my father's.

"The choice is yours, Karla. I, too, got to choose. But if you wish to return, know this: you will still belong to the Great Ones, and their tale will never leave your lips."

Eternity passed before I decided.

When I came back to my body, I was half dead. Oxygen-deprived. Bleeding. The cold of space was beginning to infiltrate my suit. Though the Temple afforded some protection, ultimately we were still in the void, and beyond my suit's lining death waited in a hundred different forms.

Without Beni, I would have perished there, and that would have been a cruel and pointless death, to have had the option of becoming one with the Great Ones, of rising above to the experience beyond comprehension, only to turn away and die guttering like a flimsy mortal.

But Beni had awoken from his programming stupor. I

clambered onto his back and he galloped like a demon horse through the Temple. And so I rode a headless centaur out of the Black Temple of *Gha'agshebla*.

There were things that came after that: scrambling into the *Rossetti;* barely making take-off due to an incoming asteroid stream that nearly demolished parts of that dark island. Then there was the torturous journey back to this waystation. Starvation. Nearly getting caught by the I.W.A. half a dozen times. Then there were the years after that, all of them passing by in a blur. I had to watch my back for a while because the Midas Clade came looking, but eventually they decided we were dead, and that the stories about a red-headed woman wandering the outer rim of the Sprawl had to be a myth. It seems I hadn't become a god, but instead a ghost. But all of that is simply the aftermath. I think the image I'd like to leave you with is me riding the headless centaur out of that lightless place. It feels fitting, somehow. Like a glimpse of freedom.

CHAPTER 14

I'VE TOLD MY story more times than I can count. And always, it's the same outcome. You see, I'm telling you this tale because I never want you to go to that place, never want you to have to feel that pain, that loss, that bliss . . . But I can see in your eyes that you're going. That's my real curse, see?

I'm cursed to give warnings that only entice people more.

I'm cursed to wander the galaxy spreading the message of the Great Ones, drawing more people to their Holy Temple, like moths to the proverbial flame. And O, how sweet that flame is! Like my father before me, I have become an emissary, an apostle of the new creed. Hear my words, foolish wayfarer, and try only if you dare:

"A floating temple lies beyond the veil,
where mortal and immortal worlds are shorn;
across the battlefields of black Algol,
the Great One's Treasure waits to be worn . . . "

THE STATION

LEE MOUNTFORD

MISSION LOG
DATE: 0334 (N.I.C.)
LOCATION: UNMAPPED SPACE
SHIP: "THE ARGENTO." FORMER DESTROYER CLASS
SHIP. REPURPOSED AS PATHFINDER.
MISSION: CHARTING UNKNOWN SPACE.

CHAPTER 1

"How is she?" Crynn Zaballa asked his childhood friend, Sona Tycho.

"Stressed and running on empty," Sona replied. The two Martians were discussing Sona's partner, Miko Goto. "She barely gets a break, and I can't remember the last time she had a full night's sleep. I don't see it changing anytime soon, not since Trenor threw himself out of a fucking airlock. The coward."

Crynn only nodded. His first instinct was to remind Sona that Trenor—the former joint-head of engineering—had succumbed to Astraecy. The cabin fever of being stuck on a ship in the deepest parts of space, with no way to escape, had broken many minds since humanity had ascended from the rock of Earth, though many believed there was more to it than that, and the affliction was actually a disease of some kind that could spread. Trenor wasn't the first it had happened to during the mission, and he wouldn't be the last. While Astraecy had never been Crynn's problem, he had once come close to running a laser cutter over his throat, though that wasn't down to madness. He had just been tired of living.

"Well, you've been non-stop a lot yourself," Crynn said. "This must be the first break you've had in a while."

The engineer shrugged. "Just trying to help. Plus, I get to see her more that way. She's had a lot of slack to pick up with Trenor gone."

Crynn gave another nod. He felt uncomfortable. He was happy to listen, but wasn't good at offering advice, and often struggled to accurately vocalise the thoughts in his head. As he had his whole life, he kept things basic. "I'm sure she appreciates your help."

The two Martians were in the mess hall of the Explorer class vessel, the Argento. The ship started life as a light-destroyer ship, but given it had served beyond its expected lifespan, it had now been repurposed to be pushed out to the deepest part of space until it finally stopped working.

Both Crynn and Sona, like everyone else on board, had been stuck on the ageing ship for five years. Crynn took a slow sip of the warm water from his metal cup. He wished it was something stronger. He'd been wishing that for over five years, and still felt the pull. And not just for alcohol, but also the euphoric blast of Dust. Though he was technically five years sober now, most of his waking days were spent dreaming about having the opportunity to indulge again. Substance abuse had ruined his life and got him a dishonourable discharge from the Sol Military Alliance after a promising early career, but he still couldn't find it within himself to purge the desire for more release.

He had Sona to thank for his continued sobriety. Had she not vouched for him, he would never have been able to transfer over to the Interstellar World Alliance and would instead have been shipped off to the metal mines on Venus. People who went there rarely came back. That, or he would have carried through with his suicidal intentions. He often wondered if it had been fate, or just good luck, that Sona had contacted him by chance and ended up talking him down.

Or . . . maybe it was bad luck.

Because in truth, being assigned as a low-level technician and security officer on the fringes of known space wasn't *too* much better than the mines of Venus. The mission of the Argento, and most vessels in its class, was to explore beyond the edges of what had previously been mapped out. Pathfinders, they were called. For the first few years, the Argento was able to ping messages back to the nearest outpost, but the ship had broken range for that over three years ago. Now, the crew collected data, which was to be handed over *if* they ever returned. That was far from a guarantee. In fact, the odds were against them. If any explorers did return, it was usually seen by command as something of a bonus, rather than expected.

Crynn and Sona sat opposite each other, hunched over one of the mess hall's long tables, both seated on the accompanying metal benches. Coming from a long line of Martians, with its reduced gravity compared to Earth, they bore the usual traits of their kind: taller and thinner than Earthlings. Sona kept her black hair short, clipped close to the scalp but leaving about an inch of length. Her slightly almond eyes had a pale-blue glint that stood out against her pale skin. Crynn could certainly understand what Miko saw in his friend, having had certain thoughts about her himself for many years. It could never have worked, of course.

He was the same height as Sona, a touch over six-five, and carried slightly more bulk, though not as much as those from Earth on board the ship. Both wore cotton jumpsuits, Sona's being the blue of an engineer, and Crynn's a dull orange colour assigned to lower ranks who, while holding an official role, were seen as little more than dogsbodies.

The mess hall they sat in could hold around thirty people, though they were the only two present. The floor beneath their feet was a mix of metal panelling and access grating that covered cables and pipes. The walls were a mix of metals and carbon fibre sections, as was the ceiling above, much of it lined with ductwork. To their right was an external wall. A row of drop-down seats with security belts were fixed to it, to be used for crew to strap themselves in should the ship need to pick up speed. Beside those seats was a large viewing window that Crynn kept glancing out of. He couldn't look out of it for too long in one go, as the infinite blackness, broken only with the small pinpricks of stars, made him feel somehow empty, like he didn't matter.

Which was true. He didn't. No one did. Not when you considered the vast emptiness all around them.

Careful, he told himself, *or you'll follow Trenor out of an airlock.*

Crynn was drawn back to the window. "When I was a boy, I always thought being on an Explorer ship would be the biggest adventure there was. But it seems charting out new space is pushed onto the fuckups."

"Because of the risk," Sona explained. Not that Crynn needed it, he was simply voicing his thoughts. "I heard over half Explorer ships are lost and never return. They malfunction or something happens and they are just gone. Sending help is too expensive and too risky. So the oldest rust-buckets are repurposed and labelled Explorer class, and the outcasts are packed in and sent off to 'further humanity,' which, in reality, is 'good luck, but we'll probably never see you again.' It's not too far removed from a prison sentence."

"I get that," Crynn said. "I just . . . I don't know. I thought it would have had more importance attached to it. I mean, what if we actually find something worthwhile out here? Beyond just more places to mine."

"We won't," Sona said. "Space is death. Emptiness. Nothing. The same thing over and over again. Unless you believe the ghost stories of the Agoul."

Crynn chuckled. "The Alliance believes it. A whole section of space we won't access because the higher-ups think something is out there. And word is, no one that goes out there comes back. Don't suppose we're a million miles away from it ourselves."

Sona shook her head with a smirk. "We're *well* over a million miles from it."

"You know what I mean," Crynn said.

"It's horseshit, Crynn," Sona stated. "You know it is. Yes, the brass is keeping everyone out of that sector of space, I'll grant you that, but I'm damn sure it ain't because of some old alien ghosts. Don't tell me you've been taken in by the stories?"

Crynn shrugged. "If it's not true, why have they built a defence grid?"

"The Chaos guns?" Sona asked. "More stories. I don't buy that they are real."

"Well, we don't get much in the way of facts all the way out here. All we have is gossip and stories."

"Don't tell me you've been taken in by all this crap?" Sona asked with a raised eyebrow.

"I haven't," Crynn said, though in truth, he wasn't certain. Part of him *wanted* to believe it. "But it's a shame there is no one else out here. Just us. You'd think we'd have met other civilisations or something by now."

"There are none," Sona replied with a shake of her head. "Just us."

Crynn took a breath and ran a hand over his shaven head. "I guess. Just depressing to think about."

"So don't think about it," Sona told him, flatly. She swung her legs back over the bench and stood up, lifting her tray that contained the remains of her meal: rations of tasteless, mostly synthesised beans and rice that was dispensed in small packs. "I'm going back on duty," she said. "See if I can help unload some of Miko's strain. Good catching up."

"Don't work too hard," Crynn told her with a grin.

Sona smiled. "I wish that were an option." She narrowed her eyes as she looked down at him. "You gonna be okay?" she asked. "You seem a little . . . I dunno . . . in your head."

"I'm always that way," Crynn replied. "You know that."

"Well . . . more than usual," Sona said.

Crynn looked back up at her. "I'm fine," he told her. "Honestly. We're all in the same situation, just doing the best we can."

"True, but if you feel like things are getting too much, come find me," she said. "Don't take Trenor's way out."

"I won't," Crynn said. "Don't worry. I'm past all that. Have been for a long time."

Sona studied his face, before eventually nodding. "Good. I'll see you later."

Crynn watched his friend leave the room. The door slid shut behind her and the silence and emptiness of the room began to weigh heavily. He looked out of the viewing window once more, feeling utterly alone.

CHAPTER 2

CRYNN SWUNG HIS legs from his lower bunk and placed his feet on the floor. The dormitory was awash in blinking amber light as the alarm sounded. The groaning sounds of those woken from their sleep surrounded him.

What now?

While the amber alarm wasn't exactly a common occurrence, Crynn had seen plenty. The reason was to signal everyone's attention and get people to their stations. The alert was seen as important, but not serious. If the situation was deemed critical, the light around them would have been red.

Like it had been when Trenor had sealed himself in the airlock and had started the countdown for the external door.

The man in the bunk above Crynn—Taiyo Kim—dropped to the floor with a heavy thud. He started to dig through his footlocker and pulled out his jumpsuit.

"This better be important," Taiyo grumbled.

Petra Zika, who slept in the bed adjacent to Crynn, was almost fully dressed already.

"My guess is the sensors have picked up asteroids," she said. "Been a while since we've come across any, and I heard command plans to mine the next ones we find for water."

"We've got plenty of water," Taiyo said. "We have bays full of the stuff, all bottled. It's warm and tastes like shit, but it's water."

"But we've never managed to fill up the reserves. If they have found ice asteroids, expect to be here for months while the mining drones do their thing."

Taiyo shook his head as he continued to dress. "My guess is it's more problems with the ship. The fucking thing is falling apart. Probably the antimatter cores failing."

"I'm pretty sure that would warrant more than an amber alarm," Petra said.

She was correct, of course. The Argento needed the antimatter cores to survive. They were the heart of the ship, pumping energy around every part of the vessel. Particle accelerators generated antimatter and dumped it into the cores, which reacted with the matter already there. That reaction generated the power which was then fed into huge storage batteries before being pushed around the Argento.

The antimatter cores had been one of the three technological pillars which helped humanity navigate the stars, with the other two being the localised particle accelerators, as well as the warp drives. Those three things had allowed ships to move close to the speed of light. Each interstellar ship was fitted with huge drive thrusters at the back—and the Argento had three—which increased acceleration up to a point. Then, the particle accelerators would kick in, working at maximum, dumping antimatter into the cores. The only other systems online at this point were critical ones, so that most of the power could be diverted to the cores, and the warp drive. Once the ship had sufficient power, the bubble drive kicked in, which contracted the space ahead of the ship, and expanded it behind, pausing the vessel faster and hitting immense speeds.

Of course, flying at such speeds was hazardous. The risk of impact was enormous, and at that speed, any ship colliding with something would create a multi-kiloton blast. For that reason, protected space lanes had been set up, which were regulated and closely monitored, keeping them clear of debris. These lanes formed a spiderweb across charted space–what some pirates and privateers referred to as "The Sprawl"–and ships could only use the warp bubble in these channels.

The Argento had used them to reach Velliam station, one of the outposts on the edge of mapped space. During the flight, the crew were all in protected stasis pods, letting the computer handle the navigation. No human could survive such speeds outside of the pods. There had been instances of some idiots not being in their pods when the bubble drive kicked in, and all that was left of them was a red smear when the ships dropped out of their highest speed.

Therefore, since entering uncharted space, the Argento could only rely on standard propulsion.

Crynn stood up and dug out his own jumpsuit. He slipped one leg inside.

"Come on then, Crynn," Petra said, "what's your guess?"
"No idea," Crynn replied.
"None of us has an idea," Petra replied. "That's why we're guessing."
"We'll find out soon enough," Crynn said.
Petra just rolled her eyes. "You're no fun, you know that?"
I do, Crynn thought to himself.
Petra turned to Taiyo and extended her hand. "Two days rations says I'm right."
Taiyo hesitated, studying her hand. "If neither of us are right?"
"Then no one wins."
He shrugged. "Fine, fuck it." Taiyo then shook.
Crynn followed the other two as they filled in the surge of people who slowly walked out of the east crew-quarters. He was curious as to what was happening, and any potential change in monotony of everyday life aboard the Argento might have been welcome, had it not pulled him from his sleep.
He made his way to the eastern technical lab, where he served as a low-level assistant, as well as doubling up as security—a role pretty much pointless aboard the ship. The most he'd ever had to do in that capacity was break up the occasional fight.
The technical lab was responsible for studying things the Argento had found on its journey, which thus far had proven to be very little, mainly metals from asteroids. Because of that, their role often consisted of backing up the engineering department and helping sift through the ship's data files. However, the technicians were the smallest contingent on board, so the help they offered to the engineers was quite limited when taking into account the workload of Miko Goto's team.
The lab mainly consisted of many workstations linked to the on-board network, as well as some containment chambers, most of which were empty, save for a few with metal deposits inside. The team who had already been on duty were looking around in mild bewilderment.
"Heard anything?" Crynn asked one of the senior technicians nearer to him.
"Nope," the woman said. "We were running diagnostics on the cores and the alarm hit. Captain hasn't given us any more information as yet."
"The cores all okay?" Crynn asked.

The nonchalant shrug didn't fill him with confidence. "As well as can be expected," his colleague replied. "For such an old system, anyway."

Antimatter cores, while playing such a huge role in the evolution of humanity, were still spectacularly unstable. Overcharging or running them for too long could easily cause a chain reaction that would destroy a ship, and everything around it for hundreds of kilometres. They had also been known to simply stop working, leaving ships as dead husks, floating in the dark while the crew suffocated.

"Need anything from me?" Crynn asked.

"Not that I can think of," the senior technician replied. "Just stand around and look busy until we hear what's going on."

They then heard a voice come over the loudspeaker system. It was Captain Ellis. "All personnel, this is the captain. I want you to man your posts. Specific instruction will filter through all chiefs of departments. I can tell you that we have spotted a strange . . . anomaly . . . up ahead, and we are moving closer to investigate."

Crynn saw the technicians in the room turn to each other and speak in hushed whispers.

"Anomaly?"

"What have they seen?"

The captain went on. "Remain vigilant and we will keep you updated." There was an audible click over the speakers as Captain Ellis shut off his communication.

Another technician, this one mid-level, approached the more senior officer. "Ever heard anything like that before?" he asked.

The woman before him shook her head. "No. The term 'anomaly' is disconcertingly vague."

"That's what I was thinking."

"Regardless," the senior technician went on, "do as the captain said. Man your post and await further info." She turned to Crynn. "Your orders don't change. Just look busy and stay out of trouble."

"*Or,*" the other man chimed in, "Crynn could go to the nearest viewing window and see if he can see anything. If we don't need him for anything else, then why not?"

Crynn saw the senior technician furrow his brow and rub his chin. It would be going against protocol, so he doubted—

"Do it," the senior woman said with a firm nod. "Keep your head down and keep out of sight."

"Is that . . . is that okay?" Crynn asked with a frown. "The captain said—"

"It's fine," his superior insisted with a wave of her hand. "We won't miss you here. I'd be interested to know if there is anything out there we can see. If you're uncomfortable with that, feel free to stand around here and just get in everyone's way."

With that, the officer turned away and moved over to a workstation, leaving Crynn with the other technician who had first made the suggestion.

"Go," the man said. "I'd go in your place if I could. Who knows, you might get to see something interesting."

"Or more asteroids," Crynn replied.

"Perhaps," the other man replied, "but if it *was* just asteroids, the captain would have said so. But to me, 'anomaly' means something new. Just be sure to tell me what you see."

The technician had a point. Crynn nodded and turned and walked from the room. None of the others paid him any notice as he exited through the door. He made his way through the corridors of the Argento, and as he did, he felt an adjustment in the thrust of the ship.

We're slowing down.

He entered the mess hall where he'd spoken with Sona the previous day—again finding it empty—and strode over to the viewing window, one of only a few on the ship. They were seen as structural weak points and were only allowed in a select few zones that could be easily and quickly closed off from the rest of the ship.

Even before he approached the fifteen-foot long, full height aperture, he saw the light generated by the strange anomaly wash across the glazed screen. He felt a tinge of apprehension . . . and maybe even excitement. After years of charting new space, which was exactly the same as old space, the Argento had nothing of real value to show for it. Now, perhaps . . .

The flashes of light seemed to be a dull, yellowish-white that came in crackles and bursts. Crynn walked up to the window and turned his head to the left, hoping that the cause of the lightshow was visible from that side of the ship.

It was.

Crynn focused, feeling a small swelling of wonder. The last time he could remember feeling anything like it was with the aid of 'dust' and other substances. In fact, back then he'd hallucinated tendrils of pure light and flashes of electrical ladders, similar to what he was currently seeing, only now it was all real.

The phenomenon kept coming in erratic bursts, usually emanating from a point far ahead of the ship, though it was impossible for Crynn to determine just how much distance was between the Argento and the anomaly. He felt the ship eventually come to a full stop as the flashes of strange light continued, with arms snaking out from a central point, along with bursts of what looked to be gaseous clouds. It was only slightly ruined by the light pollution given off by the amber alert that pulsed within the mess hall.

A cosmic storm? Crynn thought. He'd heard the theory of them but had no idea whether such things really existed. Certainly not ones that seemed to just spring up out of nowhere. There was no way the Argento would have gotten this close to the anomaly, in relative terms, had they noticed it earlier.

And the fantastical lightshow was hard to miss against a sea of pinpricked blackness.

The captain's voice came over the ship's speakers again: "All crew, we are monitoring the situation closely. From what we can tell, there is no immediate danger to the ship, but we won't be travelling any closer. However, we do plan to launch probes and drones into the phenomenon we are seeing to try and gather more data. Everyone is to continue to monitor their stations and await further updates."

Crynn continued to watch. He saw the thruster trails from the drones and probes fired from the ship and the small objects disappeared in the distance as they closed in on the irregularity. After another ten minutes of being lost in the first interesting thing he'd seen in the vacuum of space, he noticed something. The reach of the lightning cracks and tendrils of light were growing, getting closer to the ship. And the dull clouds that were continually pumping out of the central point of the anomaly were becoming denser and pushing farther outward as well.

The lightshow crackled to life yet again, pushing ever closer, its strands weaving together like a great, cosmic web as even more light, this a brilliant white, started to ebb and pulse from the centre of the phenomena.

Suddenly, the amber alert in the room blinked to red.

Captain Ellis spoke again. "All crew, strap in. Secure what you can. The situation is changing. We need to move away from the anomaly."

Shit.

Crynn quickly darted to his side, moving beyond the viewing window and to one of the wall-mounted seats. He lowered the bottom and dropped into it before strapping himself in. From his position, he was still able to look outside at the ever-approaching cosmic storm . . . if that's what it was. Part of him was tempted to flee the mess hall and get to somewhere more secure, because if the window blew, he was a dead man, and would get sucked out into space. But he just couldn't draw himself away. To him, it felt like a moment, an opportunity to witness something completely new. Not just for himself, but maybe for humanity as well. If that wasn't worth risking whatever kind of life he had left, what was?

Soon there was a lurch and the Argento started to move forward again. While the many smaller, localised thrusters on the hull of the ship allowed for small amounts of movement in all directions, the Argento would not be able to pick up any speed if moving backwards, so Crynn knew the plan would be to pick up some momentum and then attempt to veer away from the anomaly, before trying to distance the ship from it.

The huge, rear drive thrusters began to kick in, pushing the Argento on faster, causing the entire ship to rumble as the immense beasts came to life, fed by initial fuel reserves before the antimatter cores took over.

Crynn kept his eyes on the phenomenon outside the viewing window as the ship moved forward. With everyone else on board confined to their roles, not many would be able to witness what was happening with their own eyes, other than maybe those up on the control bridge. But *he* was going to take in as much as he could for as long as he could.

The intensity of the light suddenly increased. Crynn was forced to narrow his eyes, then turn away completely. As he did, he blinked rapidly, dazzled, and shocked by something he'd noticed.

A silhouette at the centre of the light source.

He turned his eyes back to try and look again but it was simply too bright, and the room around him was now awash with an intense glare, the white of it even overpowering the red, pulsing light of the alert.

Damn it, he cursed to himself, desperate to gaze again upon what he'd seen. Crynn was certain there was something out there, in the middle of the cosmic storm. Something massive.

Even with his eyes closed, the impression of that strange object, with its many arms and unidentifiable shape, remained seared in his mind as a dark afterimage. The light around him increased, almost burning through his eyelids. The ship around Crynn began to violently shake. The sounds of grinding and screeching metal overpowered the audible alarm that kicked in to join the red, flashing visual aid.

Crynn's heart rate began to spike. He suddenly regretted the decision to stay and buckle himself into the mess hall, fearing the window could explode at any moment.

His body rocked within his restraints, and he let out a scream as the sounds of chaos around him grew. A hellish rumbling began to build.

The cores!

His head snapped back to the wall behind him, then was forced to the left as the Argento was battered by . . . something. Perhaps the arms of lightning and light, perhaps something else. Crynn was still unable to open his eyes enough to look out of the window and check. His eyelids now offered little protection, and through them everything still seemed bright.

He knew that opening his eyes now would blind him. So, all he could do was helplessly sit in his chair and scream, though he could no longer hear his own voice.

This is it. The ship is done. This is how I die.

Crynn's thoughts ran to his friend, Sona. He wondered if she felt as terrified as he did. Probably not. She was stronger than him. Almost unflappable. And at least she would be surrounded by people when she died, close to the one she loved. Crynn would be alone, as he had been so often in life. Unable to integrate and become one with the crowd and forced to the edges. The thought made his impending death seem worse.

Then . . . the light beyond his eyelids receded, fast enough to have almost blinked out. The violent shaking of the ship eased as well, as did the squealing of metal, though the concerning rumbling of the drive cores continued.

Crynn slowly opened his eyes.

His vision was initially blurry, and he had to blink a few times to regain focus, but when he looked outside, the lightshow from the anomaly was largely gone. There were still small bursts of white light, like small explosions, within the strange clouds and gases that dominated everything outside the viewing window. But the storm itself was no more. Crynn felt the ship moving, but the propulsion was uneven and the Argento still vibrated and juddered.

The alarm still blared and the mess hall was still drenched in pulsing red light, but Crynn allowed his head to drop back to the wall behind him. His body slowly relaxed. He continued to peer out of the window, remembering the image he'd seen at the centre of the anomaly.

Is it still there?

The mass of clouds the Argento now seemed lost in made it impossible to know for sure.

"Attention all crew!" Crynn jumped as the captain came over the loudspeaker again. "All engineering and technical crew report to the antimatter cores immediately. This is an emergency.

CHAPTER 3

CRYNN SPRINTED BACK through the corridors to the technical labs, passing a handful of people coming the other way as he did. The small group of personnel going the other way looked every bit as worried as Crynn felt.

After entering the lab, he stopped as he saw a number of technical personnel packing up equipment. One walked towards Crynn, who was blocking the doorway.

"Wanna move out of the way?" the tall, gangly Martian said. He had a stack of data modules and energy converters in his arms.

"Sorry," Crynn said and stepped aside. "What's happening?"

"Captain has been in touch with the team leader. Apparently, the cores have been affected. Close to overloading."

"Shit," Crynn uttered.

"Shit's the word, my boy," the Martian responded as he walked past Crynn. "A few of us are on our way over to engineering now to see how we can help."

"If you can't?" Crynn asked.

The man turned and shrugged. "We die, I guess."

Crynn nodded. He didn't know how else to respond. "Need a hand?" he asked as a throng of other technicians pushed their way through.

The Martian smiled but shook his head. "Not sure you'll be much help, but thanks." The man turned and walked along with the others. Crynn felt decidedly useless—something he was familiar with. He then moved deeper into the labs, which now looked half-empty. He studied the faces of the remaining crew members. Everyone was concentrating on their work but looked decidedly pensive. It was eerily quiet as well, with none of the normally idle chatter that he heard when on shift. Crynn approached a workstation, sat down and logged in. He busied himself by checking the ship's main diagnostics—information that was freely available to anyone. He didn't have the clearance to do anything beyond just look at the information, of course, but the flashing alerts on the screen told him everything he needed to know.

The power levels being generated from the antimatter cores kept spiking to unsustainable levels. In addition, the particle accelerators were malfunctioning, generating periodic bursts of antimatter that were being dumped into the cores.

That's why we aren't slowing down, Crynn realised. The Argento didn't have the luxury of stopping the thrusters as it needed them to burn through the generation of antimatter that the engineers didn't seem to be able to get under control. But with the cores being so unstable, the constant use could mean an overload at any moment.

If the engineers can't shut down the particle accelerators, we're fucked.

Everyone on the ship waited. Those not directly involved with the repairs could do nothing else. Minutes turned to hours. During that time, there had been a few instances where the ship began to shake so violently that Crynn thought their time had come. Thankfully, the engineers somehow got the situation under control each time.

Eventually, the constant juddering of the Argento ceased, though Crynn could tell they were still moving forward. The head technician, at the far end of the labs, jumped on a vid-call, though Crynn couldn't hear what was being said. Once the call ended, the team leader called everyone over to him.

"Okay," he began, "here's the situation. We've managed to power down the accelerators and cut the feed to the main thrusters. So the ship isn't using power anymore. The immediate danger is averted. *However*," he went on, "we are drifting. And we're moving too quickly for the localised thrusters to slow us without further power from the cores, which are close to being fried." His face looked ashen.

"There's something else, isn't there?" Crynn asked.

The head technician nodded. "There's something out there. Radar and sensors have picked up an enormous structure. We don't know what the hell it is, exactly, but it's directly in our path. If we can't stop the ship or divert our course, we'll collide with it."

A flurry of questions was launched at the technician:

"What structure?"

"How did we not see it before?"

"Then why don't we turn the fucking ship?"

At the mention of this mysterious structure, Crynn's mind jumped back to what he'd seen while in the mess hall: that great thing at the centre of the anomaly. The head technician held up his hands to calm the crowd.

"We don't know what it is," he said. "The captain said . . . he said it almost looks like a massive space station of some kind."

"What?" someone shouted. "Impossible. We haven't built anything out here."

The team leader gave a slow nod. "Right. It . . . isn't ours."

Another concerned murmur went up.

"Impossible," someone shouted.

"It's the Agoul," someone else threw in.

Yet again, the head technician raised his hands. "We don't know who built it or why it's here. And we didn't see it before because of the anomaly. There doesn't seem to be any power signals coming from it, so our superiors have a working theory that it's derelict and inoperable. Could be that the irregularity we saw was recurring, and it knocked the station out of commission a long time ago."

"Or . . . " a woman next to Crynn began, "it's still inhabited, and the power was knocked out by the same irregularity that fucked up the Argento."

"That's a possibility command is aware of," the team leader said. "Truth is, we really don't know anything."

Crynn's mind was whirling. *Is that what I saw? A fucking space station, built by another race?*

The implications made him feel overwhelmed, similar to how he'd felt when witnessing the anomaly back in the mess hall. But the impending danger of crashing into the station put paid to any wonderment its existence might have caused.

"So why don't we turn the ship?" the woman next to Crynn went on to ask. "Or why didn't they adjust course before they cut the thrusters?"

The man before the crowd hesitated before answering. "We weren't able to," he eventually said.

"Why?" the woman probed.

But the head technician shrugged. "We're not sure. Command

said they kept trying, but the ship wouldn't respond. They think the anomaly has damaged the navigation systems, even though they couldn't see any obvious faults."

Crynn spoke up. "So . . . what's the plan. Are we just gonna let ourselves drift into the station?"

"No," the head technician replied. "They are going to try and stabilise the cores as much as they can then reboot. If we can generate enough power to the reverse thrusters, we can stop the ship, then power down again. But, at the moment, the cores and accelerators are still not responding how they'd like."

"How far away is the station?" Crynn asked. "And how long do we have until impact?"

"A few hours," the man replied. "With the thrusters disabled, we're no longer speeding up, but we ain't slowing down either."

More voices of discontent started to rise up. The woman next to Crynn eventually spoke up loudest. "So . . . what do we do in the meantime?"

"Stay at your posts and assist with data transfer. Anything to help out the engineers." More questions started to come, but the head technician raised his voice. "*Look,*" he snapped, "I know you want more answers, but I don't have them just yet. This is an emergency and I need you to do your jobs. Get to work."

He then turned his back on the gathered crowd and moved away to his post. The remaining crew stood dumbfounded.

"It's the Agoul," one man said. "Has to be. It's the only other life we know of out there."

"The Agoul are just ghost stories," someone else shot back.

"Then what else could it be?" the first man asked, his arms outstretched. "Because I sure as fuck don't remember hearing of any other races out here in the black. And if it *is* the Agoul, we don't stand a chance. We're doomed."

"Just calm down," the woman who had been standing next to Crynn said. "Like the chief said, we don't know anything yet. Don't jump to conclusions. The station isn't showing signs of power. If there is life on board, and I'm not certain there is, they have their own problems."

Crynn was listening to what was being said, but it was hard to focus. They had, evidently, just discovered absolute proof of alien life. It felt like he was present for a landmark moment, albeit one clouded by impending danger. And if the Argento didn't survive, how long would it be before anyone else got out this far and found the same thing?

But if they *were* able to survive, then surely that would mean they could return to civilisation and report what they had found. The mission would be over. They might even get to retire with some sort of accolade, given a comfortable life as reward for their astonishing discovery.

It was a pleasing thought, and one that went some way to breaking the gloom of the ticking clock as they hurtled towards the mysterious station. It was also tinged with disappointment at himself, as Crynn's mind fantasied about retiring to a comfortable spot, only to again indulge the call of Dust, the thought of its effects feeling like a warm embrace.

"Crynn?"

A voice called him from his daydreaming. He looked up to see someone looking at him expectedly. It was the same senior technician that had earlier sent Crynn to the mess hall. "Yeah?" Crynn responded.

"You went to a viewing window when the anomaly hit, right?" the man asked. "Did you see anything?"

It was only then Crynn realised he hadn't relayed anything of what he'd seen, having been too caught up with more recent developments.

He didn't know where to start. "Saw a lot," he eventually said. "Strange lights, that were almost blinding. It was like some kind of . . . storm. I don't know how else to describe it."

"Did you see a station?"

"I . . . I saw something," Crynn said as everyone listened intently. "It looked to be at the centre of the anomaly. Must have been the station."

"What did it look like?" a woman asked.

Crynn paused. "It's hard to say. I was struggling to see much because of the light. But it was *big* and had these great arms coming from it, but . . . it was hard to make out a defined shape. It sometimes felt like the edges kept shifting or changing."

"So it didn't look like any of ours?" the same woman questioned.

Crynn gave a firm shake of his head. "No. Not even remotely. It was far bigger than anything we have. And its shape was just . . . strange."

"And you say it was in the middle of the storm?" the senior technician asked.

Crynn nodded once more. "Yes. Pretty much *exactly* in the centre."

"And did you notice anything else?" the technician went on. "Any other ships around it, docking or anything? Any moving parts that would have indicated it was active?"

"Why would ships dock in *that* storm?" someone asked.

"Well, they might have been caught unawares, like we were."

"I didn't see anything like that," Crynn said. "I didn't get the chance to look at it for long."

"I thought I told you to get back to work?" a voice called. It was the head technician, who was now walking back over. "What are you all talking about?"

"Nothing, sir," Crynn was quick to say. Though he had been sent to the mess hall by someone more senior, he wasn't certain if the chief would have been okay with him leaving his post—whatever that was supposed to be—and didn't want the headache of a dressing down. Thankfully, no one contradicted what he said.

"Then do as ordered and get back to it." He looked around the group. "That means everyone. We're working to save our lives here, so start acting like it."

CHAPTER 4

A FEW HOURS had passed with little in the way of updates. Captain Ellis hadn't communicated anything further over the ship's speakers, preferring instead to consult directly with heads of department, who then relayed any information seen as relevant. The only major piece of information was that the engineers had attempted to jumpstart the antimatter cores but failed in doing so.

Which meant they were still on course for destruction.

As was common for Crynn, he was struggling to immerse himself in the work going on around him, resorting to asking people if they needed help with anything, not having clear instructions from any of his superiors. He'd been given a few menial tasks, but nothing of any value.

Even at such a critical time, it pained Crynn to be constantly overlooked and pushed away. Everyone needed to be chipping in, and he knew he could help, which made things even more frustrating.

Can you really help, though? a little voice inside asked. *Or would you just get in the way and make things worse. There's a reason you're ignored.*

He tried to push aside the doubt, but it was difficult to do so. It just reaffirmed he didn't really have a place on the ship. A place *anywhere*. Maybe if they needed someone to shoot or fight, he'd have more utility, but even then he knew he'd never been the best soldier in his squad.

At one point, he'd been sent briefly down to the mess hall again to see if he could see anything. There were other people present that time, all peering out the viewing window, but the angle the ship was travelling at—head on to the space station—as well as the heavy blanket of clouds around them meant they couldn't make anything out. Beyond, that was, the continued and sporadic bursts of light that exploded at seemingly random locations.

Crynn didn't stay in the mess hall long the second time and soon headed back to relay the disappointing news.

As he continued to watch everyone else work, Crynn began to feel more and more restless, with nothing to take his mind off what was coming. He wondered how Sona was doing.

Eventually, the head technician spoke out to everyone. "Okay, listen up," he bellowed. "Time is running out, so we've been told engineering are gonna try and start up the cores."

"Are they stable?" someone asked.

There was a brief hesitation before the answer came. "No, not particularly," the chief replied. "But we're running out of time and we need to stop or change course. Command says we've left it as long as we can, so . . . we have to try."

Crynn picked up on an almost defeatist tone in the head technician's words, as if he didn't agree with the decision and was resigned to failure. It seemed the others noticed this as well, as everyone remained silent.

The chief went on. "It's going to happen in ten minutes. Stay at your posts and help engineering with data however you can."

That was all he gave before returning to his own station. A few of the crew cast each other concerned glances, then carried on with their own work. Silence reigned once more. Crynn considered asking whether everyone should strap in, as they had when the anomaly hit, but soon decided against it. He realised they needed all hands on deck to give them the best chance possible. Besides, if they failed and the cores overloaded, what good would being strapped into a chair do? A seatbelt wouldn't save them from evaporation.

The minutes slowly ticked by. After what seemed like an hour, the captain's voice crackled over the speakers. "All crew, we are attempting the reboot. Stand by."

The tapping of keyboards and clicking of datapads suddenly ceased. Crynn held his breath.

The Argento shook, enough to almost topple Crynn. Loose equipment and cups vibrated off their perches. A low rumble emanated throughout the ship that grew progressively louder and louder. After a few minutes, everything stopped.

"Did it work?" someone asked. Crynn looked down to the other end of the lab and saw the chief take an incoming call. After a few moments, he disconnected and stood up, facing everyone.

He looked forlorn. "They've powered back down," he stated. "The engineers couldn't get things online and the cores and accelerators were destabilising too much. They've had to abort."

After a moment's silence, Crynn found the confidence to speak up. "But . . . they're going to try again, right? We can't just let ourselves crash into that thing."

"Yes," the chief said. "They'll try again soon. But . . . we don't have long left. About an hour. If it doesn't work next time . . . "

He didn't need to finish the sentence. The crew were expecting maybe a little more from the head of their department, but the chief simply returned to his work. No words of encouragement or a rousing speech in their hour of darkness.

Nothing.

Crynn wasn't able to distract himself or avert his thoughts to focus on anything except their impending doom. He'd never particularly enjoyed life, not since he was a child, but he certainly wasn't ready to die.

The wait for the next announcement was excruciating. When it came, only thirty minutes remained on the clock.

"All crew," the captain said. "Brace yourselves. We're going to try again." He hesitated, before following up with: "this time, we won't switch off the cores. We either stop or turn the Argento, or . . . " He trailed off, before eventually adding, "It's been a pleasure serving with you all. Let's hope we have a few more years left with each other yet."

Crynn looked over to the chief technician. Everyone did. He gazed back, eyes close to being blank.

"Good luck, everyone," he eventually said, then lowered his head back down to his control console.

The others got back to work, tapping on their keyboards with worry evident on their brows.

"Can I help with anything?" Crynn asked. His voice, not much more than a whisper, cracked as he spoke.

No one responded. Barely anyone looked back at him, save for the person who was closest, and that was only a brief glance. A feeling of restlessness grew. He couldn't just sit and do nothing while waiting for the end. He needed *something* to distract himself.

Fuck it, Crynn thought to himself. He got to his feet and walked towards the door, half expecting someone to speak up and stop him. No one did. He then walked back to the mess hall once more.

If I'm going out, I'm going to see as much of it as I can.

No sooner had he made it to the window and strapped himself into the chair, than the ship again started to shake and roar as the cores burst into life. Now, however, Crynn *did* have something to distract himself with the wondrous and slightly terrifying sight outside of the viewing window.

As the rumbling and savage vibrations around him grew stronger, Crynn gazed at the station's enormous arms that ran off into the distance, eventually becoming lost in the thick cloud that engulfed the section of space they were in. Those small explosions of light, which were much more frequently close to the massive station, helped illuminate the strange, alien structure.

What Crynn could see of the station made little sense to him. Those huge arms looked more like thick tendrils, running off in strange directions, with bends and turns in them. Crynn couldn't understand what purpose such shapes could serve. It certainly wasn't an ergonomic use of materials to build in such a way. Rather than a structure with a specific function, the alien space station more resembled something organic in form.

Crynn wasn't able to make out what material the station was constructed from. It was dark in colour, and he assumed some kind of metal, but couldn't really be sure. The surface of the station was smooth, however, with no visible joints, welded parts, or abutting materials that would have indicated different pieces of the station knitted together. Nothing so big could have been made in a single section, Crynn knew, but any connections—say where the arms began to bend and twist—were simply not visible. That in itself spoke to how advanced the strange race behind the station was.

The great arms outside dominated Crynn's view, blocking out just about everything else. They were so huge he couldn't really comprehend how close the Argento was to impact.

His shoulders ached where the belts dug in. His body was bouncing around in the seat as the Argento struggled, sounding like it was going to rip itself apart. He just hoped the other crew around the ship had managed to get secured in good time, otherwise there might be some pretty severe injuries on board. Not that it would matter, the way things seemed to be going.

We might not even make it to impact, Crynn thought, such was the ferocity at which the ship was shaking and vibrating. Even so, the Argento didn't seem to be slowing down.

After a few more minutes, Crynn noticed a change in the vibrations around him. He saw a plume of blue light come from somewhere ahead of the window, close to the ship.

No, on *the ship.*

It was the localised thrusters, those mounted around the hull of the Argento to change course or halt momentum. There was one fitted to the ship down from the window he looked out of, and the blue plume of light he saw was the burned energy residue being pumped from the thruster.

Crynn couldn't be certain if engineering had finally gotten control of the cores and were able to supply power safely to the thrusters, or if it was just a last-ditch attempt to stop, while pushing the already unstable cores. Regardless, he kept his eyes on the window as more of the station's form came into view. The Argento grew closer and closer, with the reverse thrusters seemingly having little effect.

How can that be?

With his fists clenched, Crynn held his breath as the ship came up onto a vast stretch of the station's hull.

This is it!

Crynn was tempted to close his eyes but managed to find the strength to keep them open. He watched as the Argento reached the surface of the hull . . . then kept going. With a frown of confusion, Crynn leaned close to the window and realised they had passed into an opening within the structure.

We're inside the station!

With little light to see, other than that afforded by the thrusters, Crynn couldn't see much of the internal space. In an instant, Crynn's body was thrust to one side as he felt a sudden arrest in the ship's forward momentum. The reverse thrusters burned and the Argento continued to shake, rattle and vibrate. Crynn heard a troubling low rumble over the squealing of protesting metal, indicating the cores still weren't quite stable. Still, The Argento continued to slow down.

It took a few minutes more, but eventually all forward momentum had halted. Crynn heard the localised thrusters turn and adjust their position as the ship lowered, followed by the sound of the many landing gears coming down from the underside of the

Argento's hull. He felt the impact as the ship touched down. The light from the thruster extinguished and the ship grew still . . . and silent.

No more rumbling or shaking, or the screeching of metal.

Crynn could scarcely believe what had just happened. *We've* docked *in the fucking station!*

CHAPTER 5

CRYNN STOOD SHOULDER to shoulder with the mass of people gathered in the largest cargo hold aboard the Argento. The only people not present were the skeleton crew needed to run the ship.

The last time this many people had been gathered in the hold was back when the Argento was about to leave Velliam station to undertake its mission. Back then, Captain Ellis stood on an elevated platform and gave a semi-rousing speech about the importance of the work ahead—not that most believed it. Now, the captain was again on the same platform, with the rest of the crew standing before him. Everyone had questions, and rather than pass information to the heads of department to disseminate, it seemed the captain was going to brief everyone at the same time, and in person.

After looking around, Crynn soon spotted Sona, and wove his way through the crowd, muscling in beside her. She turned to him and smiled. She looked exhausted.

"How are you?" he asked.

"Don't ask," she replied with a small laugh. Miko was next to her and looked even more dishevelled.

"Well, whatever you two have been through, it looks like you saved our lives," Crynn said. "So, thank you."

"Saved them for now," Miko replied in a low voice.

Crynn didn't get the chance to ask a follow up question as he heard the buzz of the speaker system activate. They heard Captain Ellis give a cough through the headset he was wearing.

The captain had a broad, squat physique, thinning grey hair that was brushed back, and the beginning of hanging jowls either side of a letterbox mouth. He put his hands behind his back and pushed out his barrel chest.

"I know you all have questions," he began in his gravelly voice. "And I wish I had more answers. As some of you may be aware, we have docked inside the unidentified space station we discovered after the recent anomaly damaged the Argento. Despite our best efforts, we were unable to change course after we started drifting towards the station, which we think was down to an engineering fault with the thrusters."

"Bullshit," Crynn heard Miko whisper.

"The malfunction, coupled with the instability of the cores, should have meant our end. However, navigation was quick to spot an opening in the station, which we think is a hangar of sorts. The flight team were able to bring the Argento into the hangar, where we were able to regain enough control of the thrusters to successfully land and power down, thus resting the cores again."

Crynn caught Sona's eyes, then nodded to Miko who looked furious. He raised an inquisitive eyebrow.

"The thrusters were fine," Sona whispered to him. "But we still couldn't pull away."

The captain continued. "The magnetic locks on the landing gears are keeping us in position, and from what we can see, there is no life aboard the station. No power. Nothing. I believe it to be derelict. Nonetheless, it seems we have stumbled upon an extraordinary find, and—if you can look past the serious situation we are in—a most exciting one. If we can get the Argento flying again, we can return to occupied space and send word out, that the Argento and its crew were the first to discover irrefutable proof of an advanced alien species. This is *exactly* the reason we are out here in the first place."

"It's the fucking Agoul!" someone yelled. "We need to get away as quickly as we can."

Other shouts rose up, some agreeing, others shouting down the hysterical warnings.

"Enough!" Captain Ellis bellowed as he slammed the meat of his fist down onto the platform railing before him. "I *demand* calm. We won't let our imaginations get in the way of our duty. Understood?" He took the silence from the crew as affirmation. "The Agoul have never been definitively proven. Regardless, if this station *was* theirs, then we have an opportunity to find out more about them. Or whoever it was that built this thing we sit inside. The engineering team will need time to get the ship and cores back up and running, and that gives us an opportunity. One I don't intend to pass up. With that in mind . . . I'm looking for volunteers."

"For what?" one man yelled out.

"To make history," Captain Ellis replied with a grin. "I want a team to go outside the Argento and see what they can find. I'm not expecting them to go too far from the ship, but if we can record some usable data from the station: material composition, the atmosphere inside the hangar, any evidence of consoles or user panels, that type of thing, then it would be huge for us. It will obviously be zero-g outside the Argento, so the team will be suited up. They'll also be equipped with some weaponry, though I don't think they'll need it. Our engineers will be exempt as they're needed, as will our more senior technicians, but . . . do any of the rest of you want to write your name into the history books?"

Crynn thrust his hand straight up in the air without hesitation. He could feel all eyes suddenly turn on him, including those of Sona and Miko.

"What are you doing?" Sona asked.

Captain Ellis' face lit up as he focused on Crynn. "Excellent," the captain exclaimed. "You wasted no time there, son. What's your name?"

"Crynn Zaballa, sir," Crynn replied. "Low level technician. But prior to coming aboard I served in the military and have previously worked in zero-g. Given that experience, I'd be happy to lead the team."

After considering Crynn's proposal for only a matter of seconds, Captain Ellis gave a firm nod. "I'll approve that," he said. "Thank you, son." He then looked around the room. "Anyone else? Not much more we can be doing until the ship is fixed, so it's an opportunity you might not want to pass up."

A few more hands eventually went up from some of the braver members of the crew.

"Fantastic!" the captain said as he clapped his hands together. "It's decided. All volunteers can meet with me and the command team in the control room close to the eastern airlock. Be there in ten minutes. Engineers and senior technicians . . . you already have your orders. Everyone else, just assist as best you can."

More hands went up and a flurry of questions were launched at the captain, who just held up his hands to quell the voices.

"Again, I know you have questions," he shouted, "but I've told you as much as I'm able to for now. You are all dismissed and I will update everyone as soon as possible." He then walked from the podium, leaving the crew to begin talking amongst themselves. Crynn felt a slap on his arm and turned to Sona, who looked furious.

"What the hell was that about?"

"What?" Crynn asked with a frown.

"Volunteering to go outside," Sona shot back. "Are you nuts? It'll be dangerous."

"Why shouldn't I?" Crynn replied. "There's nothing else for me to do on this fucking ship. I might as well be of use. I'm not a child, Sona. I used to be a soldier, in case you've forgotten."

"No, Crynn, I haven't forgotten. But the captain is blinded by becoming famous for making this discovery. Like Miko said before, the thrusters were working previously, but something was *pulling* us towards the station. Miko told the captain that but he doesn't want to hear it."

Crynn looked to Miko and she nodded in confirmation. "It's true," she said. "I can't explain how, but we *should* have been able to turn or stop the ship."

"And that means something brought us here, Crynn," Sona said. "It brought us here on purpose."

Crynn hesitated, before following up with: "You don't know that. The captain said the station is—"

"Is deserted," Sona said, cutting him off. "Yes, I know. But the captain knows about as much as the rest of us. Crynn, listen to me, there might be something here. So going out there is dangerous."

Crynn thought about that for a few moments. "You're right," he eventually said. "And that means those who leave the ship will need help. I could be useful here, Sona, for the first time since I came aboard the Argento. I could actually add real value. Plus, if something *did* bring us here, like you say, then we might be fucked anyway. At least I can help buy us some time so you can fix the ship."

Now it was Sona's turn to hesitate. "But . . . "

Crynn placed a reassuring hand on her shoulder. "It's okay," he said with a smile. "Go do your job . . . and let me do mine."

CHAPTER 6

THE GROUP OF fifteen stood inside the airlock, all in their spacesuits, with Crynn at the front. Amber light swirled around the room as the countdown ticked down to zero. When it did, Crynn could hear the sounds of gears working in the airlock door ahead. There was a hiss.

"Keep breathing, everyone," Crynn ordered to the others. As far as he was aware, no one else amongst them had his experience, so he knew their safety was his responsibility. He surprised himself with how calm he was about that, and rather than wilting under pressure, he was relishing the chance to prove himself and to become part of the team, part of the whole, rather than someone on the outside looking in.

The door opened, revealing only darkness outside. With a few taps on the display screen mounted on his forearm, small lights affixed to the rim of his helmet blinked on, pushing out four separate beams. However, they revealed nothing but more darkness.

"Lights on, people," he said to the others through his built-in radio. More lights came on, spreading multiple beams out before them.

With the magnetic locks in the boots the team wore keeping them grounded, Crynn was able to take a step forward. Pulling his feet away from the surface underfoot took more effort than walking normally, and he hoped all those with him were at least relatively fit, otherwise they might start to struggle in short order.

Crynn heard a female voice come over his radio and he stopped in his tracks. "I didn't think it would be this dark. We won't be able to see more than a few feet ahead of ourselves."

She sounded worried.

"It'll be fine," Crynn reassured. "There's nothing out there. Just keep together and move slowly. There's a ladder just outside the airlock. We'll use that to climb down. Move slowly and keep your breathing steady."

"What happens if we slip off the ladder?" someone else asked.

"In zero-g," Crynn replied, "you'll just float. We have small thrusters in our suits that you can use to move yourself. But remember, they use bursts from your air supply, so don't go crazy trying to fly around all over."

"I think I made a mistake," one man said. "What if I can't use the thrusters correctly. I'll end up—"

"Relax," Crynn said. "If you need it, I'd just come get you. I know what I'm doing. So, again, the most important thing is to keep control of your emotions and anxieties. You'll only get in trouble if you panic. Okay?" He got a few affirmative responses, which was more than he expected. "Then let's go. Follow my lead."

Crynn then moved forward with slow and deliberate steps. Once at the threshold of the airlock, he looked out, but could see very little straight ahead. To his right and left, however, Crynn was able to make out some of the vast hull of the Argento, which had lights of its own to help push away the oppressive, dark gloom within the hangar. When he looked down towards the front of the ship, which was mostly hidden by one of the ship's outcroppings, he saw massive spotlight beams pointing forward that the navigation team would have used to land safely. Those massive lights were able to fight off the surrounding darkness more substantially; therefore, Crynn was able to see some of the hangar floor, and even some of the roof, which looked to be miles above them. The material of both the floor and the roof was a dark grey, close to black, but he wasn't close enough to make out any details or consistency. Still, he knew there had to be at least *some* metals used in the structure of the hull, as the Argento was being held in place by the magnetic locks within the landing gears.

After leaning forward and looking to his left, Crynn quickly saw the iron ladders fixed to the hull. He moved carefully, taking hold of the top rung, and turned, planting both feet on rungs beneath him. He had a rifle secured to his back, strapped horizontally just beneath his in-built air tank. The rifle was in its 'safety' state, with the butt and barrel in a compressed configuration, and it would release to its full length when drawn and pulled from its magnetic holding. He also had a sidearm strapped to his leg. The firearms assigned to the Argento all utilised projectiles rather than laser fire, thanks to a recent technological development that allowed a distance to be set before firing, and the projectiles would explode if they didn't hit a target before that point. They were cheaper to build and maintain than lasers, but didn't pack the same punch. However, they were less likely to punch a hole in the hull of a ship.

Four others in the squad were equipped with weapons as well. Crynn had been concerned about untrained personnel using weapons, which might have been more dangerous than anything they might find out in the darkness. Command had compromised, letting those with some basic training carry guns. None had Crynn's experience; they'd only shot on one of the ship's ranges—one of the few recreational activities on board—but at least it was something.

Crynn manoeuvred down the ladder, pulling his body down by each run, using his feet only to keep his body straight. Eventually, after reaching the floor of the hangar, he reactivated the mag-lock in his boots and felt them take hold. He took a few steps back and looked up at the hull of the Argento, spotting some of the team leaning forward and peering out of the airlock. He gave a thumbs up.

Looking up at the height of the ship gave Crynn a small sense of vertigo. The Argento was an impressive thing to behold, and he realised he hadn't seen the outside of it since he was on Velliam station, where he'd peered out of one of the viewing windows to take it all in.

The once-white hull, which had been repainted just before the ship left Velliam station for its final mission, had dulled due to the constant solar radiation it had been subjected to, as there were a great many dents and scratches across its surface. It was close to two-hundred meters long, and its head was a rectangular section that folded in on itself somewhat at the very end, with the bridge area situated at the top of that curve. The rest of the body was made up of blocky outcroppings, and the back end of the ship fattened up somewhat to house the three massive antimatter thrusters on the back. Crynn could also see the many heavy weapon turrets and torpedo bays that showed the Argento's former classification as a destroyer.

As the team in the air lock began to descend, Crynn backed up to take in more of the ship, but his gaze soon turned to the back section again, where he saw the great, circular opening they had come through. Beyond that, the vastness of space; the great and yawning black. It made him feel miniscule.

Look away, he told himself. *Keep focused.* So, he bent down on one knee and inspected the floor underfoot, illuminated by the lights on his suit. He pressed his hand down onto it. Though he couldn't feel much because of the glove, he did detect that the dark surface wasn't as hard as he had initially expected, and it yielded slightly under the pressure he exerted. Not by much, but more than the metallic floors he was used to on the Argento. It confused him. *Is there a metallic layer beneath that the mag-locks are attracted to?*

Another thought occurred to him while peering at the strange material. On the Argento, the floor of each deck had built-in gravity plates fitted, which ensured gravity where they were activated. However, given they used a lot of energy, and antimatter cores weren't the safest technology, all space stations in the Interstellar World Alliance had rotating sections that used centrifugal force to create gravity in habitable areas. Hangar bays and things like that were all zero-g. Ships, the alliance had decided, were somewhat disposable, but space stations were too important.

The form of the station Crynn now stood on, though, was unbelievably vast, and there were certainly no rotating components in the strange structure. Which begged the question: had the station simply functioned in zero gravity, or was there a technology similar to their own that created artificial gravity? If so, Crynn couldn't imagine a power source big enough to supply it to a station of this size. The technological advancements needed for that would put the creators of the station far beyond humanity.

Which posed yet another question: where were the creators? He couldn't imagine why they would leave a huge station like this behind. *And surely they would have been too technologically advanced to succumb to extinction, or be caught off-guard by a solar storm the same way the Argento was?*

Crynn tried to stop thinking about such things. They wouldn't really aid him at present, so he concentrated on making sure he took in as much as he could, hoping the in-built camera in his helmet was recording useful footage. Some of the crew, now lowering themselves down the ladder, also carried equipment that would take atmospheric readings, which would all add to the data they were compiling. Crynn stood, but toed the ground with his boot, thinking someone should cut some of the material away to take back aboard the Argento for further testing.

The rest of the hangar was just too big for their lights to penetrate much of the dark, so there wasn't much to see. He decided that if the expedition was to be worth a damn, he would need to lead some of the team into the darkness to explore a little more. A tingle of excitement ran through him.

He let everyone gather at the base of the ladder and spoke to them through the radio.

"Okay," he began, "we'll walk a few hundred paces away from the ship and those of you with sensor equipment can set it up to begin recording." He noticed many of the team looking past him to the void of space outside the station. "Don't look at it," he said with a smile. "It's easier to try to ignore that view, impressive as it is. It can mess with your head too much. As I was saying, once the relevant equipment is set up, I'm going to lead a group farther outward to see what we can find here. I'll take volunteers, but I want at least half to stay with the equipment and monitor results."

The group looked at one another. From behind the glass in their helmets he could see some were full of doubt. Those, he knew, would remain with the equipment. Some other hands did go up, however. Thankfully, a few of those people were carrying guns, which would give comfort to those left behind.

"But isn't it stupid to split up?" one man asked.

"Potentially," Crynn replied, honestly. "But the whole point of us coming out here was to find out what we can. We won't know much by just standing around. If anything happens, those back at the equipment should just get back to the Argento as quickly as possible."

He didn't get much back in the way of a response, but given there was no dissent, he took that as an approval of sorts. The team spent roughly a half hour setting up their equipment and sensors. It shouldn't have taken as long, but the crew were unpractised using the instruments, and were constantly looking over their shoulders into the darkness around them, clearly on edge.

Once complete, Crynn addressed everyone. "Good job. Now, those who are still keen to come with me, fall in behind. Those that want to stay behind and monitor the equipment, you can do just that. You'll be able to see us moving because of the lights on our suits, and I'm guessing we'll find a wall or something before we fall out of view. The hangar can't be *that* big. If at any point you feel the need, go back to the Argento. The equipment here should be fine running on its own. I'd rather it left unguarded than people lose their cool and do something stupid. Is that clear?"

There were nods of affirmation. Crynn looked over them all. While most looked worried, some had an excited determination etched onto their faces, which was pleasing as it mirrored how Crynn felt. In fact, it was the most alive he remembered feeling in a long time.

Without the aid of Dust, that was.

"Good," he eventually said. "Alright, those that want to, follow me."

He unclipped his rifle from his back and swung it around, clicking the release button so the weapon extended from its compact form. He felt all parts lock into place and checked it over. He then turned and walked away from the equipment, taking steady steps, every so often turning back to see how many followed. Six people fell in behind, only one of whom had a weapon, which meant those back with the equipment were at least well defended.

That might make them feel a little better. While Crynn had considered arming more of those in his group, he kept going back to the notion that having more weapons was even *more* dangerous if they were in untrained hands. Besides, they had been outside of the Argento for over half an hour so far with no incidents at all. If anything had detected them aboard the station, they'd certainly done nothing about it.

All of that made Crynn think that the captain may have been right, that the station might have been abandoned, but he still remembered what Sona and Miko had told him.

Something was pulling us towards the station!

As they walked, Crynn looked again towards the front of the Argento, to keep his vision away from the dizzying opening in the station to his left. The powerful beams at the head of the ship were still on, pointing ahead, and while they couldn't push the darkness back far enough to see the end of the hangar, they were bright enough to illuminate some of the ceiling structure. It was dark in colour, like the floors, but the illuminated area was slightly concave, coming together at a point, with shallow ridges that ran down the length of the surface at regular intervals. It reminded

Crynn of the inside of a great mouth, looking up at a palate, and the great dark beyond disappearing down a gigantic throat.

Don't think like that, he admonished. *You'll scare yourself.*

After a few hundred feet of walking, the beams of light emanating from Crynn's helmet revealed something up ahead.

It was a wall.

"Looks like we've found the edge of the hangar," Crynn announced over the radio. The team behind him spread out a little as they moved closer.

The wall was a very dark grey, the same as the other surfaces in the station, and predominantly flat, though Crynn did notice undulations on its face. As he turned his head to look farther down, he saw some sections of outcroppings, and even vertical tubes that ran from the surface of the wall up into the darkness. Those tubes were somewhat translucent, save for thin fleshy veins set within the outer material, which to Crynn resembled a membrane. He moved down towards it, with the others following behind.

"What the hell . . . " he uttered.

"What are we looking at here, Mr. Zaballa?" It was the captain's voice on the radio. Command was obviously watching progress via the feed on the team's cameras.

"I . . . have no idea," Crynn replied as he stopped directly before the tube. At the point the strange conduit connected to the wall, Crynn noticed a webbing of black, seemingly organic material clinging to the membrane of the tube, running off from the surface of the wall itself, holding it in place. Crynn was tempted to raise a finger and touch it, but realised that would be stupid. Still, it would probably be a good idea to collect some as a sample.

"Get some of this stuff bagged up," he said to the others, while pointing at the thick black webbing. Initially, no one moved. Crynn had to stop from rolling his eyes. "You," he said to the closest man, "get on with it. Get as much as you can."

Before anyone moved, however, a sound drew everyone's attention.

Crynn turned to the large opening at the back of the hangar upon hearing the low rumble that emanated from that space. His breath caught in his throat.

"Shit!" someone said over the radio.

"What is it?" the captain asked. Then, after picking up what was going on via the feed, added, "What the fuck."

The great opening before them was . . . closing.

The edges were pulling inwards, spiralling towards a centre point as the stars outside were slowly blocked out. Crynn's heart began to beat faster.

What do I do?

In the end, Crynn did nothing but watch as the great doorway finished closing, pulling itself shut like flesh melding together.

Leaving them all trapped inside.

CHAPTER 7

"BACK TO THE SHIP!" Crynn shouted over his radio. "Move!"

This time, instead of being head of the line, Crynn held back, ushering those in front of him onwards to make sure no one was left behind. The group jogged as fast as the mag-locks would allow back over to the others who were gathered at the equipment, looking horrified. As the two teams merged, Crynn felt another vibration underfoot.

"What's happening?" someone called, as the vibrations increased, becoming stronger and stronger, until it felt like the whole station was shaking. Crynn was reminded of the feeling and sensations on the Argento when the anomaly hit. He again pointed to the ship.

"Keep going, leave the equipment!" he ordered everyone, and the whole team began to run back to the Argento.

On route, Crynn's legs wobbled beneath him and he stumbled, feeling a surge of light-headedness that stopped him in his tracks. Had he been in gravity, it would have caused him to drop down to a knee. His vision spun, though he was just able to make out the others ahead of him, and they had all stopped as well, all swaying on their feet and clearly feeling the same effects.

"What's . . . what's going on?" one of the women in the group slurred over the comms. The shuddering all around Crynn continued and he was thankful his feet were locked into place; his equilibrium was so shot he could now barely summon the mental capacity to lift his own arms.

"Com . . . command?" Crynn managed to call out into his helmet. "We're . . . in . . . trouble."

It took a few moments for a response to come back over the radio. "Stand . . . by." The voice that came back through sounded as groggy as his own, meaning those aboard the Argento were afflicted with whatever was happening as well.

"Nobody . . . move," Crynn told the others. "Wait . . . it out."

There was nothing else they could do, he knew. Even if they managed to stumble back to the ship, there was no way they would be able to climb the ladder back up to the airlock. Not in their current condition. The only hope was that whatever was happening to them would pass.

The level of vibrations coming up through the floor grew so severe Crynn became worried his boots' magnetic lock might shake loose. His vision became a palette of colours all blurred together and it was a struggle not to vomit; that was the last thing he needed floating around inside his helmet.

Thankfully, after a few more minutes, things began to settle. His nausea receded, his vision came back into focus, and the shaking around him subsided. Crynn took deep breaths to calm himself down.

"Is everyone okay?" he asked.

"What the fuck was that?" someone shot back.

"We need to get back," another added.

Finally, a third man screamed: "I need to get out of this fucking suit!"

After turning to face him, Crynn could see why. Globs of yellow vomit floated behind the glass and sloshed into the man's horrified face. If the situation hadn't been so serious, Crynn might have found the sight funny.

Crynn quickly glanced over the equipment that had been set up. To his surprise, it all seemed to be functioning correctly. He spent a few more moments making sure the rest of the team were fine.

"Command," he eventually said into his radio, "we're coming back aboard. What's the situation there? Is everyone okay? We experienced something . . . strange out here."

It took a few moments for the response to come through. "Hold your position," the captain said. "We experienced the same thing. I'm still getting reports through but I think everyone is okay. *However*," he went on, "I've just had word from engineering. The vibrations have caused a mechanical fault with one of the landing gears and the mag-lock there is malfunctioning, to the point we might not be able to retract it when we need to."

"Would that stop us taking off?" Crynn asked.

"Potentially," he said. "So a crew is going to come out there to fix it. I want you and the others to look after the engineers and help any way you can. Your priority now is getting that damn landing gear fixed. Understand?"

"I do," he said, looking at the gloomy expression of his team. "But that won't take all of us. Surely most people out here can—"

"It's going to be a manual task," the captain said. "We might need all the bodies we can get, so everyone is to stay outside until ordered otherwise."

Crynn took a breath. "Understood, sir," he replied.

"Command out," came the reply.

Crynn then addressed his team again, knowing full well someone from command would still be monitoring the situation. "You heard him," Crynn said. "We have our orders. I know some of you are unsettled—"

"Unsettled?" one man cut in, sounding incredulous. "That's a fucking understatement. We're *terrified*. And we're just getting left out here on our own, like worms dangling on a hook. That fucking door," he pointed to where the great opening once was, "closed on its own, trapping us. Then whatever-the-fuck it was happened and almost made us pass out. We *can't* just sit out here. There's something still on this station, clearly. Doors like that don't just close—"

"I get it!" Crynn said in a raised voice but with his palms raised. "I won't pretend to know what's going on, but we have our orders. If we can't repair the landing gear, then we're screwed as we won't be going anywhere."

"We *aren't* going anywhere, genius," the man shot back, again pointing to where the huge opening once was. "Our way out is blocked. Besides, since when did we all have to take orders from a fucking low-level technician?"

Crynn clenched his teeth together. The comment stung. Just as he'd started to feel useful, to feel part of the group, it was again made obvious to him he wasn't really one of them.

Always on the outside looking in.

"Since Mr. Zaballa has the experience we need," the captain's voice replied over the radio. "Regardless of your position on the Argento, *he* is your ranking officer out there. Get used to it and do your jobs. The engineering team will be out shortly. Does anyone have any problems with that? If so, I'd be happy to let you think them through in the brig once we get the Argento fixed. Three weeks with nothing but your own thoughts should do it. Any questions?"

Silence.

"Good. Command out."

Crynn felt a pang of anger course through him. While the input from the captain had put the dissenting man back in his place, Crynn hated that he'd needed help to do it.

So much for proving your worth.

Nothing else was said for the next ten minutes, not until one of the group pointed over to the Argento's airlock and said, "They're here."

A line of six people started to descend the ladder, rather unsteadily. At one point Crynn thought one was going to lose their grip and go floating away from the ship, meaning he would need to go after them. Thankfully, however, they managed to keep their grip on the rungs.

As the engineers approached and got close enough for Crynn to read their faces through the glass of their helmets, he was surprised to see Sona and Miko among their number.

He walked over to them and, using the console panel on his forearm, sent a request to the two women to access a private audio channel just between the three of them. They accepted.

"I didn't think the head of engineering would be out here," he said to Miko.

She gave a scowl, though it didn't seem to be directed at Crynn specifically. "I shouldn't be, but the team has surprisingly little hands-on experience working on ship externals. And I don't have time to write up a detailed set of instructions for people to follow. Quicker to just get out here and oversee it myself."

"Think you can get it fixed?" Crynn asked.

"I hope so," Miko replied and walked off, trailed by some of her team.

Crynn turned to Sona. "How were the repairs going inside?" he asked. "Any closer to getting the Argento flying again?"

"We'd made some progress," Sona said, "and would have had everything operational again soon, I think. If it wasn't for this interruption." She nodded to the huge landing gear in question, which sported no obvious signs of damage from that distance.

"Not sure it would matter too much. There's no way out anymore."

Sona turned to the now solid wall behind the Argento. "Command has an idea about that," she said.

"Which is?"

She gave Crynn a tight-lipped smile. "The ship used to be a destroyer and has some pretty heavy weaponry at its disposal."

"They're going to shoot their way out?!" Crynn asked in shock.

"They're thinking about it."

Crynn looked back to the wall, which was just about visible. He wasn't convinced it would work, not without blowing up the ship at the same time. Unless the hangar was deep enough to keep the Argento far enough back to avoid any impact explosions.

"Shit," was all Crynn could think to say.

"Indeed," Sona agreed. She then started to walk off after Miko.

Crynn flicked his radio to the universal channel and turned to the rest of his crew. "Okay, everyone," he said. "We escort the engineers and follow their instructions. *Everyone* is expected to pitch in and help as needed."

He led his team over to the landing gear as well. On route, however, Crynn felt his body drop somewhat as weight was returned to it. He saw the hull of the Argento sink down into the landing gears a little. The people before him all paused and he saw their poise change; arms suddenly falling down by their sides and knees bending to instinctively compensate for the sudden influx of gravity. One person fell to their back, with their feet still planted on the ground thanks to the mag-locks in their boots.

Confused voices rose up over the radio.

"What the fuck?"

"What happened to zero-g?"

"We need to get back to the ship. Something's happening!"

Crynn took a breath. "Quiet!" he barked and looked around, aiming his spotlights off into the darkness. He sensed no movement. However, that didn't stop him from panicking. The great door closing, and now gravity being introduced, was not likely the result of some automated system. "Everyone carry on with their jobs," he commanded. "The quicker we get things repaired out here, the quicker we get back aboard. Because if we *don't* finish up what we're doing, we're going to be stuck on this station for a long time. Now move, double-time. And for fuck's sake, remember to disengage the mag-lock on your boots."

After a few taps on his forearm console, Crynn's boots were powered down and he felt them release the hold from the floor. He gave his body a moment to adjust then began to trot forwards. "Everyone move," he said again, towards the engineering staff as much as his team. Everyone responded and picked up the pace.

The entire group soon converged at the landing gear, which was taller than the people around it. Movement was now much easier with the introduction of gravity, with the only hindrance being the spacesuits, but even they were as slim-lined as possible.

Miko directed the crew efficiently, initially relying only on the engineers to identify the problem, which they did in short order. It was impressive watching her work. If anyone was capable of getting the ageing ship flying again, it was her, and that gave Crynn a renewed sense of hope.

He kept stealing glances out into the darkness, on edge in case something stepped forward into the light. He gripped the stock of his rifle tightly.

Relax. Breathe. Keep focused, he told himself. *And don't panic.*

Minutes passed, then a half hour. Crynn ordered one of the other men with a gun to follow him as he started to walk the perimeter of the crew, keeping to the edges, hoping it helped people relax knowing their backs were covered. After an hour, Miko spoke over the comms.

"I think we have it," she said. "Everything else we can do from inside the Argento."

Crynn let a smile slip. "Everyone pack up and get back aboard." One of the team near to him turned to face him, grinning with relief. However, as she turned to Crynn, her expression quickly changed, with eyes widening and jaw dropping, forming a look of horror.

She's looking behind *me.*

Crynn spun around and raised his gun, just in time to see a nightmare he could scarcely describe come bounding out of the darkness.

CHAPTER 8

CRYNN HAD THE rifle up in position immediately, with the end of the stock tucked into his chest and shoulder and cheek pressing down into the weapon allowing him to gaze through the sight at the advancing . . . monstrosities.

There was no other word for it.

The telescopic sight only enlarged what was up ahead by a small margin, but it was enough to make out the horrible detail of the creatures that lumbered and towards them.

For a fraction of a second, Crynn refused to believe what his eyes were showing him.

An hallucination, surely.

The . . . *things* . . . were twisted and deformed, covered in disgusting tumour-like growths. Of the four Crynn could see via the light cast from his suit's beams, only one was vaguely humanoid, though its face—actually embedded in its chest—didn't resemble a human at all. The other three were multi-limbed, with three and four legs, multiple arms, with one even sporting curling tentacle-like appendages.

The exploded flesh—as none were wearing clothing of any kind—was a mix of browns, greys, purples and sickly yellows, all meshing together with angry reds around the clusters of growths. Crynn also noticed their mangled bodies were interlined with wires, tubes, and metallic parts; a mix of cybernetic and organic.

Crynn was certain that, whatever had happened to these things to make them look like this, none had ever been human before. Which meant . . .

Alien?

The many mouths he saw opened and closed silently, with no air around them to carry any sound, making silent screams that looked angry.

"Weapons ready," Crynn suddenly bellowed through the radio. "Fire at the incoming targets."

He squeezed the trigger and released a burst of fire, hurling a stream of bullets at his target, the nearest creature to him. His aim was true and the metallic projectiles tore through the sickly flesh, which in turn burst through with puss and a dark liquid he assumed to be blood. He fired again and caused an explosion of flesh and more dark fluid, ruining the creature's already hideous features, popping its milky-white eyes and eviscerating one side completely.

Still the monster kept coming. Crynn backed up a few steps and fired again, taking a second to glance behind him at the rest of the group. He saw horror on the faces of those that looked back. Some with weapons had them raised, but were cumbersome with their aim, and had not yet opened fire, obviously panic-stricken.

"Fire!" Crynn ordered.

"What's going on out there?" the captain's voice commanded over the radio.

"Targets incoming," Crynn shouted back as he continued to move away from the advancing threat. At least, he assumed them to be a threat. They had no weapons of their own to fire back with, but given they were honing in on Crynn and his team, he doubted it was to try and make some kind of peaceful first contact. On top of that, the firing of his weapon only made them move quicker. "We're engaging but . . . the bullets don't seem to be stopping them, sir."

"What *are* they?" the captain asked. He heard other voices as well over the channel, shouting in fear and confusion.

Crynn had no time to try to describe what he was seeing. "We don't know," was the only answer he gave. Crynn then aimed lower, at one of the many thin legs supporting the creature closest to him, adjusted the setting on his gun to increase the fire rate, and let fly with another stream of bullets. He kept his aim steady and it was enough to completely sever the limb, chewing up the flesh first before finally splintering the visible bone completely. The lower section of the leg, with a two-toed foot at the bottom, dropped to the floor and the creature stumbled.

Without pausing to think about it, Crynn repeated his attack with another leg, causing the creature to topple completely, though it still dragged itself forward on its tentacle-like limbs.

He then saw small impact explosions on some of the other shambling monstrosities as well, and turned to see that, finally, some of the others had opened fire as well. He made a mental note not to sidestep. With no sound to help signal to him where friendly fire was coming from, he realised it would be very easy to accidentally walk into a barrage of shooting coming from behind him. So, he continued to back up, more quickly this time, still firing on the enemy, and quickly changing his now-empty magazine with one of the spares strapped to his utility belt.

In his peripheral vision, Crynn saw two people fall in beside him, helping him gun down the still-approaching creatures. The muzzle-flashes were startling in the relative-darkness around them, but not so much as to make Crynn look away.

"Aim for the legs," Crynn ordered. "It's the only way to slow them down."

The trio of shooters continued their assault. Eventually, after taking enough bullets, Crynn noticed the enemy on the ground, the first one to have fallen, now remained motionless, its body a mess of mangled flesh from the hail of bullets that had cut through it. Eventually, the other three creatures joined it on the floor, also becoming still, with the only movement caused by the impact of more bullets that chewed them up.

"Cease fire!" Crynn ordered and the shooting stopped. He gazed at the smoking bodies on the floor, taking deep breaths to calm himself.

"What the fuck were those things?" the woman to Crynn's left asked. He could hear the fear in her voice but was pleased that she had handled herself so well when it mattered.

Before Crynn could answer the question, however, he heard a scream over the channel. The single cry was joined by more.

Crynn turned to see more of the creatures emerging from the darkness, coming through further to his left, making a bee-line for the huddled crew, rushing past him and the two people flanking him. The monstrosities continued to pour forward in a steady stream, with three, four, seven, ten . . . scores of them stepping into the light, each as twisted and misshapen as the one before it, though there seemed to be some small differences: multiple limbs on some, animalistic faces set into the chest on others, and tentacle-limbs on a few.

There were cries of horror over the comms as the creatures

swooped into the large crowd. One of the people next to Crynn raised his weapon but Crynn was quick to bring up his arm and bat the rifle to the side.

"You'll hit our people!" he barked.

Crynn brought his own rifle up and began to fire ahead of the crowd, where the monsters were appearing from the dark, in an attempt to slow down those to the rear—with the two people flanking him soon joining in—but the creatures were relentless, taking hold of anyone they could get their hands, claws or tentacles on. Crynn expected to see his crewmates torn to shreds by the creatures; they stood around two feet taller than their human counterparts. However, the men and women of the Argento were instead . . . dragged away.

"Help!" some of them screamed as they were pulled back into the darkness. Crynn could make out around twenty or so of the monstrosities amongst his own people, grabbing hold of anyone close. Those that were able to escape fled, running back to the ship or off into seemingly random directions.

As Crynn pushed aside his fear and started forward to help, he sensed something to his side, turning just in time to see one of the abominations appear from behind and take hold of the woman next to him.

The glass on her helmet shattered as one of the grotesque arms with three fingers at the end of its hand forced its way in. Crynn saw the woman's mouth open in a scream; her eyes went wide and she desperately tried to draw in non-existent air. Thick, yellow, tumour-lined arms wrapped around the poor woman, pulling her into the body of the beast, engulfing her as she gasped in vain. Her eyes locked on to Crynn's. They begged for help.

But Crynn had none to give. If he opened fire, he would hit her, without question. Though, as she was dragged away and swallowed by the shadows, he suddenly realised that might have been a kindness.

Keeping his rifle up and ready to fire, Crynn quickly moved to re-join the crewmates who had fled the attack, accompanied by the remaining man who had been flanking him. No further creatures spilled from the darkness. Instead, all of them drew back, each with a claimed prize. He could hear multiple, desperate screams coming through the radio, a cacophony of panic that blended together in one loud and distorted explosion of sound.

As the last of the monsters pulled its struggling prey away and out of sight, the remaining crew members quickly banded together.

"Back aboard the ship!" Crynn shouted, ignoring the captain's renewed demands for an update. His eyes desperately searched out Sona, praying she was still okay. He heard her voice through the comms before he saw her.

"We need to go after her," Sona's voice called out in desperation. Crynn saw her run forward, fighting through the crowd. He breathed a sigh of relief; but that quickly caught in his throat when he saw the distressed expression on her face.

"What do you mean?" he asked her.

"They took Miko!" Sona cried. "They have her! We need to go after her!"

Crynn's heart sank. He felt bad for Miko, someone he truly liked, and he felt worse for Sona, knowing what kind of anguish she would be in, but there was no way . . .

He put a hand on her shoulder, but she quickly shrugged it off.

"We need to get everyone back onto the Argento," he told her, as soothingly as he was able. Crynn's heart still hammered in his chest.

"We can't just leave her!" Sona exclaimed.

"More of those things might come back, Sona," Crynn explained. "For now, we just need to get everyone back aboard so we don't lose any more people. Then we can regroup and think about our next steps."

Sona's jaw fell. "How could you?" she asked. She started to say more but it was difficult to hear anything over the other voices on the channel as people began running back to the ladders that led up to the airlock. Crynn again switched to their private frequency and motioned for Sona to do the same.

"I'm not leaving her, Crynn," his friend stated with a look of defiance. "I'll go alone if I have to."

Crynn slowly shook his head. As painful as it was, the situation meant the only option was a full retreat. They knew nothing about the enemy, or the environment they found themselves in, so going out there into the unknown was suicide.

"I'm so sorry, Sona," he said, "but I can't let you."

"*Let* me?" she asked, giving him a look of disdain. "Since when are you able to give me orders?"

The barb stung, especially coming from Sona, but Crynn

understood why she was lashing out. He was the one stopping her from saving her lover.

"I'm sorry," he repeated. Crynn then saw Sona's eyes dart down to his weapon. She quickly tried to snatch it, but he pulled it aside before she was able to take hold.

"So, you're just going to let her die?" Sona asked through gritted teeth.

"I'm going to get everyone back aboard and then see what we can do," he replied, calmly. "Sona . . . I don't have any other choice."

"Yes, you do," she snarled. "You're just too much of a coward to take it."

He again let the comments go.

"Back aboard, Sona," he ordered. "We'll speak with the captain. When I know everyone here is safe, I'll offer to lead a team and go looking for those that were taken."

"It'll be too late!"

"It's the best we can do," he said. "If you want to help Miko, then please, just do as I ask."

She held his gaze for a few moments, a frown still etched across her brow, then finally relented, wordlessly turning away and moving back toward the ladder. Crynn followed close behind, checking back over his shoulder after every few steps, making sure he was last to reboard the Argento.

CHAPTER 9

"WILL THE REPAIRS be completed without her?"

Crynn could feel Sona bristle next to him as the captain referred to Miko in such a dismissive way.

For the first time since coming aboard the Argento, Crynn found himself on the bridge of the ship, along with the command team, Sona, and some of the other surviving engineers. They were informing the command team about what had happened out in the hangar. The mood in the room—which had a narrow, horizontal viewing window at the front, multiple workstations and consoles, and an elevated position for the captain's chair—was understandably fraught and glum.

"I think so," one of the engineers replied. Everyone in the room, save for some of the navigation team who continued to man their posts, monitoring the ship's sensors, was gathered around a large table. The table had a holographic projector built into the top, which cast a blue image of the Argento upwards, hovering about two feet above the table's surface. The image slowly rotated and, with the externals of the ship hidden, everyone present could see the inner structure of the ship. The same engineer that had answered the captain went on: "We think the landing gear was fully repaired before the attack, and the work on the cores and drives is relatively close to completion. We'd estimate a couple of hours or so."

"And then we should be ready for flight?" the captain asked. He received a firm nod in response.

Crynn heard Sona sigh next to him, then pull in a deep breath. He knew she was about to speak up, and would be angry when doing so.

"I'd like to lead a team out there," Crynn said, before his friend had the chance to get herself in trouble.

The captain, who was leaning forward on the table, raised his eyebrows in surprise at Crynn. He paused for a moment, then shook his head. "I'm sorry, but now there is far too much risk and we would likely lose more crew."

"But—" Sona began, but the captain gave a dismissive wave of his hand.

"I'm truly sorry about what happened out there. We're all trying to wrap our heads around the situation and no one wants those lost crew members back more than me. *But* we have to do what's right for the ship and the rest of us. We'll soon have the chance to leave this place behind and we have to take it."

"By blasting your way out?" Sona asked, not bothering to mask the scorn in her voice.

"If it's our only option, then yes," Captain Ellis replied. "And I won't have you second guessing that, understood." It wasn't a question.

"Sir," Crynn went on, "if I could just explain my reasons for wanting to take a team—"

"I understand your reasons, Mr. Zaballa," the captain said. "People we know have been taken by things we don't understand, and you want to go help them. I get it. Really, I do. But I can't allow—"

"That isn't it." It was Crynn's turn to interrupt now. "Chief Miko Goto was among the people taken."

The captain paused for a second. "Yes," he eventually said, "I'm aware of that. I have a full list of the people we lost."

"And you're also aware that, since we lost Trenor, she is the last chief of engineering we have left."

"Yes, and a huge loss," the captain conceded. "But we can't risk—"

"No one knows the Argento like she does, sir," Crynn cut in. "She's the one that has been holding this ship together. I know the other engineers we have are talented, but—speaking frankly—they aren't on her level. So, say we do escape, then what happens the next time the ship is in danger and our systems are failing? I'm sure we'd have a better shot if we had Miko Goto to rely on."

Captain Ellis began to chew the inside of his mouth, clearly deep in thought. "You have to know the chances of getting her back are slim at best."

"Yes, I understand that, sir. I just want a small team, no senior engineers or personnel, to go out and try. We'll be in radio contact and can come back as soon as we're ordered. If we fail and are lost as well . . . is the ship really any worse off? It has to be worth the risk."

Captain Ellis straightened up, keeping strong eye contact with Crynn. After what seemed like a half a minute, he finally spoke.

"Do it. But the team can only be ten people, no more, if you can wrangle up that many volunteers. But I have to warn you, we won't wait around, Mr. Zaballa. If you aren't back here when we have the chance to leave, then this station will be your final resting place."

"I understand, Captain," Crynn replied. "Fully."

"Then you almost have my permission to round up a team and go out there."

"Almost?" Crynn asked, confused.

The captain nodded. "When you get out there, I need you and your squad to do one thing before you start your search."

"Which is?"

"The equipment you set up last time you were out there? That needs to be packed up and brought back aboard."

Crynn's eyes widened. "You can't be serious."

"Deadly," Captain Ellis replied. "I want to know what data it captured. Could be important should we break out of here."

Crynn couldn't believe it. Even after what had happened to their people, the captain's focus was still on the plaudits he'd receive if they took back evidence of their find. Wasn't the video footage taken by the suits enough?

"Sir," Crynn began, trying to keep his cool. "I understand you want the info, but time—"

"It's this or you remain aboard, Mr. Zaballa. Understand?"

"But—"

"But nothing," the captain said, sternly. "Time is a-tickin'. Get the equipment back straight away. I'll have a team waiting in the airlock to collect it. Then you can begin your search."

Crynn let out a slow breath through gritted teeth. He cast a glance at Sona, who looked enraged.

But what choice did they have?

"Understood," Crynn eventually said. "I'll go round up a team."

Captain Ellis broke out into a grin. "Good man. Get to it."

Crynn turned to leave and felt Sona fall in beside him. When they were through the door and out of earshot, his friend quickly said, "I'm coming with you."

"We need all senior engineers to stay aboard," Crynn began. "Captain Ellis would never allow it."

"He doesn't get a choice," she replied. "Neither do you. My partner is out there, and I'm going to do everything I can to get her back. You want me to stay, then you're going to have to knock me out or tie me up. Otherwise, I'm coming with you."

Crynn knew it was pointless arguing. "Understood," he said with a small smile.

CHAPTER 10

THE PACKING UP of the equipment and getting it back to the airlock took roughly an hour, which was an hour they didn't have. Sona had worked like a machine: relentless and hurrying people on. Crynn had tried to match her energy. While the team had completed the task as quickly as possible, Crynn felt Sona's mounting frustration exuding from her. When they were finally done, Crynn again took charge.

"We'll walk out to the far wall again," he said to the group. "The things we saw seemed to move in that general direction, so we might find a door or something or a corridor we can follow."

"Not much to go on," a young man, barely older than a teenager, said.

"No, it isn't. But it's the best we have."

Crynn walked forward and Sona came up beside him, with the others following behind. There were nine of them in total. A call had been put out asking for volunteers, and at first only three people had turned up. Sona had asked for permission to put out a ship-wide communication to implore for more help. It had been granted, and Sona's speech had certainly been moving and passionate, if a little desperate. She stressed to everyone how much they needed their head of engineering back, and how much those taken would be relying on the crew to rescue them. "Imagine it was you out there . . . wouldn't you want help?"

It had worked to an extent and given Crynn almost the maximum number of personnel the captain had permitted him to take.

Every person on the team had been given a rifle, but few people had much experience firing them, so Crynn gave some brief instructions after the last of the equipment was put away. One of the main points he stressed was to make sure no one fired unless he gave the order and the line of sight was clear. He just hoped everyone remembered that in the heat of battle.

The team moved cautiously, all eyes trained ahead, but Sona kept trying to quicken the pace, getting a few steps ahead to force the others to speed up. Crynn accepted it the first few times, but when she came close to jogging, he put his hand out to the side to move her back.

"Don't get too far ahead," he said. "We need to be careful. Those things came out of the shadows quickly before and we don't want anything getting the drop on us. Just . . . slow down a little."

Crynn saw her shoot him an incredulous look. He understood: how could she be expected to slow down when the woman she loved was out there somewhere. Unfortunately for Crynn, he had to make sure Sona fell in line. If they all died, then no one would be rescued.

Not that he harboured any real hope of finding anyone. And if they did, Crynn doubted they would be alive.

Still, for his friend, he was willing to put his life on the line to try.

The wall ahead came into view again. With the beams from their lights illuminating the surface, Crynn ordered the team to walk down its extent to the right, keeping perpendicular to it. He knew they would either reach the end of the hangar that way, or ideally an off-shooting corridor. He turned and cast a quick glance back towards the Argento, feeling it was the last time he would see the ship. The scale of the station they were now on was unimaginable, and the creatures that took the crew had a good head start, so there was very little chance of finding their lost crew mates. There was, however, a good chance of getting lost, or killed by the same monstrosities.

He thought of those alien creatures again: a mix of organic and synthetic tissue, with strange wires, metallic parts, and thick tubes sewn into diseased-looking flesh. He remembered their forms, which weren't human in the slightest.

They had encountered true alien life. It had been a terrifying confrontation, but the dreams he'd harboured as a child of crossing the galaxy and meeting new life had been fulfilled, much as he now regretted it.

One thing that struck Crynn was how savage and unthinking the alien life had seemed. They had attacked without any kind of weaponry and technology, instead swooping in like animals, taking away their prey for . . . who knew what. To feed on? And while it looked like there were two or three different kinds of species among their number, none showed any real intelligence beyond acting on instinct. It struck him that such beings would be unable to operate a complex space station like the one they found themselves in.

So, why were they here? Were they all that was left of the original inhabitants? The awful condition of the flesh could mean they had been infected with something that turned them feral. But the mechanical implants and additions didn't exactly look well implemented in terms of aesthetic design. Humanity's own augmentation capabilities, back when augmentation was more widely used and accepted and not the domain of pirates, looked more refined, which made Crynn question if their implementation on the beings aboard the station had been consensual. None of it made any sense to him.

Not that it mattered. He didn't have to understand it. He just had to try and find Miko and the others and get the hell out of there.

The team continued to move down the hangar alongside the wall. They saw more of those translucent tubes, but there didn't appear to be anything flowing inside. *Maybe some kind of gas?* Crynn thought. As they walked, Crynn tilted his head for a moment, almost certain he could pick up sound outside of his helmet.

Impossible. Without air molecules around them, sound couldn't travel. He kept listening and became certain he could detect a steady and low-level hissing sound.

"Anyone else hear that?" he asked. There were a few negative replies, but Sona replied to the affirmative.

"I can," she said. "Sounds like a gas leak or something."

"How can that be?" one of the women in the group asked.

The beam's from Crynn's helmet soon picked up a section of wall filled with holes, all perfectly circular and around two inches in diameter. The holes were stacked together in a regular pattern, stretching out a few feet in length and running up the height of the wall out of sight. Crynn walked closer to them—now hearing the faintest of his own footsteps as well—and leaned in. He could make out hazy distortions just beyond the holes, reminiscent of a gas being forced free.

"Something is being pumped in," he announced as he stood back up. It suddenly made sense why they were able to hear things beyond their helmets, and he didn't doubt there would be many more pockets of holes spread around the huge space of the hangar.

"What do we do about it?" one of the men with them asked.

Crynn shrugged. "Nothing. We have a few hours' worth of air in our tanks and whatever is coming in through these holes shouldn't penetrate our suits. For now, we ignore it." He set off walking forward again. "Come on," he said. "Let's keep going."

The team followed the wall down the length of the hangar. There were outcroppings to the surface, as well as alcoves, but no control panels or lights or any other signs of technology. After approximately ten more minutes of walking, Crynn picked something up in his torchlight that broke the plain expanse of the wall.

An opening.

It was wide and arched, shaped like a shallow semicircle but the apex was around ten feet in height. The edge of the curved opening was ribbed, and a sickly yellow colour, contrasting against the almost-black of the walls around it. Crynn scanned the ground and saw a stain streaked across the floor, running into the tunnel. It was a reddish brown, still wet, and around half a meter long, with smaller streaks ahead. While he initially thought it could have been human blood, he quickly realised it was more likely to have come from one of the creatures that had taken away their crew mates.

Which meant they were on the right track.

Those with Crynn examined the stain on the floor as well, but said nothing, and soon turned their attention to the way ahead.

The corridor before them was wide, around fifteen feet, and arched in shape like the opening. However, the walls here looked to be of a different consistency than those in the hangar, and this became more evident the further the group progressed into the hallway. Instead of the plain, dark-grey texture, the walls changed to take on a dull mix of colours: browns, yellows, pale greens. And instead of being flat, the surfaces were uneven, with creases, bulges, and even growths similar to those Crynn saw on the monsters.

"Organic matter," Sona stated as she walked closer to one of the walls. She leaned closer to it.

"Careful," Crynn warned, "don't get too close."

Sona gave him a brief glance, then backed up.

"How can organic matter grow on the walls?" one of the team asked.

Sona shrugged. "Maybe it's some kind of outbreak. The same thing that caused the things we saw in the hangar to be so deformed."

Crynn couldn't be certain the monstrosities were deformed, because he had no frame of reference, though he conceded it was a good, educated guess.

"Let's keep going," Sona said. "All of this is interesting, but we don't have time to study it."

"Agreed," Crynn added. They kept moving forward, with Crynn again at the head of the line with his weapon ready.

They eventually reached a point where the corridor split right and left, the walls and ceiling there heavily lined with the strange, organic substance.

"Which way?" Sona asked, looking to Crynn.

Before he could answer, Crynn detected an alert on his arm-mounted console. There was a voice on one of the audio channels, the same one they had been using when repairing the Argento. He frowned and flicked his eyes to Sona. Given she had been using that channel back then, she'd received the alert as well. Crynn tapped into the frequency.

He was met with moans of pain.

The crew that were taken.

"Hello?" he said. "Can you hear me?"

It seemed like multiple voices were coming through, groaning in obvious agony, but no actual words were vocalised. At least . . . not at first.

"Hellllp," a voice eventually wheezed, little more than a strained whisper.

"Who is this?" Crynn asked. "Do you know where you are? Which way do we need to travel? We're here to get you. Give us something." His questions tumbled out in quick succession, leaving no time for the mystery person to answer. The single word uttered wasn't enough for Crynn to recognise the voice and all he could tell from it was that it was male.

"Miko?" Sona suddenly shouted into the comm. "Miko, are you there? Talk to me, please!"

Both Crynn and Sona waited for a response to come over the faint moans that still continued.

Nothing did.

Crynn flicked back to the main channel. “I’m not sure how many of you heard that,” he said to the others, “but we picked up voices. Our friends and crewmates are still out there but . . . things aren’t looking good, from what I can tell. Transponders aren’t picking anything up.”

“That means we should go back,” one man quickly stated. There was far too much eagerness in his voice.

“No, it doesn’t,” Crynn snapped back. “It means we need to move quickly.”

“But to where?” the same man replied. “We’ll just get lost out here. It’s a fucking maze.”

Crynn searched the surrounding area. As he did, the lights from his suit picked up something on the ground to his left. Small objects littered the floor, glinting. He walked towards it and bent down.

Shards of glass lay at his feet. He picked one up. It was thick, and as he looked closer at the shattered edges, he realised it wasn’t actually glass, it was strengthened polycarbonate. The same material used in their helmets to view out of.

“They were brought this way,” Crynn stated, pointing down the hallway to the left.

“Miko!” Sona shouted again. Crynn was quickly up to his feet and over to his friend. He grabbed her gently by the shoulders and pointed at her console. She flicked back to their channel.

“We need to go after them,” he told her. “If you want to help Miko you need to keep it together. Understand?”

She took a moment, then nodded. Crynn then addressed the others. “I want everyone on their guard and at the ready. Our friends are this way and at least some of them are still alive. Let’s go save them.

CHAPTER 11

THE TEAM PROGRESSED at a jog. Crynn wanted them to move as fast as possible but knew there was a chance they could spring straight into trouble, so led them forward at a steady pace. As they continued, he noticed the walls and ceiling around them became thicker with that strange, organic substance. In a few areas, Crynn was certain he saw it shift and pulse. The ground started to become coated with the same material, making progress slower on the uneven floor beneath them. Crynn then heard someone call out behind him.

"What the fuck is that?!"

Crynn immediately stopped and spun, bringing up his weapon. One of the men had stopped and was facing the wall, arm raised and pointing.

"What?" Crynn asked as he jogged forward. However, after moving a few feet, he saw what his crew mate was referring to. "Fuck . . . " he uttered.

Everyone else gathered around as Crynn stepped close to the wall. It was completely covered in that strange organic substance, but bedded within it, was something else, something more discernible.

A face.

Not human, but Crynn recognised it from the earlier attack, set within a torso that became lost in the surrounding matter of the wall. The mouth of the alien face slowly opened, and its yellow eyes gazed through those gathered before it in a dead stare.

"Is . . . is it alive?" Sona asked.

Crynn studied the strange creature for a few moments before shrugging. "No idea," he said. "It doesn't seem aware of us if it is."

Crynn also noticed small wires and tubes protruding out from the mass of flesh on the walls and feeding into the torso. He suddenly had a horrible idea of what might be happening to the crew that was taken.

Sona had clearly come to the same realisation. "Miko," she uttered in a quiet, terrified voice.

"Come on," Crynn told the team. "We need to move."

He took off again, travelling as fast as possible over the ground, slipping on occasion on the squelchy surface underfoot. Some areas, however, were much harder, and almost caused Crynn to trip as well.

Careful, you idiot, Crynn admonished himself.

"Wait!" someone cried behind him. Crynn again spun around to see one of the women in the group pitching forward after her feet got tangled up in the organic matter. In an instant, Crynn saw where her helmet would strike the ground, at a point where a hard section of the matter jutted upwards. She held a rifle in her hands and was unable to drop it in time to brace herself.

Crynn watched helplessly as the viewing panel of the woman's helmet crashed into the protrusion, which crumpled beneath her weight. There was a burst of fire from her gun as the woman rolled to her back. Crynn flinched and ducked as bullets whizzed past him. He noticed a huge crack across the panel in her helmet before turning around to make sure the involuntary fire hadn't hit anyone . . . but was horrified to see one of the team standing motionless, their helmet punctured, and the screen coated in red gore from the inside. The person dropped lifelessly to the ground.

No!

"Nola!" someone yelled and one of the team ran over to the downed person.

"My helmet's cracked!" cried the woman who had tripped. "There's a hole!" Crynn cast his gaze back to her to see the girl helplessly clamp her gloved hands over the large hole and long crack in the polycarbonate.

Crynn allowed himself a second to take stock and assess. The person who was shot was dead, no question, which meant the woman clutching her helmet was the priority, as was calming the others who were already starting to scream and cry out in shock. As fucked up as the situation was, Crynn knew it could get worse if everyone panicked and the scene descended into chaos.

"Everyone keep calm!" he barked as he ran over to the woman

on the ground. As he moved, he rifled through his utility belt and pulled out a small gun that fired silicon expanding foam. Everyone on the team carried one for this very scenario, though it would wreck the girl's visibility, meaning someone would have to take her back to the Argento.

Crynn just hoped she hadn't lost too much of her air. The woman's hand was insufficient to cover the entire hole in her visor, so it would be spilling out all the time. In fact, he wasn't even sure the foam would be sufficient to plug it.

"Hold still," he told her as he knelt down beside her. "Move your hands so I can apply the foam."

"I'll suffocate," she cried back, and Crynn realised he could hear her actual voice through his helmet and not just through the comms.

"You'll suffocate if you don't," Crynn shouted back and tried to wrestle her hands away and aim the gun at the head of the crack. The woman fought against him for a moment, then she paused. Her brow furrowed.

"Wait!" she said.

"Listen," Crynn went on, desperate for her to listen. "If you don't—"

"No, *you* listen," she snapped. Crynn noticed some of the panic was gone from her voice. "I . . . I can breathe."

Crynn paused. "What do you mean?"

She pushed him away and sat up, looking around in confusion. He saw her chest slowly expand beneath her form-fitting suit. "I can breathe," she repeated.

"There's still air in your suit."

"That isn't what I mean," the girl told him. She waved a gloved hand in front of the hole in her visor. "There's . . . air. I can breathe without the suit. I can feel it drifting in." He watched her take in another slow and steady breath. Her eyes then met his. "The gas that we saw pumped in earlier," she began.

"It was air," Crynn finished, now furrowing his own brow in confusion.

"Why would air be pumped in?" Sona asked.

Crynn didn't have an answer. There was another question as well, equally as unanswerable: *who* was supplying it.

He helped the woman up to her feet, glad of the turn of events, as seeing the size of the gap in her visor up close, he was certain the foam would have been insufficient to stretch right across it, meaning she would have died. Still, she needed to get back.

He turned as he heard the gentle sobbing of one of the team kneeling down next to the person who had been shot. He walked over to see the person sobbing was male and looked to be in his fifties. He couldn't make out the sex of the dead crewmate, as most of their face, and the top of their head, had been obliterated by the shot.

"I'm . . . I'm so sorry," the woman with the hole in her helmet said. "I . . . I didn't mean it."

"You shot her!" the sobbing man cried as his head suddenly snapped up. "You fucking killed my daughter!"

He was suddenly up on his feet and made to dive towards the woman. Crynn quickly put his body in the way, letting his rifle fall and dangle by the support strap as he grabbed the man's wrists.

"Stop!" he shouted, feeling the whole situation slip away from him. If they lost control and everyone had to return to the ship, then those who had been taken would be lost forever, including Miko. And Crynn knew Sona wouldn't just leave the love of her life behind without going on alone if she had to.

The man continued to struggle. Crynn could take him down if needed, he knew, but the last thing he wanted was to cause another accident.

"She didn't mean it," Crynn went on.

"My daughter is dead!" the man cried. Crynn saw the pain etched on his wrinkled face. His pale blue eyes burned with fury. Crynn felt bad for him but couldn't allow the situation to spiral any further than it already had.

"I'm sorry," Crynn said and forced the man a few steps backwards. "I really am. I can't imagine what you are feeling but we can't turn against each other."

"Then *she,*" he seethed and jabbed a finger over to the woman, "shouldn't have killed Nola!"

"It was an accident," Crynn said in the most soothing tone he could muster. He was aware everyone else was just standing and watching on, useless, and still coming to terms with what had happened. It wouldn't take much to send them into a state of panic. "I'm sorry about your daughter, I really am, but what do you propose you do? Are you really going to try to kill the girl who caused it?" He felt the strain in the man relent ever so slightly. "She killed your daughter by accident, but you'd be killing her in cold blood. Then what? I didn't know Nola, but would she really approve of that?"

The man's eyes suddenly met his own. "Don't tell me what my daughter would have wanted," he snarled. Even so, Crynn sensed some of the man's rage ebb away. His body sagged and he stepped back. He then walked over to his daughter again and knelt down. He began to cry again.

"I didn't mean it," the woman behind Crynn said again.

"I know," Crynn replied. In truth, she should never have had a firearm in the first place. The same could be said for most that currently held them. The mission was fucked from the outset.

Keep it together, he told himself. *Everyone is counting on you.*

"What's your name?" he asked the grieving father, who took a moment to respond, like he hadn't heard the question at first.

"Aziel," the man replied, gazing at his daughter. Crynn could barely bring himself to look at the mess within the poor woman's helmet, so he had no idea how Aziel continued to stare.

"Aziel," Crynn went on. "I want you to go back to the Argento."

The man gave a firm shake of his head. "I'm not leaving her," he insisted. "I . . . I can't. She can't stay here. I won't have her left behind."

"Crynn," Sona interrupted. "We need to keep going. The others need us."

He took a breath. "I'm aware of that," he said. "And we'll move as soon as we can." He turned to Aziel. "Sir, I know this is hard. Actually, scratch that, I have no idea. I've never suffered what you just have. *But* . . . there are others that need our help. I don't want to just leave you here, but we need to keep going. Please, go back to the ship. If we can, I promise I'll try to collect Nola when we come back."

The older man's head snapped up, eyes burning, and he snarled. "I already told you, I'm *not* leaving her here!"

Crynn withheld a sigh. He knew he was going to have to leave the man behind as well. However, the woman who had inadvertently killed Nola stepped forward with tears of remorse in her eyes.

"I'll help."

Everyone's attention turned to her. "What do you mean?" Crynn asked.

"It's my fault," she said, looking directly at Aziel. "All of it. And I'm so sorry. But I need to go back, so I'll help you carry your daughter, get her back home."

Crynn watched Aziel's face through his visor and could see the conflict etched there. He obviously detested the woman responsible, but if it meant getting his daughter back . . .

"Fine," he eventually said. "But this doesn't mean I forgive you."

"I know," the woman replied, softly. "I don't forgive myself. I never will."

Aziel moved to the head of his daughter. "Get her legs," he ordered the woman. Crynn took her rifle from her and she duly obliged the order, hooking the dead woman's legs in her arms. Aziel shifted Nola's body around as he grabbed hold of her under her arms and Crynn grimaced as he saw some of the blood and gore within the helmet shift around. The two people then heaved Nola up.

"You know the way back?" Crynn asked.

"Of course," the father replied. "We haven't come that far."

Crynn nodded. "Then be careful. Keep alert and also watch your step."

"Think you are capable of doing that this time?" Aziel asked the woman opposite him. She didn't respond and lowered her eyes. Crynn felt bad for her but chose not to say anything. Not given what Aziel was going through and how fresh his pain was. The pair carrying the body slowly made their way back, carefully navigating their ground as they disappeared around a corner.

Crynn turned back to the rest of his team. All eyes were on him. Most people looked shocked and horrified, which was to be expected, but at least they had stayed quiet while Aziel's situation had been dealt with. Now, he needed to make sure they were committed to what lay ahead. He could ill afford to lose any more numbers.

"I know what just happened will have shaken you," Crynn said, addressing them all. "It should serve to remind us of the dangers we face out here, not just from whatever might be lurking in the darkness, but from our own lack of concentration. Because, make no mistake, what happened there could and should have been avoided. Everyone with a weapon, make sure the safety is on until you need to use your rifle. And be fucking careful where you are walking. I don't care if there is air around us now. We don't know how easily it can be taken away so I want helmets and visors on at all times." He was speaking sternly, to focus people's minds back on the task at hand. "We don't have the luxury of sending anyone else back, so you are all in this until we complete our mission. Our friends and family are still out there and we're going to help them." He then turned his attention to one of the group who was without a weapon. He handed her the spare rifle he was holding.

"Remember what I showed you back at the Argento?" Crynn asked her.

She eyed the weapon with a look of trepidation, but nodded. "Yes."

"Good. Safety is now on. Take it and only use it if you need to."

He handed it to her then, and again made his way to the head of the group. "Now . . . follow me."

Thankfully, he was met with no resistance, and everyone fell in behind.

CHAPTER 12

THE TEAM HAD carried on down the corridor ahead of them, seeing more of those strange alien creatures bedded into the walls and ceiling. They noticed that many of the bodies were not whole or intact, with the head of some a few feet away from the torso, connected by synthetic-looking tendrils, wires, and tubes.

"Why are they here like this?" Sona asked. No one answered. Crynn turned to see his friend tapping on her forearm console. He knew exactly what she was doing and hopped on to the same comms channel they'd used before. It was still showing some low levels of audible activity and when he connected, he heard it was the same pained groans from before.

"Sona," he said, "don't torture yourself. Come off the channel and keep focused."

"Miko?" Sona said, ignoring Crynn. "Honey, can you hear me?"

No clear reply came through, though Crynn was certain he heard a quiet sobbing amongst the moans of pain.

Eventually, they came across an open doorway, just to their left. The opening was around eight feet square. Crynn slowly moved towards it and peered inside, letting the torch beams push back the darkness.

His heart froze.

In an instant, he brought up a closed fist next to his head, indicating for those following behind to halt in their tracks.

Crynn then put both hands on his rifle and aimed it at the mass of creatures stood within the dark space.

None of those things moved, all standing stock still, like nightmarish mannequins, arms and limbs down by their sides and no signs of life in their eyes.

There were scores of the alien creatures, all huddled in the centre of the large space that had a slightly curved ceiling around ten feet above. The room was deep, and Crynn's lights managed to illuminate past the motionless life forms, where he saw something else that caused his throat to tighten and stomach to drop.

Crynn was able to make out the back wall. Like many other surfaces, it had a layer of organic sludge coating it, though here it isn't quite as thick as in other areas. Through the matter, Crynn could make out the actual structure of the wall, only this time it wasn't the same dark material he had noticed elsewhere. There were many blinking lights, tangles of wires and tubes, as well as shifting parts that he couldn't identify. There was also a secretion that came from an unknown source, running out and into the surrounding matter.

All of this was secondary, however, to the true horror Crynn laid his eyes upon. There, fused to the wall, were his crewmates.

Or what was left of them.

The poor souls were encased in the organic matter, with only parts of their bodies showing. Some limbs were positioned many feet away from the main torso, connected by lengths of tendons and strange fibres and wires. The head of one poor man was half a meter above his body, linked by those stringy red veins, tendons and wires, as well as a length of his spinal cord.

The crewman *should* have been dead. But he wasn't. Though his wide-open eyes had a dead stare, his mouth slowly opened and closed as if he were silently screaming. After a moment, Crynn noticed the man's glazed eyes slowly move around before falling still again.

"What the fuck . . . " someone on his team muttered.

As he turned his head, Crynn saw that there were scores of people stuck to the walls to their sides as well, some with their stomachs open and intestines spread out like a gory web, snaking into the strange matter around them. In all cases, the poor people showed some signs of vacuous life. Ruined space suits were strewn on the floor, torn and ripped, with smashed helmets sitting next to them.

Those creatures stripped the crew down before eviscerating them and stringing them up, Crynn realised.

"Miko!" Sona suddenly yelled.

Crynn saw her sprint forward before he was able to grab her. She weaved through the motionless creatures before them, moving too fast not to make contact, and ended up shoulder barging one or two, but kept going. Crynn winced, expecting the strange entities to converge on Sona in an instant . . . but none of them moved.

"Sona, stop!" Crynn barked into his radio, but his friend kept going, breaking through the alien crowd and sprinting over to a section of the wall. Beyond her, Crynn saw Miko. His stomach lurched.

Sona's lover was in perhaps the worst state of all.

Her head and all her limbs were detached from the main torso, spread around in a disorganised fashion, with one leg up above the main body, her head off to the left, and both arms off to the right. Yet again, all limbs were connected, though Crynn could also see metallic plating infused with Miko's various body parts. What's more, the matter around Miko was shifting, resembling a sludge as opposed to the hardened organic substance elsewhere. It moved Miko's body parts around, and Crynn watched as the substance totally covered her torso just as Sona reached it.

Sona then began clawing at the dark brown goo, screaming her lover's name over and over: "Miko, Miko, I'm here! Miko!"

As soon as the first handful of the substance was moved, revealing a metal plate with blinking red lights now attached to Miko, Crynn saw the idle creatures huddled in the centre of the room suddenly come to life.

"Sona!" Crynn shouted. "Weapons up!"

But his friend didn't respond and continued to claw helplessly at the sludge that replaced itself just as quickly as it was removed.

Damn it, Sona.

Crynn had the stock of his weapon anchored to his shoulder as the monstrosities before him turned.

"Everyone with a rifle, ready to fire!" Crynn commanded. "Arc left and right and circle around. Make sure you hit your targets. Aim low. I don't want any fire getting through and hitting Sona or . . ." He was about to reference the crew members fused to the wall, but the words wouldn't come. "Ready?"

As those with him spread out as ordered, Crynn hesitated. He was terrified some of the team would fuck up and kill his friend, but he had no other option. Through gritted teeth, he eventually gave the order.

"Fire!"

The team around Crynn unleashed a hail of bullets. Crynn opened fire as well, keeping his aim low, cutting into the legs of the shambling beings as they lurched forward towards Sona. Thankfully, the others kept their aim away from Sona as instructed, and caught the creatures in a crossfire, the bullets cutting through the flesh of their legs. Unlike the firefight out in the hangar earlier when some of the crew had originally been taken, the one taking place in that awful and macabre room was *loud* thanks to the air around them allowing the deafening sound of shooting to travel.

Now under the threat of attack, the alien beings turned as one, and advanced on their attackers.

Sona was still too focused on her lover to pay much attention to what was going on around her, so Crynn sprinted forward, racing around the mob and his team in a wide arc.

"Keep them occupied," he ordered as he reached his friend. He grabbed her arm.

"We need to pull back," a man in the team shouted. Fear and panic were evident in his voice. Crynn ignored him, shaking Sona as she clawed at the wall. He didn't even want to look at Miko, but could see her jaw slowly work in his peripheral vision as her face was etched in a look of terrified agony.

"Sona!" he shouted again. "Fall back. We can't stay here." A volley of stray bullets whizzed past Crynn's head and buried themselves into the wall beside him. "Watch where you're shooting!" he snarled at the others.

Sona shrugged Crynn's hand off her shoulder. "I can't leave her," she said. Crynn's heart broke for his friend at hearing the sadness and desperation in her voice, but he didn't have time to show sympathy.

"Look at her!" he shouted and pointed towards Miko's detached head. "You can't save her, Sona. Just fucking look at her."

Sona's gaze, which had been concentrated on the covered torso, slowly drifted over to Miko's head as Sona's frantic clawing slowed. Crynn watched through the glass of his friend's helmet and he saw the look of pain cloud her face as her heart broke. Tears flowed as Sona clenched her teeth together. Her body began to shake.

"We need to go, Sona," Crynn gently said, as gunfire continued around them. "We can't stay."

"I . . . I can't leave her like this."

Miko's mouth continued to open and close like a fish out of water gulping for air. Crynn took hold of Sona's rifle, which was dangling down by her side by the strap. He looked around to make sure they had time, then put it into her hands and raised the barrel for her, pointing it towards Miko's head.

"I'm so sorry," he said. "But this needs to be quick. End her suffering, then we need to go."

Sona looked at the gun, then turned to Crynn as horror washed over her face. "What . . . what do you mean?"

"We don't have long, Sona," Crynn replied. "We can't save her, but you don't have to leave her like this."

He hated to put such pressure on Sona. Putting a bullet into your life partner was an unthinkable thing to do, and Crynn was pushing Sona to do it moments after seeing Miko in that horrific state. But it was this or nothing. He turned and trained his weapon on the other monstrosities that were all busy with his team, who themselves were slowly falling back.

Not that he had given the order for it.

Two people at the front of the crowd fell as the creatures sprinted forward into the hail of bullets and managed to take them down.

We need to leave! Panic filled Crynn.

He turned back to his friend and watched as Sona took a breath, readying herself for what needed to be done. Then, her expression changed as her jaw dropped. Crynn quickly turned to see Miko's eyes had now locked onto Sona. There seemed to be something there, a kind of focus. Miko's eyebrows raised.

"She . . . she can see me," Sona uttered.

"Impossible," Crynn replied. *How could she? Her fucking head wasn't even attached.*

But Crynn saw it himself. There was recognition there. Miko's mouth opened as if she were trying to speak, then an expression of pure pain and anguish.

Does she even realise what kind of state she's in? Crynn had to wonder.

"She sees me!" Sona repeated, as if the development changed anything. There was no way to help Miko, no way to fix what had happened to her body. They'd tried for her, and for the others who now found themselves desecrated by the strange space station, but now Crynn and the others had to concentrate on themselves.

"Pull the trigger, Sona," Crynn said.

Sona lowered her gun. "What?"

"You heard me."

"I can't! She recognises me! She's in there, somewhere."

"Then put her out of the hell she's in!" Crynn snapped back. It pained him to think that way, but the whole thing was taking too long. The swarm of creatures behind them would soon advance. "Because if you don't, I will. And frankly, I'd want you to do the same for me. Do you really think you can save her from . . . *this?*"

He motioned to Miko on the wall, with her body resembling a horrific and disconnected jigsaw, waiting to be put back together. Sona looked back to her as well. Crynn saw the battle taking place inside her as the woman clenched her jaw and let out a stifled sob.

Crynn turned and raised his gun. The team had filtered back out of the room, forced away by the alien creatures, who were following. However, those at the back slowly turned, for the first time directing their attention towards Crynn and Sona.

"Please, Sona, do it now. For Miko, as well as us."

Crynn held off firing for as long as he could, fearing as soon as he unleashed his first volley, it would spur the monsters into a quicker advance. In his peripheral vision, Crynn saw Sona eventually raise her gun again. He heard her weep.

"I'm so sorry, my love," Sona whispered. A burst of fire erupted next to Crynn causing him to jump, despite him having expected it. He instinctively looked back at Miko. The top right section of her head had exploded, disintegrating her eye and everything above it.

But the single eye that remained was still focused, and Miko's mouth continued to scream its silent cry.

Sona began to howl. "I've hurt her! How can she still be alive? I'm so sorry."

Crynn grabbed Sona's arm as he noticed the organic matter around Miko's body shift and move, starting to cover the dismembered woman.

"No!" Sona cried as her lover disappeared completely. Crynn pulled her along beside him.

"We need to go."

The straggling monsters weren't pursuing the rest of the team; they sprinted forward towards Crynn and Sona. He squeezed the trigger of his rifle, again aiming low to cut the legs of the creatures out from under them. There were six in total. One fell as Crynn successfully mangled one of its lower limbs.

He quickly allowed himself a glance over to his two fallen comrades. One had his helmet ripped off and there was a bloody hole where his face used to be. The man was clawing at his ruined head, but his movements were slowing. The other was split in two at the waist, with ropey intestines running out from the exposed midsection.

Fire erupted next to Crynn again as Sona stepped forward with her rifle up. She unloaded shot after shot into the five approaching creatures.

"You evil fucking things!" Sona seethed as she continued to fire. However, her aim was unsteady, and she waved the barrel of her gun in slow arcs both left and right in an attempt to hit as many of the monsters as possible, which meant she missed more shots than she landed.

"Aim for one at a time," Crynn ordered. "And take out their legs to stop them advancing." Almost as soon as Crynn had finished his explanation, Crynn put another enemy down after concentrating his fire on its lower extremities. The downed creatures still pulled themselves forward across the floor, but at a much slower pace.

Sona continued her wild firing, screaming as she did. Crynn placed a hand on the top of her rifle and gripped it firmly, stopping Sona from sweeping the weapon any farther. The gun vibrated savagely under his palm. "Aim for one at a fucking time, Sona. You wanna put some down to avenge Miko, then make your shots count."

Thankfully, his friend listened this time, and began picking her shots. Crynn pushed her to the left as he started to side-step right. "We'll go around and catch them in a crossfire, then bolt for the exit. Stop shooting when we're opposite each other; I don't want to eat one of your bullets." Sona didn't answer and kept up her fire. Crynn slapped the back of her helmet. "I mean it. We're going to get back to the ship, get off the station then nuke the place. *Then* you will have paid them back for Miko. But if you don't start listening, we'll just end up joining her."

Crynn immediately regretted saying that, knowing that in her state of shock, that might be just what Sona wanted, to go down in a hail of fire.

However, to his eternal relief, Sona complied and began to move around the monstrosities. Crynn followed suit, moving in the opposite direction, with both of them cutting down more of the deformed alien creatures. Two more fell. Then a third.

"Get to the door!" Crynn shouted just before they reached the halfway point of their arcs. The two sprinted to the open doorway. Crynn could still hear pained sobs coming over his comms from Sona and hoped she could keep it together long enough to do what was needed. Once they were safe, he would then concentrate his efforts on being a good friend and provide a literal shoulder to cry on.

As he joined Sona's side, Crynn quickly checked the display panel at the head of his rifle, checking the ammo count.

Still good.

The projectiles hurled forward from the weapon were extremely small, but propelled at a frightening rate and exploded on impact using microscopic tactical explosives on the tips. That way, the rifles were able to hold thousands of rounds of ammunition. Rather than fleeing immediately, Crynn wanted to take out the remaining two creatures, so they could not follow. After a few well aimed bursts, they fell.

"Let's go," Crynn shouted, taking one last glance back at his crew mates, fused to the walls around him. He grabbed Sona and ran back into the hallway. Up ahead, he heard gunfire and screaming.

The pair ran down the corridor as fast as possible, being careful not to trip, weaving their way back to the hangar. It was there Crynn saw the rest of his team trying to fend off the horde that had followed.

A volley of bullets hit the wall next to Crynn, causing him to grab Sona's arm and pull her to the side so as not to get caught by friendly fire. Crynn and Sona circled the creatures in the hangar, who were beginning to overwhelm the rest of the team. Men and women fell, letting out shrieks of pain as limbs were torn free.

"We need to get back to the ship!" Crynn commanded and quickly changed his comms channel to connect with the Argento. "This is Crynn. Open up the airlock and let us back inside. The mission is finished."

"Afraid we can't do that," came the reply. It was the captain. "We've been monitoring your comms during the mission and can see what's happening out there. We can't risk any of those things getting on board the ship."

Crynn looked over to his team. He saw one man lying on the ground, arms raised in panic, as the heavy foot of an alien fell and smashed through his visor and helmet, crushing his head. Those with weapons were missing most of their shots, and some even hitting each other.

"We're dying out here!" Crynn shouted back.

There was a short pause. "I'm sorry," the captain said. "But you knew the risks."

Crynn was about to argue back but the entire hangar was soon washed in a white light.

CHAPTER 13

"WHAT THE FUCK is that?" Sona shouted as the hangar around them suddenly lit up. Crynn squinted as he looked up, now able to see the ceiling above him. The light shone out from huge, flat fittings that were not covered by the organic matter around them. Turning to his side, he saw some of the huge floodlights lined the walls as well, these areas similarly unobscured by the strange flesh.

The amount of light suddenly generated in the huge space was considerable, dousing the whole area with a clinical white sheen.

With more of the hangar now revealed, Crynn was even more in awe of its size. The Argento looked lost in space, which stretched on for hundreds, if not thousands, of feet. There was a concave shape to the ceiling above, with repeating ribbed sections, making the hangar resemble a long mouth. Deeper, he could make out other ships as well: alien vessels covered with the strange organic matter that infested the rest of the space station, a graveyard for those ancient husks.

Awful shrieking sounds immediately alerted Crynn to something happening on the other side of the Argento. He ducked, looking beneath the vessel, and his heart caught in his throat.

Hundreds of creatures poured out of doorways on the far side of the hangar. Then, they began to filter through openings closer to him and his team as well. He noticed some were of the same species that they had seen already, but there were new variants in the hordes as well, including some that were over fifteen-feet tall: great, shambling beings with small, flat heads on hulking bodies.

We're fucked.

"Sona," Crynn said, switching his comm back, "is there a way to get back aboard the Argento if they don't want us to get in? The captain said—"

"I heard what he said," she replied through gritted teeth. "The fucker wants to leave us out here to die."

Crynn allowed himself a panicked look around to make sure they weren't about to be swarmed. "And we will if there isn't a way to get aboard."

He saw Sona set her jaw within her helmet. Her eyes were still wet and red. The team beyond them now were all-but decimated.

"The landing gears," Sona eventually replied. "If we can get to the front one and climb it, there is a way to get inside. It'll be tight and a difficult crawl until—"

"Good enough," Crynn said, interrupting her, and grabbed Sona's hand.

It was a few hundred feet to the front of the ship, and specifically the landing gear at the nose of the Argento. However, with both Crynn and Sona sprinting as fast as they could, Crynn felt confident they would reach it before any of the creatures could catch them. The monstrosities were relatively slow moving, even at their fastest, moving with the stifled grace of, well, a reanimated corpse.

However, the problem was the mass of creatures on the opposite side of the Argento that were closing in. They already had a head start and seemed to be making a beeline for the ship.

Crynn thought those monstrosities had just taken note of him and Sona and were coming for them, but then he saw where their eyes were really looking . . . straight at the Argento. They were going for the ship.

As Crynn and Sona got closer, Crynn heard the sound of mechanical releases coming from the Argento. He frowned at first, not sure what the noises signified, but then he saw a number of gun turrets lower from the belly of the ship. They rotated around to face the advancing aliens.

That'll buy us some time.

The ship's guns opened fire. The turrets boomed, the sound enough to knock Crynn's equilibrium and almost make him lose his footing. He pushed through but then noticed some of the guns spinning to face his direction.

He barely had time to widen his eyes in surprise before he felt himself knocked to the ground by Sona, who had thrown her body into his, just in time to avoid the hail of fire that was launched at the creatures behind them. He turned and saw scores of the alien entities obliterated by gunfire; their bodies exploding on the spot, blown to bits and leaving smouldering scorch marks in their wake.

Bastards! Crynn thought. *They didn't care if they hit us.*

However, Sona was soon up to her feet, dragging Crynn alongside her. "Hurry!" she shouted, as she hauled Crynn over to the large landing gear. It was taller than they were, almost double their height; a latticework of thick metal and cables with a substantial hydraulic cylinder at its centre. Horizontal panels hung down from the ship around the landing gear—doors that had opened to allow the gear to drop.

The sheer numbers advancing towards them was terrifying, and the small army was accompanied by a cacophony of awful screeches and wails that carried through the air. Sona, however, wasted no time in climbing the landing gear.

"Hurry the fuck up!" she barked, prompting Crynn into action.

The guns on the Argento continued to fire, and the power of the shots was enough to slowly rock the gigantic ship, making it sway slightly from side to side as Crynn and Sona climbed upwards. Above them, the form of the landing gear disappeared into a dark void as it ran inside the main structure of the ship. There was enough clearance around the metallic shaft for Crynn and Sona to squeeze through, and the torchlights from their suits quickly illuminated the space.

Sona led Crynn to their immediate right after climbing inside, where a small passageway had opened up, which was large enough to crawl through. Thick rubber wires surrounded them, and Crynn noticed metallic tracks above and below them that the landing gear would use to run along when retracting. He just prayed those aboard the Argento didn't try to take off and lift the gear anytime soon, or they'd both be squashed flat inside that small space.

Then, over the continued gunfire outside, he heard something that gave him pause: the clanging of metal and the sound of those awful shrieks growing closer.

"They're climbing the gear as well!" he exclaimed to Sona. "Shit, they're coming after us."

"Or they're trying to get into the ship."

Shit, Crynn thought. *Either way we're fucked.*

"Keep going," he urged. "And make it quick."

The pair made steady progress, and Crynn kept looking over his shoulder and aiming his gun behind himself to make sure the creatures weren't behind them. It didn't take long for the alien monstrosities to clamber inside the crawl space as well, squeezing their large bodies inside, pushing against the cables and wires around them. Crynn let off a few shots, striking the entity at the head of the pack. The first few shots obliterated the creature's face, which was buried into its upper torso, and others tore away one of its thick shoulders.

"Watch where you're shooting," Sona suddenly shouted. "If you damage the cables we won't be able to retract the gear, meaning we'll struggle to fly out of here."

The faceless monster continued to slowly move forward, however, driven by something keeping it alive long after it should have died. Crynn took more precise shots, trying to connect with the strange, alien technology grafted to its body, and succeeded in destroying a metallic panel on the side of its chest. Eventually, the creature grew still, though some of those behind it forced their way through.

"Up here," Crynn heard Sona shout. He saw her roll to her back and pull some tools free from her utility belt. There was a large access panel above her and a small console next to it. "Keep them busy," she ordered, and began to remove the cover plate of the console panel. Crynn kept up his fire as Sona worked.

"What are you doing?" he shouted.

"Overriding the access panel," she said. "With the landing gear down and the gear doors open, this panel is sealed shut so there is no air leak."

"Will it take long?" Crynn asked, panicked. However, he soon heard a hiss and then a metallic release.

"Done," she replied. Sona then pushed against the panel above her, moving to her knees as she struggled with the heavy door. It eventually moved and swung upwards. "Come on, let's go," she called to him as she disappeared into the ship.

However, Crynn turned his attention back to the approaching enemy. The large creature he'd put down at the head of the line was causing a problem for the others, and they were finding it difficult to squeeze past, though some of the smaller ones had.

"We don't want these things following us," he shouted back.

"What do you mean?"

But Crynn didn't answer. Instead, he took aim with his rifle again, aiming it down between his feet, and started to open fire.

"Don't hit the cables you fucking idiot!" Sona snapped.

But Crynn was careful with his shots, and aiming wasn't difficult as the alien bodies before him had nowhere to move to and couldn't avoid his fire. After a few more minutes of fire, Crynn had managed to kill enough of the slowly advancing enemy that the crawlspace had become completely bottlenecked. Only then did he haul himself out to join Sona.

He found himself in a corridor on the lower decks of the Argento, though couldn't place exactly where they were, not familiar with that part of the ship. Crynn panted heavily and was relieved for the momentary let up. After closing the panel once more, Sona reached up and released her helmet, which was accompanied by a small hiss as the air from her suit bled free into the atmosphere around her. Sweat coated her skin. Her face was flushed and her eyes still red. He was about to ask her if she was okay, but Sona cut him off.

"Come on," she told him, pointing down to their right. "This way."

"Where are we going?" Crynn asked, removing his own helmet.

"We're going up to the command deck," she said. "And we're going to force the captain to get us the hell out of here."

CHAPTER 14

"HOW THE HELL did you get back aboard?" the captain snapped at Crynn and Sona after they entered the command deck unannounced.

The pair had sprinted up to the top deck after entering the ship, using access ladders and stairways rather than lifts, and had thankfully found the main door to the room open as senior staff were frantically running in and out of the room while carrying out their duties. Red lights flashed around them, signalling a state of high alert.

The command deck was oval shaped, and around ten meters in diameter at its widest point. Windows around the room gave a panoramic view of the hangar. Captain Ellis jumped down from his seat, which was a large, padded chair suspended from the ceiling on a vertical strut, allowing it to swivel to see all areas of the deck. Workstations and screens lined the edges of the room and there were floor-mounted consoles dotted around the centre. The area was a hive of activity and noise, which only fell silent once the captain strode up to Crynn and Sona.

"I'll ask you again," he snarled. "How the hell did you get back onto the ship?"

"Would you rather we stayed out there and died?" Crynn snapped.

Sona raised a hand and placed it on Crynn's chest, signalling for him to back down. "Through the front landing gear," she explained.

The captain raised an eyebrow. "There's a way through there?"

"Yes, but I resealed the access panel," Sona explained.

"And I clogged up the crawl space pretty good," Crynn added. "If we manage to take off and retract the landing gear, that should finish off whatever else is still down there."

"Sir," a woman stationed at a console interrupted, "those . . . things . . . are climbing the hull. Hundreds of them."

"Can they get in?" Captain Ellis asked.

The woman considered the question for a moment, then shook her head. "Unless they can break some of the viewing windows—and those things are thick—then I doubt it."

While the discussion was taking place, Crynn drifted over to one of the windows and looked out, keen to know what had happened to his team. His stomach dropped as he saw what he'd expected: they had all been wiped out. Bloody remains and body parts littered the ground where they had made their last stand. The swarm of creatures had left their bodies on the floor and all alien life in the hangar was now surging towards the ship.

Crynn took a breath. He and Sona had abandoned the others and left them to die. Granted, the pair would have no doubt been killed as well had they chosen to stand alongside the team; instead they'd saved their own skin and fled. It might have been the sensible decision, but that didn't bring Crynn any comfort. He'd been trusted to lead the team, to finally prove his worth, and he'd failed.

"Sir," Sona began, "we need to figure out a way to get free of this station."

"You have a talent for stating the fucking obvious," the captain shot back. "We do, however, have a plan of action." Crynn turned, eager to hear it. The captain went on: "The crew are readying some of our heaviest weapons. We're going to blow through the wall that closed up earlier. Then, we're going to fly out of here and head back to known space."

Crynn looked out of the windows behind them, to the section of wall in question. "Will our weapons penetrate it?"

Captain Ellis gave a shrug. "No idea. But we have some pretty powerful guns on this ship. I should think so."

"But what about the damage it might do to the Argento?" Crynn replied. "We're not that far away from the hull. Any explosion could—"

"I'm aware of that," Captain Ellis snapped. "Which is why we're going to start small. We don't have a lot of choices here. *Something* closed the hole up behind us, trapping us inside, and has now unleashed those things out there. If we don't do something to get free, then this place will be our graveyard."

Crynn couldn't argue that point. Better to die trying than to sit and wait for death to claim you. He looked outside again and saw more and more of the alien creatures pouring inside the hangar and descending upon the ship. *How many are there?*

"Is there room inside here to take off before we fire?" Crynn asked. "To move us away from the wall?" He was also concerned about the route he and Sona had used to get inside. Eventually, the creatures would pull out the bodies blocking the crawl space, and if there were enough of them, it was *possible* they could force their way through the access panel, strong as it was.

"It'd be tight," the captain said and looked over to one of his pilots. "Simmons, what do you think?"

The man swivelled around in his seat and Crynn saw the blood drain from his face. "I've . . . I've never done anything like that before,' he said. 'Manoeuvring in such an enclosed space—"

"Is. It. Possible?" Captain Ellis sternly repeated.

"Maybe," came the delayed reply, as the pilot looked to his colleagues. They offered him blank stares in response.

"Ready yourself to try," the captain ordered. "We are almost ready to open fire with some of our heavier weapons. I want us to be airborne when—"

The captain trailed off as he gazed out of one of the windows overlooking the left-hand side of the hangar. Crynn followed the direction he was looking and frowned himself.

"What the . . . " he uttered.

On the far wall, there was a large, circular area where the organic substance lining it was beginning to . . . glow. A strong blue hue seeped through the matter, eventually burning it away. Crynn wasn't able to see the surface beneath, only the circular light that grew stronger.

"What is that?" someone asked, as if anyone aboard could possibly give an answer.

"Is it coming from inside the wall or something?" Sona asked as she stepped forward.

Then a blue beam exploded from the light source, shooting forward and striking the Argento in its side. The ship rocked from side to side, causing Crynn and others to stumble. The beam, which looked around ten meters in diameter, continued for a few seconds before disappearing in an instant. The Argento then grew still.

“What the fuck happened?” the captain demanded, to no one in particular. “Was that a weapon of some kind?”

“Sir,” an officer at one of the consoles interrupted, “it’s punched a hole through the hull. Decks four through eight.”

There was a moments silence as everyone took the information in.

“Can we still fly?” the captain asked. “Is there a way to seal off the areas affected?” There was a rising panic in his voice.

“We’d need to evacuate the starboard side of those decks and lower certain blast doors. It should be enough.”

“Do it,” Captain Ellis commanded. “Put out the evacuation order. I want those areas cleared in a matter of minutes. Anyone not out in time is on their own.”

The officer nodded and began to make the announcement. The captain then addressed his navigation team. “Get us up in the air and turned around,” he shouted. “Now. Then bring the weapons online and punch a hole in that fucking wall.” He pointed out of a window behind them. As Crynn followed the captain’s gesture and looked through the window, he narrowed his eyes and frowned. “Erm . . . Sir,” he said and pointed as well.

“What now?” Captain Ellis asked.

“The wall,” Crynn replied as he walked across the command deck over to the window. “It’s . . . opening.”

Everyone fell silent. Those standing drifted over to the window as well.

“What in the hell . . . ?” Captain Ellis muttered.

The back wall of the station was indeed beginning to open. Starting at a point in the centre, a hole formed that expanded outwards, pushing away the structure that folded in on itself like a gelatinous substance being penetrated by an invisible force. Crynn had watched a similar effect when the same wall had initially closed up, and still couldn’t understand how it was possible, given from the outside the station’s hull appeared to be metallic. Regardless, the opening kept widening, like a great yawning mouth, encompassing the full width and height of the hangar and providing them with a view of outer space. And what Crynn saw out there made him draw in a sharp breath.

For the longest time, everyone on the command deck simply stared ahead in stunned silence. Nothing about what they could see made sense. The area of space outside the station had changed completely.

No longer were they looking at an endless void of black pin pricked with stars and the odd swirl of distant galaxies; now the view was dominated by something that threatened to fracture Crynn's mind, and around it, great, vast crawling things that moved through space. He couldn't tell if the titanic, multi-limbed monstrosities were ships or space-dwelling creatures of some kind.

Beyond these entities was the void of space itself. No black canvas, but rather a storm of angry reds and purples that swirled together, interspersed with great spikes of light that resembled enormous streaks of lightning. Behind everything was a great light. It was hard to tell how many million miles away that enormous source of pure white light was, but the chaotic streaks of lightning were expelled from it, thrust forward and covering millions of miles.

However, the thing that Crynn couldn't draw his eyes away from was the gigantic form that floated centrally in the view outside. Again, it was difficult to judge the titan's distance, but its sheer size was terrifying, easily bigger than a planet or sun, but to Crynn, it resembled a kind of foetus, the form curled up and hugging itself. It was in no way human, however, with stumpy legs and fat, three-toed feet. Its bulbous head was enormous in comparison to its torso, and what Crynn assumed to be its titanic mouth resembled more a cephalopodic sucker.

Just staring at the still, alien foetus infused Crynn with a terror he had never known before, and he couldn't stop his body from shaking.

"What . . . " the captain began in a quivering voice. "What the hell are we looking at?"

No one offered an answer, but Crynn followed up with. "Where did that . . . *thing* . . . come from? And those entities around it?"

"They didn't come from anywhere," Sona eventually answered.

"What do you mean?" Crynn asked, turning to her.

Sona was starting dead ahead, eyes wide. "We're not where we were before. Think about it. We only noticed the station after the solar storm. But it wasn't a storm. The whole phenomenon was just the station appearing in our space."

"How can you know that?" the captain asked.

Sona shrugged. "I can't, for certain. But once the Argento docked, the wall closed up behind us, and we felt something, remember? Like the station was shaking itself apart. Well, what if it was transporting us back to where it came from. To this place . . . " She pointed out to the nightmarish scenes outside the station.

"And where *is* this place?" Captain Ellis demanded.

"Damned if I know," Sona replied. Her shoulders slumped. "But we can't get home. If we leave the station, we fly into that hell."

While it was true Sona couldn't be sure she was correct, Crynn was inclined to believe her. It made a strange kind of sense to him.

"But why take us?" one of the command crew asked, panicked. "Why drag us out here?"

Something clicked in Crynn's mind as he thought of the initial crew members that were taken and imprisoned within the walls of the station. "They're experimenting on us," he said.

"Who's *they?*" Captain Ellis asked.

Crynn shrugged. "Whoever or whatever controls the station. Maybe the station itself. But that's why it swallowed our people and fused them with the structure. I don't know how, but the station is studying us, learning about us." The more he spoke, the more confident he became in his assertion. "Before our crew was taken, we needed our suits to breathe out there. Then, we noticed air fill up the corridors and hangar. Why else would that happen if the station hadn't learned we needed it to breathe?"

"Why let us breathe at all if the station wants to kill us?" one of the pilots asked.

"Maybe it doesn't want to kill us. Not all of us," Crynn answered. "Like I said, maybe we're being studied like bugs." He thought of the alien creatures outside swarming over the ship. "Those things out there probably suffered a similar fate before being repurposed by the station. Who knows how many species encountered this place."

"So, you're proposing this station is . . . what . . . a giant, floating Venus fly trap?" the captain asked. "Preying on space-faring species."

Crynn nodded. "Why not? Only when it breaks us down, it studies us. Learns about us."

"For what purpose?"

Crynn shook his head at the captain's question. "Who knows. Maybe so they know how to beat us."

"When you say 'they', you mean the Agoul, don't you?" one of the crewmen asked.

"I don't know," Crynn replied. "It could be. But I've heard stories about the Agoul, we all have, and somehow this doesn't line up." A few people nodded in agreement. "There are other stories though, like the one about the red woman . . . "

"You don't believe that old tale? Temples and magic and all that gibberish?" Captain Ellis said, sneeringly.

Crynn shrugged.

He again looked to the chaos outside, specifically at the titanic entity. "Whatever is behind the station, I'm guessing it's linked to *that,* somehow."

Crynn continued to stare at the huge entity. *Is it some kind of god?* Just looking at it made him feel minuscule and utterly irrelevant. Less than a bug, but a microbe, completely beneath notice or concern of such a thing.

A beeping from one of the control panels alerted the attention of one of the command crew, who turned to the screen before then addressing the captain.

"Sir," he began. "Those things outside are getting into the ship. Through the hole that was punched in the side." Crynn noticed his voice was flat and defeated, the man delivering the news like a robot. He understood what Crynn did: it was impossible for them to get free now, because even if they did, there was nowhere to go.

They were doomed.

The massive opening in the wall of the station then began to slowly close up again; the hole retreating on itself and the terrible view being swallowed up. Crynn was at first confused as to why it had opened up in the first place, before a thought struck him.

We're being taunted, he realised. *Whatever is controlling the station is just showing us how helpless we are, and the kind of things we're facing. It's crushing our hope and desire to survive.*

Crynn then looked around the room and realised the station had succeeded. The expressions on the faces of his crewmates varied between horrified and forlorn. Many had tears in their eyes.

"What . . . what do we do?" one of the command crew asked.

Silence. Everyone looked blankly around at each other, everyone hoping someone else had an answer, and could provide a miracle idea that would save their lives and get them home. There was no miracle answer, but Sona spoke up with an idea of her own.

"I know what we can do," she said, her own voice sounding empty and hollow.

"What?" the captain asked, wide eyes with an expression of hope.

Sona locked eyes on him. "We blow ourselves up. And we take as much of this fucking station with us as we can."

CHAPTER 15

"GET OFF MY command deck!" Captain Ellis snapped in response, but only after being left momentarily stunned into silence. "I won't hear such nonsense." He then looked around at everyone else. "I want reasonable ideas on what we can do."

However, despite trying to appear calm and authoritative, Crynn could see the fear and panic in his eyes. A vein bulged from the captain's temple as he clenched his jaw. No one offered him anything.

"Think!" he shouted and slammed his fist against his chair which stood next to him.

"We could stick to the original plan," a navigation officer suggested. "Take off and try to blow our way through the wall. Then just . . . I don't know . . . fly and try to get free of this whole zone. It can't go on forever, maybe we can get back to normal space."

The captain gave a manic smile. "That's more like it," he said. "It's not much, but it's something."

"Even if we get out of the station," Sona said, "we'll never get free of what we saw out there. Did you see the conditions? Those streaks of . . . *lightning* . . . or whatever it was. Not to mention those gigantic things crawling around, and the fucking huge foetus-looking alien."

"I thought I told you to get off my command deck?"

No one moved to eject her from the room, so Sona went on; "And even if you do get free of this madness, we have no idea *where* we are. We'd never be able to find our way back to known space."

"Then we'll survive in the black for as long as we can," Captain Ellis shot back. "Better than being torn apart by those things that are getting into the ship. Or worse, swallowed up by this fucking station."

"Sir," a woman at one of the consoles chimed in. "I'm getting reports that the blast doors we closed are being forced open. We're being overrun."

"They can't have been forced open. Do you know how strong they are?"

"Do you know how many of those things have gotten on board?" Sona responded. "Some of them are huge. The blast doors aren't impenetrable. Enough force against them and—"

"Then we need to get airborne quickly!" Ellis shouted. He then pointed over to the navigation team. "Get us in the fucking air now, you idiots!"

Crynn understood why the captain was clinging to hope, but he was overlooking a pretty big problem. "How are we going to fly with a hole in the side of the ship?" he asked. "And we're already overrun with those monsters. They're inside and there's no way we could take them all out. We don't have enough weapons on board. I mean, just *look*." Crynn pointed through a window to the hangar beyond, which was now teaming with thousands upon thousands of those things. He could even see some of the crew being taken from the ship, tossed down to the masses below to be hauled away. He sighed. "Captain, there's no way out of this. Everyone on the lower decks is now either being killed or dragged off into the station. We don't have a crew to operate the ship."

The captain slowly strode over to one of the windows. As he peered out, Crynn saw tears form in the older man's eyes. A renewed expression of pain broke over his face. "There has to be a way," he said in a voice that was little more than a whisper. "There has to be."

"Sona has given you the only option we have," Crynn said, gently. "I know it isn't easy to hear, but it's that or we all get dismembered and strung up to the walls of this station like broken marionettes. I know which fate I'd rather have."

Crynn didn't feel good admitting that. In fact, the thought of blowing themselves to kingdom come terrified him. But knowing what would happen to them if they didn't scared him more. He thought again of the crew they had seen that had been fused to the wall, with heads detached, connected only by spinal cords and tendons, still alive in some unknowable way, but no doubt suffering. He refused to end up like that. The quick death of incineration would therefore be welcome, but they were running out of time.

"Captain," he prodded. "You need to give the order."

"The ship doesn't have a fucking self-destruct button, you idiot," Captain Ellis said, though Crynn knew he was buying for time.

Time they didn't have.

"No," Crynn agreed, "but you know as well as I do it can be done."

"We can just override the weapon locks and fire them while holding them in place," Sona suggested. "They'll detonate. The explosion would be massive, too. Who knows how much of this station we'd destroy as well. A little payback for the people it took from us."

Crynn turned to her. There was a determination there, evident by Sona's curled lip and the frown on her brow. He wondered if she would have preferred this option rather than being able to get away completely, and if avenging Miko was more important to her than survival. Not that it mattered now, given survival wasn't possible. He then looked back at the captain.

"If we're gonna do it, we need to do it now," Crynn said. They could hear the echoes of roars and screams drifting up from the decks below. "What's it going to be, Captain?"

More tears fell down Captain Ellis' lined cheeks. After what seemed like an eternity, with everyone on the command deck awaiting his answer, he took a deep breath.

"Fine," he said. He then turned to Sona. "Do you know how to get it done? Can we do it all from here?"

"If enough of the weapons were prepped and ready to fire before we were overrun, then yes, we can."

Captain Ellis slowly spun around and stared out of the window ahead of him, watching the horrors that continued to spill into the now-crowded hangar. "Then get it done," he sai

CHAPTER 16

CRYNN HAD OFFERED assistance to Sona, but she'd declined, politely telling him she didn't need his help. A good portion of the heavier weapons on board the ship had already been prepped and were almost ready to fire. She just had to set a timed detonation on them, then override the locking mechanisms that held the missiles in place, ensuring they wouldn't release.

So, he simply watched the chaos outside the window, as many of the other command crew were doing. There were quiet sobs in the room. Everyone looked broken. One man had spoken up, insisting there had to be a way, clinging on to the hope that the captain had earlier shared. But no one responded to him, so his protests faded to silence.

Outside, Crynn saw one man among many being passed along the crowd of monsters, like a twig flowing down a river. However, when one huge creature took hold of him and passed him to an equally large one, it didn't release its hold in time, and the screaming man was subsequently ripped in half, his body putting up no more resistance than a wet tissue. His two halves were then quickly discarded and attention was turned to the rest of the steady stream of people being brought out of the Argento.

In addition, the horrific growls and roars that they could all hear on the ship were growing closer. An army of those monstrosities were marauding through the ship and making their way right to the top, where the last remaining survivors were hiding away.

From the sound of it, Crynn knew it wouldn't be long before they had broken the door to the command deck down and swarmed inside. The door itself was another blast door, so was certainly strong, but the horde had already proven they were capable of getting through such things. He cast his eyes to Sona who was tapping furiously on one of the consoles, her face a picture of concentration.

Hurry up.

He walked over to stand beside his friend, watching her fingers dance across the surface of the console display.

"I don't like people watching over my shoulder while I work," she said without looking up.

"I'm not checking up on you," Crynn said, "just don't know what to do with myself. I feel jittery and . . . I don't know . . . "

"Scared?" Sona asked, finally glancing at him. He nodded. She gave an understanding smile. "Me too," she said.

"I always thought a ship malfunction would kill us," Crynn went on, speaking quietly so the other crew couldn't hear. "Just a random moment as we drifted pointlessly on our mission. I never imagined we'd find anything like this."

"Yeah," Sona replied as she worked. "Hard to process what we've seen, isn't it?"

"I'll say." He took a moment, then added: "Sona, I'm sorry about Miko. I wish we could have done more."

Sona paused. Her face hardened and her jaw clenched. Crynn saw her eyes grow wet, though she was clearly trying to fight back the tears. "It's fine," she eventually said, though her voice cracked. "We did all we could. Thank you for trying. But I'm going to make sure she isn't suffering anymore. I won't leave her to exist like . . . like . . . "

The tears flowed. Crynn put a hand on her shoulder. "I know," he told her in a gentle voice.

Sona shook her head to steel herself and her fingers resumed their dance. "Almost ready," she eventually said.

After a few more moments, she looked up. "Captain," she said, drawing the attention of Captain Ellis. "I need you to input your command codes to approve the use of weapons. You can do it from the console on your chair."

"I know how it works," he replied, his hands behind his back as he stared out into the hangar. The creatures on the ship were close now, tearing at the blast door. He then turned, moved to his chair, and sat down. Swivelling the adjustable console toward him, the captain stared at the screen.

Crynn and Sona cast each other a glance. The captain continued looking but didn't move. The sounds outside the door grew louder and more excitable. There was a screeching of metal and some people within the command deck continued to cry softly.

Come on, Crynn silently pleaded.

Eventually, with obvious reluctance, Captain Ellis tapped on the screen of the console. He then batted the unit away from him. "It's done," he said and lowered his head.

Finally.

"I'll launch—" Sona began but was cut off by one of the crew as a metallic squeal rang out around them.

"They're getting through!" the crew woman said. Crynn snapped his head around to the blast door and saw that it had been bent outwards, the bottom corner pulled away, and one of the monsters was squeezing itself through.

"Hurry, Sona!" Crynn barked.

Sona didn't reply, instead too focused on her screen as she tapped away. The first creature got through and Crynn opened fire on it as people screamed around him. But his one gun wasn't enough to hold it out as the door was continually forced away and other abominations slipped through as well.

"Ready!" Sona shouted and a cold smile crept over her face. She lifted her hand, pointer finger aimed down to hit the final key . . .

There was a flash of blue light all around them that pulsed inside, coming from the hangar and passing through the walls of the ship as it washed over the crew. Crynn felt a strange sensation as the area around him seemed to swell, though he put it down to the pulse effecting his equilibrium and he struggled to maintain his balance for a few moments. The lights inside the command deck instantly blinked out. Computer and console screens snapped to black. The hum of the engines ceased in an instant.

Crynn looked over to Sona with confusion.

"What the fuck just happened?" Captain Ellis demanded. Crynn had an idea. *The station.* It *stopped us.*

Sona looked back to Crynn, tears in her eyes. "The ship lost power," she said. "Some kind of EMP or pulse or . . . I don't know. But I can't fire the—"

She was cut off as one of the monsters dove on her, knocking her to the ground.

"Sona!" Crynn shouted, as he felt alien hands and limbs take hold of him as well. Everyone on board started to scream in panic as they were overrun and dragged away.

CHAPTER 17

CRYNN'S BROKEN MIND once again temporarily restored enough to form coherent thoughts. It wouldn't last. How long had he been here?

Years? Decades? Centuries?

Once again he was filled with an urge to scream, but could succeed only in moving his jaw, opening and closing his mouth like an infant searching for milk.

He felt his hands twitch and his toes flex, even though his limbs were separated from his body, plastered to the wall and connected only by the strange wiring imbued in him by the station and the organic matter that surrounded him. His dismembered body was being kept alive long after it should have been dead. He didn't understand how, but he wished it would stop and he could be granted death.

The momentary reprieve granted to Crynn served to shut out the billions of voices in his mind: those of others on the station and, most terrifyingly of all, the things *outside* of it. He was even touched by the great, stillborn infant, that which was at once life and death, its comatose mind still more powerful than anything Crynn could imagine.

And the things around the infant, that were trying to wake their god, were on course to achieve their goal.

Life was the key to their success.

The lives of others. Species that spanned the length and history of the galaxy. All fed into the thing that had many names, which Crynn had heard spoken by the multitude of voices.

Bishma.

Gha'agshebla

Ashklaar.

Crynn's reprieve wouldn't last. He knew that. Soon his mind

would be flooded again and plunge him back into insanity. Which only made things worse, as he was terrified of what would soon come. He was now part of a cosmic whole and it terrified him. He didn't want it. He didn't want any of it.

He squinted. Narrow beams of light cut through the near dark around him. Though his hearing was muffled and had been since he'd been taken, Crynn was certain he could hear some kind of movement. He turned his eyes to his left, looking down the long corridor.

The lights swept left and right, before landing on him, blinding him. He tried to close his eyes but couldn't, his body wouldn't respond, so instead he had to simply bear the pain that burned in his retinas. Eventually, the lights grew somewhat dimmer, and a shadow fell over him. Crynn's vision, though spotty, soon returned.

Someone stood before him. Crynn wasn't certain if it was human, given it was clad in a thick suit, but it was at least of humanoid shape. It leaned forward, studying him, its face lost behind the visor of a large helmet.

Help! he tried to scream. *Please, help me!*

He knew no words escaped him. The person before him stood upright and began to look around. There were others there as well, all taking in the surroundings of the hallway, no doubt horrified at what they'd found.

They wouldn't help, no more than Crynn had helped the strange life forms stuck in the walls of the station that he'd found.

Suddenly, the strangers before him all turned and focused their attention farther down the hallway. Crynn saw them begin to back up. Some raised their hands defensively and others drew what he assumed were weapons, but they looked strange to him. The crowd quickly began to advance, though the beams of their lights were still focused in Crynn's direction.

He soon saw why, as the misshapen and disfigured bodies of the space station's sentinels lumbered past him. Some had once been human, his crew mates, though now more resembled horrific patchwork imitations. Others were of alien species he had never known.

The one closest to Crynn angled its body slightly and their eyes locked for a moment.

Human. Female. He felt a flash of recognition, and saw the same in her pale-blue eyes as well.

A name started to swim to the surface of his fractured mind.

Sona.

He suddenly remembered his life-long friend. It broke his heart to see what had become of her; her body twisted and mangled, infused with strange technology that looked painfully grafted to her skin. Even so, he knew he must look far worse to her. At least she was in one piece.

The eye-contact was soon broken as Sona turned and slouched down the hallway to chase after her prey.

Crynn was again left in darkness. He felt his mind slipping again, ready to be plunged back into chaos. He was allowed one futile thought before succumbing to it.

Please . . . let me die.

GRAVEYARD OF STARS

DAN SOULE

MISSION LOG
DATE: 0432—NEW INTERSTELLAR CALENDAR
LOCATION: THE BORDER OF EARTH-ALGOL SPACE
SHIP: REG-G13, ECHO CLASS ENGINEERING SHIP, BRITISH CONTINGENT OF THE INTERSTELLAR WORLD ALLIANCE (IWA)
CREW: 7
MISSION: DEFENCE NET MAINTENANCE, CHAOS-GUN K32,171 OVERHAUL

CHAPTER 1

'MURPHY, NEED YOU back inside to attend to your patient, Baby Girl,' Captain Valentine's voice came through the comms in Murphy's helmet. Controlled as a robotic extension of her own hand, the welding torch was a white dwarf star going nova. She shut the torch down and the universe went dark, before she flicked up the gold sheen of the welding shield.

'Ito's awake?' Murphy asked, floating inside the Fat Boy, small thrusters keeping her in place on the undercarriage of the chaos-gun. It was an exosuit for heavier welding jobs or lifting manoeuvres that required a sailor to be untethered. An engineer could drop inside the Fat Boy's big bulbous head wearing their space suit and take on the robotic exoskeleton.

'Affirmative,' Valentine said. 'He's complaining about room service.'

Murphy checked the time readout projected on her helmet visor. Ito should have been out until they finished this final shift, and then they'd be heading home. Maybe she got the dose wrong. Could be his metabolism. Maybe he was taking something she didn't know about. His tox-screen was clear though. At the back of it all was that fear that this wasn't just a case of cabin fever or a pre-existing neurological condition that somehow got missed. What if it was Astraecy? What if that contagion of the void was on their ship? No, the precursors were clear. *Yeah, and you got Ito's dosage right too,* Murphy thought, trying to shrug off the self-doubt of her first tour as ship's field-medic. Christ! It was her rookie tour straight out of basic.

'I'm heading in now, Captain.' Murphy pulled the Fat Boy away from her welding job. It was done anyway, and she manoeuvred over the undercarriage of the chaos gun. She glided across fifty metres of its armour-plated fuselage up to the main deck between the twin guns. Magnetising the feet in place, Murphy popped the Fat Boy's dome, which yawned back on a hinge, like that hungry yellow character that ate ghosts, in that ancient videogame Kohl loved to play. Pulling herself free she dropped to the deck and reattached her tether.

There was a slink of movement to her right, a silent slash of white falling through the blackness of space that made her jump. Her hand knocked a stray bolt, and it floated off into space. Wu reached out gracefully intercepting it with his gloved hand. He'd dropped down from the gun placement above her—although on a spacewalk, above was a relative thing.

He smiled, a thin uncomfortable movement. 'You go. I finish here for you.'

Wu's Chinese accent was thick, and she couldn't blame him for feeling uncomfortable. After all, she was being called back in to check on Ito who'd tried to stab Wu three days ago and accused him of being a spy. This was a British rig, but like all the crews working maintenance on the defence grid, there were always two spots for international liaisons. Ito was Japan's, Wu China's. They as easily could have been from France, America, Brazil or any goddamn place. The roll of the official dice put representatives from two of Earth's fiercest rivals together. Shit! The whole world was an uneasy alliance in defence against the Agoul. That's why they were all out here on this long-ass tour doing routine updates to the defence grid.

Murphy clunked silently along the deck, her magnetised boots keeping her attached to the main hull of the chaos-repeating plasma cannon. Effectively, it was two big-ass guns attached to a resonance energy core and the onboard wetware to connect with the rest of the grid.

The void of space was a vertiginous drop in all directions. They teach you in basic to keep your eyes on the only fixed thing on your spacewalk: the object you're working on. But it's like telling someone not to look down. And even when you learn not to, your brain continues to chatter nervously about how there is absolutely *not* a descent into infinite nothingness all around. Nope, nope, nope, nope, nope!

The REG-G13, or Reggie as they lovingly referred to her, was docked on the cuboid main-hull of the gunnery placement. The Reggie looked like a squashed robotic turtle: stout, flat bodied, with four engines hung below the hull at the four corners, and the bridge poking its head from the prow. She was cramped in terms of crew quarters and operations, with most of her internal space taken up with the cargo bay, carrying equipment and spare parts, which were almost used up. That at least gave them a makeshift combined basketball court and football goal. A chance to blow off steam and have fun.

Murphy reached the open airlock and pulled herself in and switched her carabiner over like the wet-eared rookie she was. She'd noticed the seasoned vets often skipped that part of the protocol, but the horror stories of airlock accidents from basic were fresh in her memory.

Behind, the doors shunted closed with a clunk and the hiss of pressurisation. It was an audible one-two that after a double tour of six-months without a break still produced a flutter in Murphy's chest. They were the twin sounds of relief and safety. She wasn't yet like Wu, Hendrix, or Grover. Salty space-dogs who look as though they are in their natural environment when they're outside the ship. Grover was a grumpy old bastard most of the time, but she saw him sometimes on a break, sitting at the edge of a gun placement they'd be overhauling, staring out into the starry abyss. It was like one of those old-school black and white pictures from the twentieth century of the men building New York skyscrapers. Hundreds of feet above the city, they sat on girders without even a rope, eating their baloney sandwiches. Murphy couldn't ever imagine being like that. It was all she could do not to puke in her helmet on a long walk outside.

The light above the internal door to the Reggie turned green in time with the chime in her helmet. She unclipped it and took a breath. It wasn't exactly fresh, but it was that familiar smell of the Reggie and its recycled air. It perennially carried that not-so-faint whiff of Eau-du-grease-hounds: UML (AKA universal mechanical lubricant), burnt rubber, rust and farts. It's amazing what you can get used to. Murphy had come to associate the smell with feeling back home because the Reggie was more of a home than she'd ever known, replete with her very own dysfunctional family. She loved it, even with its tensions and downsides.

'On the double, Baby Girl. Our guest in the penthouse suite is getting rowdy.'

'Aye, Captain. I'm on my way.' Murphy said, stepping into the cramped suit room on the other side of the internal airlock.

Valentine always called her Baby Girl when she was on a walk. Murphy didn't mind. It reminded her and everyone else she was the rookie, but it also reminded her and everyone else out here; they were family. They only had each other to depend on.

Murphy hastily stripped off her suit and stowed it with her boots and helmet in her locker. Sickbay wasn't far, located on the foredeck behind the bridge and mess hall, which on a ship the size of the Reggie was less hall and more cramped New Tokyo street-food kitchen. The rubber soles of her trainers squeaked as she jogged along the corridor. Low, green, fluorescent strips lit the way. She came into the empty mess hall.

Kohl leaned back in his chair on the bridge, bringing his long face and ruffled mop of brown hair into view. He gave her one of his goofy grins. 'Yo, sailor!'

Murphy was pleased to see him. Of the seven crew, Kohl was her closest friend, probably because they were a similar age, though he was a couple of years older. She thought maybe he fancied her, but he was too shy and awkward to do anything about it. That and Valentine might blow them both out of the airlock if she caught them so much as locking lips. On-tour relationships were strictly prohibited. Besides, Murphy didn't know if she felt that way about him.

'How's my patient?' she asked.

Ito answered for himself with a piercing ululation, a sound more like a trapped animal than a human.

Kohl's bonhomie quavered into a frown above his black rimmed spectacles—a retro-throwback but one that suited him, along with his beloved paperback books and something he called a record-player he'd jury rigged into the Reggie's comms. 'Waiting for your house call.'

Murphy rubbed the back of her neck, where her 'Fro remained short from the last buzz cut Valentine had given her. An act of equal parts ship's discipline and bonding exercise. She and Hendrix buzzed and cut their way through hair and festering squabbles—most of the time. Putting her shoulders back and chin up she strode over to med bay, relieved most of the crew were outside. Ito was one problem they'd not managed to clip and sweep away.

Murphy paused for a moment, girding herself. The clear glass porthole revealed only a full moon of medical supply cabinets.

Eclipsed from her sight, the rest of the room suddenly felt like an uncharted sector of space. Except, her trepidation didn't come from the unknown.

Ito wailed. Murphy tensed. Palms sweating, her hands unconsciously bunching and flexing, not as much at Ito as at her own potential shortcomings. He should still be sedated. Had she got the dose wrong? As if an additional three-month field-medic rotation at the end of basic made you a qualified clinician.

Another peel of rage came not from behind the door but from above. Murphy yelped and ducked. Hand to her chest, heart thundering.

Weaver howled with laughter, which echoed down the squat shaft up to his gunnery post. His leering pate mooned above her, his two canines a fraction too big and pointy. Fucking Marines! Shavy-headed, hand-humpers.

'You asshole, Weaver.'

'Aw, don't cwy, baby.' He mockingly turned his smile upside down. Then he burst out laughing again and disappeared back to his post. A Marine can't take his hand off his gun for a second; he might forget where his brain is.

There came a squeal of muted feedback overhead. Weaver cried out, and Murphy heard him briefly thrash in his seat as he pulled out his comms link. 'Fucking wanker, Kohl. I'll kick your skinny-weirdo ass.'

'Sorry,' Kohl said, but he didn't sound it. He scooted back on his chair's runners and came into view in the bridge door, all goofy grin and eyes twinkling behind his glasses.

Murphy made an okay sign and mouthed the word, 'Perfect!'

While Weaver carried on cursing and threatening, Kohl's eyebrows waggled, and he slid back to his post.

'That's enough, Weaver. Take what you give, big boy, or get off my ship. You okay, Murph?' Valentine said over the comms, her voice a reassuring tonic.

'Aye, Captain. I'm going in now.' Murphy pressed the access button and the door to the med-bay sighed open.

Ito looked like he was building up to scream. His thin but muscular arms strained against the restraints, cording the muscles all the way up through his neck. At Murphy's entrance, he froze, eyes a feral glare. Murphy hoped her anxiety wasn't playing across her face. She was trying to project a mix of calm and caring concern. Maybe she managed it too because Ito slumped back on the gurney. The wild craziness melted away as Murphy approached him, only for his eyes to mist. He broke into tears.

'It's all right, Ito.' Murphy checked his stats on the screen behind the bed.

Heart rate was elevated but coming down. Blood pressure was up too. Neither thing was at odds with his stress levels. She was sure being tied up and sedated didn't help matters. They had little choice this far out. Even if he hadn't been raving about a spy on board, they had no other option but to restrain him after trying to kill Wu with a ceramic kitchen knife.

The rendezvous with the carrier ship wasn't for another two days. Until then, they were on their own. Ito's problems clearly went deeper than three months of medical training could handle, and of that just half a day had been devoted to mental health issues.

'Please, I'll be good,' Ito sobbed. 'Don't put me under again.'

Murphy placed a hand on his forearm. He looked at it and up into her eyes. Tears running down his face, he leaned across. Murphy fought the urge to jump away. He only wanted to tell her something. He checked around furtively before whispering.

'The spy might not be Wu. It could be anyone. Trust no one.' His eyes narrowed on her and then widened in realisation. 'It could be you.'

Murphy patted his arm. 'It's not me.' As soon as it was out of her mouth, she knew she'd framed that badly.

'You would say that,' Ito whispered, with a knowing tilt of his head.

'It's not anyone, Ito. What would be worth spying on out here? We're all on the same team.'

'That's what I thought.' Ito's pupils had shrunk to pinpricks, little black holes staring into her. 'But . . . ' He caught himself. Eyeing her suspiciously, he slumped back and turned his head away. 'I'll be good,' he concluded in a murmur.

Weaver's voice came over the comms. 'Ladies, gentlemen and augment fetishists—I mean you Kohl.'

'How is that even an insult?' Kohl countered.

Weaver continued, 'We have incoming on the scope.'

'Vector?' Valentine asked.

'Algol space, heading straight for us.'

'Hendrix, Wu, Grover: get your asses back home,' Valentine ordered.

Murphy found herself looking back towards the bridge, her heart pounding. Unlike Wu and Weaver jump scaring her, this could be the real thing. They'd worked on the frontier with Algol space for six months. No ship had ever gone unchallenged there by the race they'd come to know as the Agoul. Most never made it back, certainly, none of the early expeditions, although their transmissions did. Wild tales of what was there. And the Agoul themselves, they were the bogeyman. They were the reason for the defence net, the reason for the uneasy alliance of earth powers coming together to build the net A common enemy no Earth power had beaten, because you can't fight what you can't see.

'Wait a second, Captain. It's moving too slow,' Weaver said. He was focused, calm even.

'What does that mean?'

'It's not moving like an Agoul ship. The course is straight, steady and very slow.'

'How slow?'

'Like docking manoeuvres slow.'

'Visual?'

'That's the thing. The shape is all wrong on the long-range scope. For one thing I can make it out. Can't do that with Agoul ships. It's . . . ' There was a pause. The sound of Weaver tapping screens and checking readouts. 'It's about two hundred and fifty centimetres long and a metre wide.'

Murphy's mouth was desert dry. She could feel the whoosh of blood in her ears. Ito grabbed her wrist. She caught a cry like a hot stone in her mouth. His grip was a vice she couldn't peel off.

'You see? Don't let it on board. This is why we are here. The spy did this.'

Murphy couldn't free herself, but Ito suddenly let go and she staggered back, rubbing her wrist.

'Have you got eyeballs on it yet?' Valentine repeated.

'That's a negative. Still long-range telemetry. Video in twenty seconds.'

Valentine again. 'Hendrix are you guys done?'

'Negative, Captain. We need another hour to finish the upgrade, and double that for a systems check and reboot. Weaver has to cover the gap in the net a while longer.'

She's thinks we need the chaos-gun to protect us, Murphy thought.

She'd been in dogfight simulations with the Agoul. They hopped in and out of sensor readings, first in one place then, impossibly, in another. Jumping unpredictably closer and closer. No one ever destroyed them or even got a shot on target. That was the whole point of the defence net. Blanket fire from a whole battery of chaos-guns. Burn an entire area of space. The best strategy for a ship was to turn and run. Agoul had never crossed into Earth's space, and the Reggie was right on that line but not over it, as was every gunnery placement making up the net.

'Weaver, are you running hot?'

'So hot I've got full wood and a spare sock. But that can't be right,' Weaver said to himself, but everyone heard.

'He's such a poet,' Kohl said.

'Explain yourself, Marine,' Valentine ordered.

'It's . . . You're not going to believe this.'

'Goddamn it, Marine. Hendrix, get your team—'

'It's a coffin.'

CHAPTER 2

THE ARRYTHMIA OF confusion produced a skipped heartbeat of silence.

'Say again, Weaver,' Valentine said.

'It's a ship's coffin.'

'Stop fucking around, Marine, or you'll be on report,' Valentine growled.

'I'm not fucking around, Captain. Get Kohl to check his sensors. I already matched it against the database.'

'Give me a second,' Kohl said.

It was a weightless and untethered second, one without the comfort of meaning.

'He's right.' Surprise didn't quite describe Kohl's voice. Incredulity, shock, maybe even a little wonder. A geek with a puzzle to solve. 'It is a coffin. US issue. Not their current model. It hasn't been in use for over two decades.'

'Is there any way to tell what ship it belonged to?' Valentine asked.

'Negative.' Both Kohl and Weaver spoke at the same time.

'Weaver, go,' Valentine said. This was the Marine's domain. He was their assigned protection detail. He ran the security protocols and risk assessments. He was the guy operating the cannon mounted on the Reggie's back, who would have to guard their rear if they had to make a run for it.

'It's too far out for a clear image. Still a dot on my vid.'

Ito chose that moment to flip out. He huffed and grunted, wrestling with his restraints. 'No!' he shouted. 'This is all part of their plan. Can't you see? We've got to go.' He thrashed his head and bucked his hips.

'Shut that fucking spaceball up,' Weaver shouted.

Murphy rushed over to a drawer and popped it open. She

worked fast, tearing off the hygiene wrapper, popping the security seal on a vial, and slapping it into the hypo-spray.

Ito writhed and snarled animalistically. 'No! . . . Can't . . . Let . . . Me . . . Go . . . ' Then words failed him, and he screamed, piercing and anguished.

'Murphy!' Valentine said, her buttery voice sizzling with urgency.

'I'm on it.'

Her patient's paroxysms were too violent to try his upper body. They'd need to add hip and head restraints later, but without them that left one option. Ito bridged up, bowing backwards from heel to head and torquing to one side. He couldn't hold it forever, and when he relaxed, hips falling, Murphy grabbed his thigh in one hand, and slammed the hypo into the meat of his quadricep. Ito bucked and the hypo fell from her grip, clattering to the floor, as Murphy took a defensive step back.

Ito twisted towards her, betrayal and hurt riven into his ashen face. 'Please!' he slurred. His eyes drooped. His body slackened, and he slumped unconscious.

On the bridge, Murphy leaned against the door, just behind Kohl's comms station, listening. Thankfully, Weaver remained in his turret, playing with is gun, keeping an eye out for Agoul activity, which seemed even more likely with a piece of Earth tech creeping slowly towards them.

Hendrix, Wu, and Grover had finished the upgrade and joined them on the bridge. Second-officer and pilot, Hendrix sat between Valentine, and Wu, who ran telemetry. Balding Grover stood behind Kohl, his arms folded above his potbelly, watching Kohl's monitor from under his perma-scowl. He occasionally moved to rub a hand agitatedly through his rough stubble.

The reboot and systems check on the gunnery placement had a few hours of waiting around left to go. Bar any last-minute adjustments, this would mark the end of their double tour on the edge. Normally, that would have meant a celebration. They'd crack open the hooch. Kohl would put on one of his funny black record disks, and they'd party to some forgotten twentieth-century music. At least, this being her first time, that's what Murphy had been told would happen. Instead, they were staring at the 3-D vid-projection in front of the flight deck's windscreen.

'Here it comes,' Valentine said.

Sensors at maximum, the dot had grown to a blob, something akin to a breath tac. It was an agonising wait; one they couldn't take their eyes off. Conversation had been sparse. Unanswerable questions had been thrown into the air, which no one knew how to catch. Speculation both wild and benign. An Agoul trap. An object coincidentally the same size but not what Weaver and Kohl had initially deduced. A thousand possibilities.

The brushed steel object grew into the undeniable shape of a coffin, along with rounded ends, and finally the lettering at its prow came into view.

'The Palatine?' Hendrix said, shocked.

Kohl ran fingers through his hair and leaned way back in his chair. 'No way!'

Grover growled something inaudible.

Murphy had unconsciously stepped onto the bridge, drawn to the growing image of the coffin. It was like finding out a legend was true.

The Palatine was a deep exploration vessel. One of the pathfinder missions that forged ahead of the growing network of Earth stations. It was also the first ship to enter the Algol region of space. That also meant it was the first to disappear, but not before it had sent back a survey scan and images that drew more ships and ultimately disaster. And now the lettering of that lost ship hovered tantalisingly close, a 3D projection of a dream or maybe a nightmare, that Murphy could reach out and touch. The thought made her want to recoil. She snapped out of her reverie and took a step away.

'I told you. Not an Agoul ship,' Weaver's voice came through the comms.

'Well done, Weaver. You want a medal?' Hendrix said.

'Six months putting up with you grease-monkeys, I deserve one.'

Hendrix ignored him. 'What's the plan, Captain? Pull it in?'

'No! No fucking way!' Grover said. He was pointing, stabbing a finger at the holographic coffin, which was about the same size of his fist, but growing incrementally larger. 'That fucking thing is an albatross.'

Wu turned around from his station. 'Albatross?'

Grover didn't like anyone; however, Wu, possibly because of the cultural barrier from a century and a half of Chinese isolationism, was the most stoical of the crew. That meant fewer words, which meant Grover didn't exactly like him, but they worked well together. Grover could bitch and moan; Wu would nod and work. So, Grover shot Wu a look, managing to frown even harder. 'Old naval superstition. Unlucky sea bird if you kill it.' He turned his attention back to the spectral glow of the floating coffin. 'That fucking thing is dead, ergo, it's a dead fucking albatross.'

Kohl laughed, excitement lighting up his face. 'Come on, big G, you can't mean that. Aren't you the least bit curious? I mean, The Palatine. Lost and never recovered. First contact with the Agoul, and we've all seen the video of what they found.'

'Exactly! A fucking graveyard is what they found, and they joined it.'

'I wouldn't call it a graveyard,' Hendrix chipped in. The second officer had an aquiline nose, pointed chin and a large Adam's apple that bobbed when he spoke. With a tall gangly body, gravity made his gait awkward and rangy, but in zero-G he moved with languid grace.

'No?' Grover snorted. 'What would you call a sector full of dead ships? Giant, fucking leviathans from unknown species—'

'Not unknown; they're Agoul,' Kohl said. 'Not just ships either. So many stories.'

'You're as stupid as Weaver looks,' Grover snapped.

'Cowgirl your monkey wrench, you old wanker,' Weaver said over the comms.

Grover barrelled on. 'At least two styles of ships. The smallest of which is thirty-times the size of the largest any Earth nation has ever built. None of them match Agoul design.'

'We don't know what Agoul ships look like,' Kohl sounded hurt. He looked up to Grover. Misanthropic as he was, the old space dog was a top-notch engineer. And he wasn't done ranting.

'They sure as hell ain't thirty-times the size of ours.'

'We don't know that either.' Kohl was crestfallen.

Grover rolled his eyes and shook his head, as if that wasn't deserving of a riposte.

'Didn't take you for the superstitious type. Didn't you meet the Red Woman at some waystation?' Hendrix said, with the hint of a smirk.

Grover ignored the Red Woman gibe. 'Superstition? Common fucking sense, more like.'

Valentine raised a fist. 'That's enough. Protocols are clear. First, we're still a science designation, which means we have a duty to investigate. Second, it's a coffin, which means someone could be inside. If so, it's also our duty to retrieve the body, let the next of kin know what became of their loved one. And third—'

Exasperated, Grover turned on the spot, throwing his hands up. 'There's a third!'

'Watch your mouth, Sailor,' Valentine warned. 'And third, we are a military ship, and that object is intel relating to an ongoing conflict. Any way we cut it, we have a duty to bring that coffin on board. Once the systems check is complete, we go fishing while it reboots. Weaver, how close will it come?'

'It's going to fly right by, Cap. It'll come within two hundred metres. Close enough to net.'

'Perfect. You hook our fish. We'll land it. Quarantine it in the storage bay. Wu, you're the senior science officer, you'll assist Murphy with opening the coffin.'

Wu nodded curtly.

Murphy hoped she'd heard wrong. Her eyes locked on the glowing projection of the coffin looming larger on the bridge of the Reggie.

CHAPTER 3

'IN THREE, TWO, ONE. Net away,' Weaver said.

Through the hull of the Reggie, Murphy felt a vibration. Waiting on the other side of the bulkhead from the cargo bay, she went to bite her nails, before remembering she was wearing a spacesuit, and had a helmet tucked under one arm. Wu was dressed the same, though he stood silent and without fidgeting. At their feet lay a combination of medical and scientific equipment, as well as a kit bag full of field rations in case they needed to enact quarantine protocols.

There was a sense of a collective breath held, a humming silence on the open comms line, until Weaver confirmed. 'Got the sonofabitch.'

'A little respect, Marine,' Valentine said. 'There could be a dead sailor inside there.'

'Aye, Captain. Pulling it in now.'

The Reggie had taken off from the gunnery placement to float nearby for the perfect intercept position. As the coffin approached, they increased their speed with manoeuvring thrusters to mirror the passing object. Once their salvage was caught, Weaver would winch it to the rear of the ship, where Hendrix could steer it into the docking bay adjoining the back of the cargo hold. Murphy was aware of the changeover between Weaver and Hendrix through the knocking and vibrations of the ship. She pushed down her nerves. A hundred things spun around her head, like the gatling chamber of a chaos gun.

The Royal Navy Interstellar Division's recruitment slogan was *Explore, Protect, Serve.* Lots of recruits were escaping a crappy family life or looking for a job to give them some direction. Murphy was a combination of both. It all sounded romantic, venturing into the stars, protecting your nation and your planet. She had found a family on board the Reggie, and as dysfunctional as it was sometimes, it was nothing compared to her own real family. She pushed those memories aside.

This was only supposed to be a three-month tour. Life on the edge could be monotonous and claustrophobic. Because the defence grid's overhaul was nearly done and command was always looking to cut costs where they could, the high ups had doubled their tour and pressed for completion. It looked like they were going to make it too, but the extra time had pushed them a little too far. Ito had snapped, and now this. She wasn't ready. She was just a kid, nineteen, a barely trained field-medic and a Royal Engineer who at the start of her tour needed guidance from more experienced crew on even the most basic of tasks. Not so much anymore, but she was still 'Baby Girl' wasn't she? *Explore, Protect, Serve*: nowhere in that job description had there been anything about opening coffins from an infamous missing ship. Must have been in the small print.

Wu's hand rested gently on Murphy's arm, calling her back to the here and now. 'Okay to be nervous. Normal,' he said.

Hendrix sounded over the comms, 'Coffin secured. Pressure and air restored.'

Then Weaver was in her ear, 'Time to work, Baby Girl.'

It was cold in the cargo bay, frosting their breath, biting at their cheeks. Murphy's sinuses ached with the freeze. Side by side, they strode the cavernous length of the cargo hold and opened the doors to the docking bay.

The blast doors were heavy reinforced slabs of riveted alloy, so that in a docking accident the ship had a greater chance of survival, but this made them into a hulking and foreboding portal. They secured their helmets before the doors' hydraulic locks released with a loud decompression. The secondary magnetic seal clunked, and the doors hissed, moving glacially apart.

A silvery capsule emerging as the shaft of light flayed aside the dark, the coffin glittered with frost. With a final clang, the blast doors gaped wide. Shadows clung to the extremities of the docking bay. Wu took the first step in, and Murphy forced her feet to follow.

Black on the silver casket, Palatine was printed in a blocky font. Murphy's heart skipped a beat as the automatic lights blinked to life and flooded the room with light. The Fat Boy, stored to one side, appeared from the dark like some hulking statue guarding the coffin on its journey to the underworld. Wu or Grover must have piloted him back in for Murphy. His giant arms hung by his sides; his vacant domed head watched blankly.

As they walked towards the coffin, each step feeling like the gravity had been increased, Murphy ripped open the satchel slung over her shoulder and pulled out the cylindrical, multi-purpose bio-medical scanner, known as a “sniffer”. It fitted in the palm of her hand and vibrated as it turned on. She touched the panel on her gauntlet’s wrist and paired the sniffer with her suit. Wu circled around to the top of the coffin, eyeballing it the way he might a fried circuit panel on a spacewalk.

Aside from the risk of infection, the spacesuits provided protection against how cold the coffin and the surrounding environment of the docking bay would be. The vacuum of space would have frozen it to minus several hundred degrees Celsius. It had been Murphy’s suggestion to turn off the heat to the docking bay to keep the ambient temperature as low as possible to preserve any organic matter. Valentine had given her a fleeting but proud look. Kohl had palmed his forehead and said, ‘Of course, good call.’ Even Grover grunted in what Murphy thought was an approving way. That didn’t stop the implication of her idea slopping around her brain like putrefying matter on a hot day.

If there was a body in there, it would be an icicle. A sudden change in temperature could shatter it. Then they’d have the universe’s most grotesque three-dimensional puzzle on their hands. If the temperature rose above freezing, decomposition would set in, and they didn’t have the means of storing or refrigerating a corpse. This was why deep space vessels, like the old naval ships of Earth, had coffins to commit dead crew’s bodies to the deep. That led to another thing that was a fly in the decomposing sludge idea. Standard protocol had always been to aim the coffin at the nearest star or to burn it up in a planet’s atmosphere. Not to have them just floating around in an infinite graveyard of stars.

Murphy shivered at the thought.

‘Any reading?’ Wu said.

‘No external bio-hazards present.’ Murphy could see her heart rate was elevated; the reading flashed in the top left corner of her helmet’s visor. She slowed her breathing and switched to an internal scan. Immediately, the sniffer pinged. Wu straightened up from examining the casket.

'What have we got, Baby Girl?' Valentine's voice sounded in Murphy's helmet as the high-res holographic image was simultaneously projected on the bridge and above the sniffer.

The body of a woman, half naked, veiled in the ghostly blue hue of the hologram, floated in the air before Murphy.

Hendrix said, 'What's that on her chest?'

'Zooming in,' Murphy said. Her skin crawled as she pinched her fingers apart in the centre of the image.

His words brittle and hesitant, Kohl said, 'Does that look like . . . what I think it looks like?'

The woman inside the coffin was naked from above her diaphragm. Her head was cocked to one side, angled down towards her left breast, and there cradled in the crook of one arm was the answer to Kohl's question.

Wu was the one to voice it. 'A baby.'

CHAPTER 4

THE BLAST DOORS closed behind them with a tolling clang. Murphy told herself the docking bay was nothing like a tomb. Nope, not a bit. It was bright and metallic, grey and cold and forbidding. The webbing on the walls was nothing like cobwebs. Service hatches weren't sepulchres. No, there was nothing charnel about the place.

They were shutting themselves in with corpses until they'd ruled out the risk of infection organic matter might carry. Organic matter—quite the euphemism for a mother and child.

'By the numbers, Baby Girl,' Valentine tried to soothe. 'Let's find out who this is and then we can work out what to do next.'

Wu was up first, using a cutting torch. Grover had ruled out the option of a drill because of the vibrations—shattered corpses and all that. Kohl was pretty sure the ambient temperature wouldn't rise enough using a cutting torch to damage the contents. Contents—another euphemism. The torch blazed white hot, sizzling the air. When he was through the lock, the lid of the coffin gave a touch. Wu killed the torch and flicked his gold visor clear. Murphy did the same.

They took up position at either end, getting their gloved fingers into position. The space suit was too cramped for this. Murphy checked there was nothing wrong with the airflow. Everything was five-by-five. *Breathe, just breathe,* she told herself.

Wu met Murphy's gaze across the 2.5 metres of brushed steel. She wished she felt as stoic as he looked. As ice cold as this place that was absolutely *not a* tomb. 'On the three,' he said, his idiom slightly off, and began to count.

They lifted together. Murphy expected it to be frozen solid or for it to resist and spring wide. It did neither and glided open on hinges as well-oiled as the day they were committed to the void.

Murphy stood at their feet, unable to see over the bundle of arms and the rise of the woman's chest. Wu had the perfect view and inclined his head to one side. There they were: mother and child.

'Something wrong?' Murphy said, thinking it was a stupid question. Of course, something was wrong. Look what they were doing. This wasn't checking that the bearings ran smoothly on a chaos-gun's rails. They weren't stripping down a plasma field generator or running efficiency diagnostics.

Wu didn't answer. He stood, gaze inscrutable.

'What the hell is that?' Kohl said. Something in his tone not sounding right in Murphy's helmet.

'Wu?' she said.

He didn't respond, but his head tilted slowly to the other side.

Confusion over the airwaves. A tumult of chatter and emotion.

'Goddamn, albatross, I told you—'

'But what is it? We've got to get a better view—'

'Wu, zoom in—'

'Get them out of there and fire that thing back into space where it belongs—'

'Calm down, old man—'

'Fuck you, Hendrix—'

'Stow that shit, sailors. Wu, move your helmet. Get us a better view.'

Murphy wanted to move back, every instinct was telling her to, but she didn't know why, and she wasn't about to make a fool of herself in front of her team, her new, hard-won family. It was the not knowing, trying to read the confusion and tension over the comms, and more than that, Wu's face.

'Wu,' Murphy called, sharp, urgent.

He heard her this time. Seemed to snap out of it, slowly righting the tilt of his head. He was the length of the coffin away from Murphy, and even from that distance she could see how dilated his pupils were. Two black holes that had eaten away the colour of his irises. Like a crystal-nova addict had just popped a brittle wafer under their tongue and checked out for something better than looking after their little girl. And now Murphy was really shitting herself, because she was in two places at once: in the docking bay of the Reggie with an open coffin and a frozen corpse, and eleven-years-old, hungry and dirty and trying to wake her mum, whose eyes were wide open, but no one was home. Someone was banging on their apartment door, and calling out, shouting, same as her crew.

Wu blinked. His eyes came back into focus, pupils contracting. He looked as confused as everyone sounded.

Murphy repeated herself. 'Wu, what is it?' she said, while telling herself his eyes were responding to lights overhead. That was all.

Muscles twitched in Wu's brow. There was an almost imperceptible movement of his helmet, as if he was going to check the contents of the coffin again but fought the urge. He wet his lips to speak in stilted English.

'Not a baby.'

CHAPTER 5

MURPHY BEGAN TO move up to Wu's end of the coffin. 'What?' she said, unable to understand his meaning.

'He's right.' Weaver sounded incredulous.

Murphy halted mid-stride. 'I don't understand.'

She had walked far enough up the side of the coffin to know there was something in their words. The baby, or rather the thing in its place, was a dark, lustrous brown. Metallic, or possibly polished stone, but the way even the small part of it she could see reacted to the light, made Murphy think it was neither. Light seemed to slip off it, as though repelled. Yet there was that sheen of reflection any highly polished object possesses. That same impossible mix of compulsion and repulsion, of simultaneously wanting and not wanting to know had Murphy's feet on the move again.

'Kohl, can you run an image search on her?' Valentine asked.

'On it. Checking for the artifact as well.'

Artifact? Murphy thought, trying to find meaning. The woman was wearing a grey flight suit, unzipped to the waist and pulled open to expose her chest. The white vest underneath had been hitched up. A Caucasian woman, her pallor was a faint blue with the combination of death and freezing solid. Her skin and curling blonde hair sparkled with the hoarfrost of frozen water vapor. An emergency oxygen mask covered her mouth and nose. The small tank of liquid oxygen was tucked down by her hip. She was smiling contently down at the thing in her arms, her lips appearing black through the transparent green plastic of the mask. Murphy followed the woman's gaze, and like the light which seemed to not want to adhere to the thing, she couldn't acknowledge what she was seeing. She had to force her mind to perceive it. Something was there. A thing of dark burnished brown. It was right there, cradled like an infant. *A baby*, Murphy thought, the words almost came out as a murmur. *It is a baby*; the idea came stronger. An idea that clutched at her heart, made it ache.

As if hearing her thoughts, Wu repeated, 'Not a baby.'

Murphy realised he was telling himself what it wasn't, reminding himself because the alternative quicksilvered in his perception. And then the spell was broken for her, and she could see it for what it was. A statue or small effigy, not as large as a baby, unless it was extremely premature. The size of her two clenched fists inside her spacesuit's gauntlets. Laying on its side, one arm folded under its chin in a palsied hook. It hunkered on squatting stumps, feet fat and three-toed, sickled in and overlapping. Hunched in form, it was possibly humanoid, though its head made up over a third of its entire bulk. Because its features were all slightly misaligned on both the X and Y axis, the head appeared bulbous and uncanny. And there was a depression in the crown, as if someone had tried to stove in its skull at birth. The woman had the effigy's lopsided anus of a mouth resting at her frozen nipple, where a single droplet of lactated milk had frozen into a tiny pearl at the tip.

Grover continued to rant in the background.

Weaver said something along the lines of, 'That's some fucked-up shit.'

Impatient, Valentine said, 'Murphy, what are the bio-readings?'

Murphy had forgotten all about them and chided herself. *Goddamn rookie!* She flicked through the readings. Ran a set of secondary tests for phage, fungal, and prion diseases, the first level being for bacterial and viral contaminants, and of course Astraecy, that madness which had consumed entire ships, but not before turning them into rabid ships of the damned. In seconds, the data materialised on the sniffer's readout.

'All clear,' she said, knowing the results showed synchronously on the bridge and tapped in for a third test.

'What are you doing, Baby Girl?' Valentine was stern.

'Just an idea.'

Before Valentine could question her further, the analysis was complete.

'What are we looking at, Murphy?' Valentine used her surname, and Murphy didn't know if this was a sign of her maturing into an established member of the team, or the prelude to a rebuke. Either way, she needed to know and traced her finger up through the readings floating above her gauntlet.

'I ran a standard health scan on the body.'

'Why?' That was Hendrix.

'Look, whoever she was, she was perfectly healthy when she went into the coffin.'

Grover scoffed, 'Apart from being dead.'

'No, actually. This was my hunch. She was alive and well, at least physically when she went into the coffin. What I mean is, she died in the coffin of hypothermia, most likely once she'd been ejected into space. That explains the oxygen tank, and there are some unopened ration packs and a water pouch stashed by her thighs.'

Grover kicked off on the bridge. Hendrix tried to shout him down. Kohl was saying something, but it was lost in the cacophony, and Wu, Murphy noticed, was transfixed by the statue.

'Murphy.' Valentine raised her voice to be heard. 'I want you to retrieve that artifact, and both of you get back to the bridge.'

They didn't meet on the bridge. There wasn't enough room, so they convened in the mess, crowding around the dining island, perched on stools. The artifact, statue, effigy, or whatever the hell it was squatted in front of them on the white countertop.

Murphy would like to have said retrieving it was the worst thing she'd ever had to do, but that wasn't quite true. It was an inanimate object, that was all. But putting her gloved hand on the thing—because that's what it was, *a thing*—felt unnatural. It created a sensation like a mental itch, something niggling at her that she couldn't pinpoint. Aside, of course, from the obvious extraordinariness of their find.

Kohl had discovered the woman's name was Dr Sue-Ann Merryweather, originally of Wallace Idaho, USA. An Astroarchaeologist from the University of Michigan, in Ann Arbor, she was seconded to the Demon Star Expedition.

Dr Merryweather's hand was a rigid claw around the thing's feet and backside. When Murphy attempted to ease the statue out, exerting pressure clock- and counter-clockwise as she pulled, the pearl of breast milk had broken off and fallen away into the coffin's interior. Suddenly coming free, the statue knocked the dead doctor's nipple, producing a muted ting, like bone China.

Murphy couldn't wait to get out of there. She felt sick and repulsed. The skin on her back prickled and crawled as they closed the casket, leaving Sue-Ann Merryweather frozen in maternal glee. Murphy stowed the statue in her satchel along with the biometric sniffer. She was glad to shut it away. It was deceptively light. But she noticed Wu intermittently turning in his suit to look at the bag, emphasising it was still there.

'You okay?' she asked. They were half-way back up the cargo bay, the docking bay doors clanging shut behind them.

Wu's pupils constricted and a false smile tugged at the corners of his mouth. 'You did good. Want me to carry?' He pointed at the satchel.

Yes, she did. Her foreboding was growing, like she was carrying a bomb. Though a scan showed no moving parts. It appeared entirely solid; however, it corresponded to no known element on the periodic table. But it was the look on Wu's face that unsettled Murphy even more.

'I've got this,' she said, bluffing.

They'd walked the corridor on the Reggie's starboard flank, back to the suit room and changed. All the time, Wu kept glancing at the satchel while they stripped to underclothes. Murphy was glad to reach the mess and hand the statue over to Valentine, who'd turned it over in her hands before placing it on the counter. Murphy noted how the captain discretely tried to wipe her palms on the hips of her flight suit without anyone noticing.

Grover paced in the background. Weaver leaned on the wall near the med-bay, not far from the ladder to his garret. The rest of them stood around the island counter transfixed by the statue, too animated or maybe repulsed to sit. Murphy backed away towards med-bay, until she found Weaver smirking at her, enjoying the show, and chewing on a toothpick.

'This should be interesting,' he said.

Murphy said nothing.

'You watch.'

Grover gesticulated from the bridge door. 'I still can't believe you brought that thing up here. I want nothing to do with it.'

'It's too important a find. People have been looking for Agoul artifacts for years,' Kohl said.

'How fucking green are you Kohl?' Weaver sneered. 'There's been a black-market trade for them for years. Piece like that on Proxima Centauri.' He whistled around his toothpick.

'It would be worth a small fortune, that's for sure. But we wouldn't see a penny of it,' Hendrix said.

Kohl stared at the statue in amazement. 'It's not about the money.'

'There'll be commendations for sure.' Hendrix said, as much thinking out loud as anything else.

Kohl shook his head, running his fingers through his hair and making it stand up like Promethean wheat. 'Commendations? Money? No, he is so much more than that.'

'He?' Valentine said, with a tilt of her head, inspecting the statue.

'Just thought he, it, looked male,' Kohl added quickly.

'Do Agoul even have sexes like we think of them?' Hendrix mused.

Grover threw up his hands. 'Don't you guys get it. This thing came from a graveyard, a forbidden fucking graveyard, hitching a ride with a woman who voluntarily climbed in a coffin and fired herself into space.'

'Maybe she was trying to escape,' Kohl said.

'Escape? A PhD in Astroarchaeology thought she could survive in a coffin, exposed to the vacuum of space? Oh, and while she's freezing to death, she thought, you know what? I should breast feed this freaky ass statue I'm running away with to my certain death. Yep, everything is five-by-five with this picture. Nothing completely insane going on here. It looks more like she went full Astro.'

'But the scans were clear,' Murphy said with no confidence in herself. She'd got Ito's dose wrong. Could she have got this wrong too?

'Enough!' Valentine raised her voice. 'It's not our call.'

'You've already relayed it back to command.' Grover was pacing again, shaking his head.

'That's just great.'

'Told you. The old man will need sedating too. You got enough Dexodrol?' Weaver said in a low voice only Murphy could hear.

Valentine looked every bit the captain. A strong Latina, with naturally smoky eyes on fire and full lips thinned by the seriousness of the situation. Murphy hoped one day she could be the same. Confident, forthright, in command.

'Nothing has changed. We have another twenty-nine hours until our pick-up rendezvous. We finish our tests and bring the gun back on-line and linked with the rest of the defence net. Then we bug out for our ride home.'

'And here it is,' Weaver whispered.

Grover stopped pacing. His jaw muscles rippled. Murphy thought he might either break some teeth or have an embolism.

'What about *that?*' Grover stabbed a finger in the direction of the strange little brown statue, the sheen of light playing oddly on his surface. But he wouldn't look at it.

Valentine seemed to think this was obvious. 'We take it with us.'

'Take it with us? Are you crazy? That's Agoul. It doesn't belong here.'

'We have our orders. Nothing has changed other than we keep the body on ice in the docking bay, bring her home at last. And that,' Valentine inclined her head at the statue, but didn't look at it either, 'it's only a statue. Okay, it is from the Algol region. Hendrix is right: that's going to mean commendations all round. Look, I know it's been a long tour. We just need to keep our heads for one more day and we'll be on our way home, sipping Martian Slam-Bams and getting ready for stasis.'

Pleased and excited, Kohl and Hendrix agreed. Murphy noticed Wu didn't react; his vacant, dilated eyes were fixed on the statue. His chin creased fractionally, twitching his lips in a manner she'd never seen him do before.

Grover still wasn't happy. 'Wait, I have to say this. We need to get that thing off the ship. The gun placement isn't back online yet. It has been a while since anyone tried, but we all know what happens when you attempt to take something from that place.'

Valentine slammed her fist on the counter. 'Duly noted, Sailor, but we have our orders. This is above all our paygrades. They point at a problem; we go fix it. They say bring a statue home, we gift wrap it and pay for shipping.'

'This isn't a malfunctioning purification unit or a corrupted gel-matrix,' Grover said, palms out. 'We're not marines.'

'I am,' Weaver spoke up, rolling the toothpick to the side of his mouth.

'Oh great, that's just wonderful,' Grover said. 'Shakespeare has climbed down from his infinite monkey cage and is going to protect us single handed against the Agoul. We're supposed to be tightening our defences not provoking an attack.'

'You all signed up to do whatever you're told. We serve and protect. You can be confined to quarters and be disciplined when we get home, or you can shut up and help. You're right about one thing though, let's get the final tests on the gun finished and start packing up to go home.'

There came a flash of orange light from the cockpit. They all turned that way to see it fading like an accelerated sunset. Seconds later the shock wave hit them, buffeting the Reggie and setting off alarms.

'Chaos-fire,' Weaver shouted, already mounting the ladder to his gun turret.

'How? The gun isn't armed yet,' Hendrix shouted over the alarms, running with Valentine to the bridge.

'Not our gun,' Weaver said over the comms. He was already in his chair and strapping in. 'Next one over. Its shock wave hit us.'

'It's them,' Grover shouted and lunged for the statue, but Wu snatched it up.

Kohl was working at a panel, trying to shut off the alarms. Murphy didn't know what to do. Help Kohl? Check Ito? Do something about Grover and Wu? Curl up in a ball and wait for it all to stop? She clung to the med bay's door frame at the rear of the mess area, watching Grover and Wu either side of the counter in a face off. Wu hugged the statue to his chest. Grover faked left, Wu went the opposite way and Grover lunged, but the old man was too slow, and without zero-G his creaking knees hobbled him. Wu slipped through his fingers, but Grover snagged a handful of jumpsuit. Like two ironball players, Wu dragged the old man off his feet, nearly lost his balance too, but regained it and broke free. Grover fell into the back of Kohl's legs, slamming his head into the frame of the open control panel, and Kohl slumped down the wall unconscious.

There was a second flash of orange, bright and searing. Murphy covered her eyes.

'Agoul, Agoul! Coming through the gap in the net,' Weaver shouted over the comms. 'Battle stations.'

CHAPTER 6

THIS WAS MURPHY'S first combat dog fight. No matter how many simulated missions you've done, it doesn't prepare you for the real thing. The main difference being, even in VR with full haptics, you know you can't die. The moment you're about to, the programme ends, and you are back to reality.

Murphy staggered across to Kohl, losing her footing and crawling the rest of the way.

Grover disappeared in pursuit of Wu, neither of them following protocol. She carefully rolled Kohl onto his back as the Reggie veered to starboard. The movement was so fast the inertial dampeners couldn't keep up and she was dumped on her backside.

Chatter over the comms was frantic.

Kohl had a two-inch gash in his brow, and head wounds always bled like a sonofabitch. Crimson rivulets ran down one side of his face. His eyes fluttered as the electrical impulses of his brain tried to reboot his consciousness.

'Guns are hot,' Weaver brayed and hooted a battle cry. The Reggie juddered with the recoil from the marine's cannon fire. White light strobed from the hole up to his gun turret.

'Shit! I missed, I missed. He's gone. Where is he?'

The Reggie lurched again, this time to port, and Murphy sprawled over Kohl. He let out a weak moan.

'Bogey at three o'clock,' Hendrix shouted.

'I see him.' Weaver's gun turret spun with a whir. Flashing white light, noise, and vibration followed in a hellish thunderstorm.

'Can't get a lock; can't get a lock.'

'Fire, Weaver, fire.'

'Where is he?'

'He's jumped; he's jumped.'

The Reggie banked hard to port and then dropped. Murphy's stomach lurched up. Kohl's head lolled; where it wasn't ribboned with red, his visage drained of colour. She needed gauze for the blood, ephedrine swabs to stem the bleeding, cellular glue to patch the wound, bandages to protect it, cortical anti-inflammatories for the concussion. In short, she needed to get her ass to med bay.

'Overhead. He's overhead.'

The gun turret whirred. Cannon fire played a rat-tat-tat percussion.

Murphy pushed herself up, groping for the central counter.

'Missed, missed. He jumped.'

'Where? He was right on us.'

Murphy clung on as the Reggie manoeuvred sharply. Kohl slid back headfirst in a bulkhead. When the ship levelled out, Murphy sprinted for med-bay. She unlocked it and dove inside for the portable med kit stored in one of the low cupboards. Asleep and strapped in with the additional head and waist restraints, Ito was blissfully unaware of what was happening.

There was another enfilade of cannon fire, followed by a sudden rise in the nose of the Reggie and a swerve to starboard. Inertial dampeners and gravity drive unable to compensate enough, Murphy found herself in free fall. It was only a drop of four feet, but she braced for the landing and slammed into the med-bay wall, cracked her head and saw stars. Their keel evened out.

She made it back to her feet and into the mess hall, where she could see through to the cockpit. Valentine and Hendrix sat side by side at the helm. They made a hard turn. Murphy held on, and the stars became streaks of fine silver.

More flashes and desperate shouts.

She looked around, trying to get her bearings both physically and mentally. Kohl unconscious and bleeding on the deck. Wu absconded with the statue; Grover in pursuit. The rest in a firefight for their lives.

The Reggie shuddered. Murphy dropped to her knees, ears ringing.

We've been hit, she thought, a beat ahead of Hendrix who yelled, 'Direct hit. Port side.'

Jets of white gas vented from one of the overhead service ducts.

'Damage report,' Valentine ordered.

Murphy struggled to her feet. Warning lights flashed red. Alarms wailed.

'Fore-port engine damaged. The hull is holding.'

'Got you, motherfucker.'

White lightning and thunder erupted from Weaver's gun turret.

'Did you get him?'

'Shit! Negative, negative.'

'Where is he?'

The ear splitting *whoot-whoot* cry of a proximity alert shredded Murphy's ears.

'Brace for impact. Brace for—' the automated warning tried to tell them.

The world of the Reggie dissolved into a maelstrom where up was down, feeling became pain, light turned into blackness, and all hope seemed lost in the churning tumult.

CHAPTER 7

MURPHY IS ELEVEN *years old and wants to cry. Her leg hurts so much where her mum's boyfriend stubbed out his joint on her bare leg. Right in the middle of her hamstring, hand clamped like a claw around her ankle so she couldn't wriggle away. But Murphy didn't cry out then and she won't now. Tears fall in fat droplets down her light brown skin. It's as though the tears release the pressure building up inside her, letting out a little bit so that she doesn't explode. Besides, it's not the worst thing he's ever done to her.*

She hides in the darkness of a wardrobe, hugging her knees. Clothes hang down and touch her face. They are the unwanted skins of a person her mother no longer wants to inhabit. Unused, they grow damp and moulder, the floating ghosts of comfort, hope and joy, lost to this life. The blackness is Murphy's cloak of invisibility. When she is old enough, she will run away to space, where everything is black. She can see herself there, floating like these ghosts around a ship or bounding in great superhero leaps across a chalky grey moon. But in her hiding place the pain is so searing, it is a monster that wants to eat her. Gobble her up with its jagged teeth. Rip her flesh and crunch her bones. It crawls all over her, inside her, searching her out, with its venomous touch and poisonous tongue. In the blackness, it cannot find her if she doesn't give into the pain and cry out. Keep quiet. Don't make a sound. But then, beyond the wardrobe, outside the safety of blackness, a baby begins to cry.

Quiet. Shush, baby Jack. Shush. Please be quiet. I can't come out. I can't or the monster will get me. Please, baby Jack.

Baby Jack won't be quiet because Murphy isn't there to help him. She's too afraid to come out. Hates herself for not thinking to grab him from his crib and bring him into the dark with her.

But baby Jack doesn't like the dark, and baby Jack always makes noise. And in her heart Murphy knows that's why she didn't bring him.

'Shut that fucking baby up,' Mum's boyfriend shouts. His words are gravel in his mouth.

Murphy knows it's directed at her and Mum, but Mum is staring into nothing, eyes glassy. She didn't move when the boyfriend let go of Murphy's ankle. Her lips were blue, her skin grey. Mum took the special medicine, the one not for children, that she needed all the time, even though the more she took it the sicker she seemed to get. So, Mum wouldn't be going to baby Jack.

There is a loud bang as the door to her and baby Jack's bedroom is kicked open. Murphy flinches and squeezes her knees so tightly a whimper squeaks in her mouth, the burn on the back of her thigh touched by her lower leg.

'Shut up, you little bastard!'

Baby Jack lets out a scream so shrill it stabs Murphy in her heart. Some part of her, stronger than her fear, opens her eyes and makes her hand push open the door a crack.

This lets in the light.

This lets in more of little Jack's screaming.

What will happen, is so terrible . . . was so terrible Murphy thinks. And as she does that mental shift it lets out the past so that the present could drag itself back from wherever it was thrown. Then again this is so real she pushes the door of her childhood apartment wider, with her leg that is singing with pain, but on the other side isn't her mother's squalid bedroom, with its bare mattress scarred with a patchwork of stains. It is the deck of a spaceship—one hiding place leading to another—and in both places baby Jack is screaming and screaming and screaming. A desperate cry, sharp enough to flay her soul.

Murphy groaned as her mental and physical-self quivered across each other like a scanner pinpointing an interstellar signal. They oscillated back and forth, homing in on their mark but forever missing each other. Until Murphy winced with a pain so acute it took her breath away and one place and time was overlayed by another. She was eye-glaringly, teeth-grindingly, muscle-clenchingly present and reached for the back of her leg.

Sparks spat. Bare electrical cables snapped. Releasing gasses hissed. And the very bones of the Reggie seemed to groan. The screams of baby Jack were an echo, bouncing far away. But she knew he was nowhere and that was a sadness wider and deeper than the universe.

Murphy looked towards the pain in her leg. A twisted sliver of metal impaled her hamstring like a cocktail stick through a party sausage, although with a lot more blood. Two further things felt off, though it was hard to make out what in her dazed state. The first was the dark red droplets floating in the air before her focusing eyes. The second was her lack of proprioception, that internal sense of which way is up. Taken together, she realised she was weightless. As she moved to feel the injury, she brushed something hard and realised she was floating a few inches from the floor.

Carefully, she felt around the wound. The blood was still slick and warm, soaking the leg of her jumpsuit, but not too much. That was a good sign. By remaining in place, the shard was probably stemming some of the bleeding. Not so good for infection, but one thing at a time. Also, it hadn't hit anything essential, no arteries or major nerves. A flesh wound. If she could get to med bay, it would be awkward, but she could sort it out. Without access to a sedative and the deep cellular stimulation of a regenerative module (the latter of which you'd only get on Endeavour class ships or bigger), the injury would hobble her for a few weeks while it healed, but apart from that she'd be okay. That almost made her laugh at how ridiculous it was given the circumstances, which brought her wider predicament back to her.

Getting her bearings, she found Kohl floating up near the ceiling of the rec room. The contents of the kitchen, plus a deck of cards, a tablet, and one of Kohl's paperbacks—a fat thing with the word *IT* and a red balloon on the cover—drifted. The bulkhead doors to the bridge were closed. Emergency lighting had kicked in, casting a green glow through the ship. Someone cussed, and Murphy twisted to see Weaver pulling himself headfirst down the gun turret's ladder. That's when she also saw med bay. The doors were half open. Medical supplies hovered in mid-air and the gurney was empty.

Weaver took a quick reconnoitre of the situation and pushed off the ladder towards Murphy. She drew a sharp breath, looking around for any sign of Ito. His restraints must have unlocked with a power surge, or maybe a brief failure, and now he was loose on the ship. As she searched to see if he was hiding in a darkened corner, a noise like the vestiges of past traumas sounded softly from down the port corridor. She must have banged her head harder than she thought, because she could have sworn it sounded like a baby crying.

Weaver reached Murphy, stopping his momentum with the deck. He looked her over, then up at Kohl, over to med bay, and back to the closed bridge doors. She'd never seen him think before, not like this, not just looking for the next lewd thing to say.

'What happened?' Murphy said.

He seemed not to hear her at first, thoughts darting like his eyes. When he looked back at her, she guessed he was going to say something sarcastic. He didn't.

'Can't say for sure, only that we were hit hard, spun out, lost power briefly. Lucky we're here at all. Gravity is offline. Life support is holding, I think. Need to check. Back-up power kicked in. But . . . '

'But what?'

'The captain sealed the bridge.'

'What does that—' Murphy strangled a cry of pain caused by trying to move.

Weaver stayed her with a hand on her shoulder. He quickly eyeballed her injury and looked up at Kohl. His limp body hung face down up near the ceiling, as if he was a drowned man floating on the surface of a pool. 'What do you need for you and the nerd?'

Okay, so he was still being a bit of a dick, but Murphy didn't mind. It was normal, one less weird thing in their little world that had been flipped head over heels. As she ran through the medical kit, he pushed off the ground up to Kohl, and then back off the ceiling to bring him down to rest next to Murphy. Then the marine pulled himself through to med bay.

'But why is the bridge sealed?' Murphy called after him.

'First things first,' he said, gliding expertly across the rec room and dining area. Murphy wondered how much zero-G work he'd done before. They were all used to spacewalks because they were engineers who had to work outside. Weaver didn't have the skills for that, or so she thought. He sat with his gun watching for threats. Occupying the same container, he was oil in their water. Murphy realised what she thought she knew about him was mostly assumption. She hadn't ever asked him about what he did before, where he'd been posted, how long he'd served.

While Weaver found what they needed in med bay, she couldn't help but worry about the bridge. Why would the captain seal it? What was Weaver holding back?

'This?' Weaver shouted over and held up a surgical stapler.

'Yes,' Murphy confirmed.

A baby's cry, shrill and demanding, came from the portside corridor. Murphy saw only the low green emergency lights curving off around the bend. She brushed it aside. A bad memory; the tatty, threadbare clothes of a past that doesn't fit you anymore, but you can't help but remember how they felt. Nothing of use to the problem in which they were currently mired. Nothing more than thoughts knocked loose by a concussion.

Weaver floated back with a medical kit, gliding to a stop and ripping open the bag. 'What do we do first?'

'Weaver, tell me why the bridge is sealed.' Murphy's heart was starting to pound and her chest felt as though it was getting tighter and tighter, panic rising.

The marine must have heard it in her voice. 'Soldier, I'm going to tell you, but we've other shit to sort first. You're the only trained field medic we have, and we need you operational so the rest of us can keep working. Right?'

'Tell me, Valentine, Hendrix, are they alive?'

Weaver looked her right in the eye, no wise crack, no smirk, dead serious, and she noticed his right eye was closing with swelling. 'They're alive, and the quicker we fix you and Kohl, the quicker we get to them. Triage, right?'

Okay, Murphy thought. They're alive. Triage: that means we're in worse shape than them. She nodded as much to herself as to show she understood. They got to work on Kohl. His head wasn't bleeding as much as before. Murphy stemmed the flow of blood, applied a couple of internal bio-degradable staples, laced with phage-based antibiotics, and used bio-glue to knit the surface of the wound back together. Next, he got a cocktail shot of drugs for his cerebral inflammation from the undoubted concussion, and enough pain meds and stimulants to raise the dead. That last injection into shallow pectoral muscle slapped Kohl into a gasping consciousness. He looked around uncomprehending, tensing and flailing in the weightless atmosphere. Murphy explained the little she understood in short, calming sentences, while Weaver tried to restrain him by the arms. Finally, Kohl relaxed. He touched the blood on his face, inspecting his fingers as they filled in more details. Then they got to work on Murphy.

It needed the two of them. That's why they'd dealt with Kohl first. They'd be able to work on the back of her leg far better than she could. Weaver used scissors to slit up the back of Murphy's trouser leg. They stabbed her with a numbing agent and drew out the metal shard impaling her hamstring. Even with the drugs, it hurt like having salt rubbed into a spliff burn. If they noticed the little circular burns on the back of her leg under all that blood, they didn't say a thing, and it was too painful for Murphy to care.

With a cold sweat and through gritted teeth, she told them how to clean and close the laceration. They were probably doing a ham-fisted job, but nothing about this was ideal. After that she could administer her own drugs. This was tricky. With Kohl, she tried to balance pain relief with the need for him to remain awake and lucid. He seemed stoned, not out of it, but dulled from his usual bouncy, sharp-witted self. So, she lowered her own dose of pain meds, and upped the stimulant. Better to suck it up and hobble around in a little agony. Even so, Murphy already felt beat up and wiped out. Like she'd played a game of ironball with a pro-team, and she was the ball.

'The bridge,' she said, pulling herself up, glad of the zero-G. At least she didn't have to load bare on that leg.

Weaver didn't resist anymore. He simply gave a single curt nod.

Kohl tried to blink away the fog of narcotics. 'Wait, what about the bridge?'

CHAPTER 8

THEY PUSHED THEMSELVES over to the bridge doors, which were latticed with reinforced alloy and topped with portholes of eight-inch-thick toughened glass. Murphy and Kohl took a window each. Weaver hung back as Murphy banged on the glass and shouted.

'Captain . . . Hendrix!'

Busy at the helm, the two senior officers sat with their backs to them, hands moving urgently over the controls.

'They can't hear you.' Kohl was bleary-eyed and slurred his words slightly, but he was pointing to the access panel.

Her toes hardly touching the floor, Murphy reached over and found the intercom. 'Captain.'

Valentine's back stiffened and she twisted in her seat to glance over her shoulder. Even with everything that had happened so far, the look on her captain's face frightened Murphy. She pushed the intercom, trying her hardest to keep her fear under control.

'What's wrong?'

Behind the toughened glass' veil of silence, Valentine and Hendrix exchanged words. Hendrix unbuckled without acknowledging Murphy or Kohl's presence. He pulled his gangly form around the consoles until he was across from Kohl's usual comms and telemetry station. It was for the ship's essential systems, engines, life support, artificial gravity.

Valentine unbuckled too, and like a spectre pushed off and drifted across the bridge towards Murphy. She opened the two-way com on her side of the door.

'Hey, Baby Girl!'

That brought tears to Murphy's eyes. Because they couldn't fall, they beaded and broke free with a blink to spin away on their own sad orbits.

Valentine put her hand on the glass. 'You've got to be strong. Hold on. Got to work together to find a way back.'

This sounded like a goodbye speech. As Murphy scanned the bridge, trying to understand it, she finally noticed the extent of the damage, how one side was misshapen and crumpled in, the windows webbed with growing fissures. 'What do you mean, Cap?'

Like frost fingers on a lake, the fissures in the glass inched forward.

'We're outside the defence grid and can't uplink to the last gun placement. You're going to have to try and get the systems back online—'

Hendrix had floated over to Valentine, interrupting. Taking her in his arms, he said, 'It's going to go.'

Valentine's hand dropped from the intercom, as behind the captain and first officer the cracks in the glass spread over the windows, dicing space into a thousand shards. Valentine and Hendrix turned to the fractured starscape and back to each other, falling into a tight embrace, heads on each other's shoulders. Valentine closed her eyes.

Murphy pushed frantically at the intercom. 'Captain, wait.'

But there was no waiting. The glass to the bridge suddenly blew out, sucking the captain and her first officer out into the freezing vacuum of space. Their bodies smashed against the window frame, jolting them apart. They spun, whirling in separate directions, to die alone, suffocating in the cold, black void.

'No!' Murphy cried, slamming her palms against the glass.

Kohl rubbed his eyes as if trying to scrub away what he'd seen through the fog of drugs in his bloodstream. 'This is messed up. It can't be happening.'

'It's happening,' Weaver said, off to the side. He was moving his way back towards the med bay.

Murphy turned, drying her eyes on her sleeve, the terrible sense of loss turning to anger. 'How can you be so cold?'

Weaver arrested his flight with a handhold on the ladder and hoisted himself up through the hole above. 'Crying isn't going to help them,' he called down, clattering around, looking for something. 'While you two were out of it, I'd already spoken to the captain and got my orders.' He pushed back down from his turret into the rec area, with a rifle slung over his shoulder. 'The blast doors sealed automatically because they had a breach. They were trying to get the ship back online, but they had limited time. If they failed, it was down to us, or more exactly you two, Grover as well if we can find the old bastard. My job is to keep you safe, and if we can find the alien artifact, get it off the ship.'

Trying to make sense of things, Kohl asked, 'What did the captain mean about the defence grid?'

Weaver came back over to them and performed a point check on his weapon as he spoke. 'The Agoul came through the gap in the defence net our gun repairs created. The big flash of orange was the next nearest guns, four of them, firing, but they were too far away. A combination of evasive manoeuvres and that last Agoul attack knocked us into their space. We're sitting ducks, and if the enemy doesn't finish us off first, then the gun placement will when it reboots back online in less than ninety minutes.'

'It won't fire on us,' Murphy said, hardly able to keep their litany of woes in any kind of order. 'It'll recognise our signature. We need to . . . ' But she couldn't finish the thought of going to get Valentine and Hendrix back.

Kohl shook his head—telemetry and comms were his domain. Murphy could see him thinking it over. What was wrong with him? How could he move on so coldly? He said, 'Not if we're sitting in a piece of space junk, not pinging back a signature because our comms and telemetry are down.'

'Bingo!' Weaver said. 'We gotta move. Where do you need to be?'

Murphy couldn't believe what she was hearing. Their captain and first officer, their friends, were sucked out into space and they were moving on as though nothing had happened. She couldn't take it anymore. 'What's wrong with you? You cold hearted bastards!' she screamed, each word burning with fury.

Weaver was still for a moment. His eyes fixed on hers and before she could decipher what that strange look meant or why he wasn't showing any grief, he moved fast. He kicked off a toppled easy chair, lying on its side, and was on her in a second. Murphy put her arms up to cover her face as he hurtled towards her, but he caught both her wrists in his fists and the momentum of his body knocked her back against the bridge doors, pinning her there.

'Do you want to die?' he shouted in her face, flecks of spit flying.

Murphy struggled, grunting with the effort. What she wanted

was to lash out at him, claw his face, knee him in the balls, make him feel what she was feeling, but he was too strong and too skilled.

'Hey man, get off her,' Kohl said, coming over to help.

Weaver spun him away with a deft tug on Kohl's shoulder, but he had to release his grip on Murphy's hand. She managed to slap the marine across the face before the big man had her restrained again. 'Do you want to die?' he repeated.

She struggled with everything, to no avail, and broke down.

'Do you want to die, Soldier? Do you?'

'No,' she cried, dissolving into a pitiful sob. With the fight gone out of her, Weaver let go. She curled up into a ball, hugging herself. Weaver didn't move far away, and Kohl floated back over. Being there with her, they let her cry, maybe for them all, maybe because they couldn't themselves.

Finally, Kohl rested a tentative hand on her back. 'The captain and Hendrix wouldn't want us to give up.'

Murphy took a deep shuddering breath. She knew Kohl was right, Weaver too. Painful as everything was, her body, her soul, she did want to live. She'd always wanted to live, even if the survivors had to carry the guilt of that with them. That was something she knew well.

She straightened up, stifling her grief. 'I know . . . ' Kohl hesitated, unsure if he should put an arm around her and decided against it. 'What's the plan?' she said.

'Is there a way to get our Reggie at least limping again? Cap said something about the docking bay,' Weaver said.

Kohl ran his hand through his hair, causing it to stand up on end and wave there like seaweed in a gentle current. The healing wounds on his forehead reminded Murphy of this boy wizard in one of the tatty paperbacks he'd lent her. He blew out his cheeks and then it dawned on him. 'There are manoeuvring thrusters there. They're integrated with the rest of the system but on a separate circuit. Could be the captain was thinking we'd be able to jury-rig them. Probably couldn't manage it from the bridge.' That last comment tumbled between them, like a falling stone into a deep well, or a pair of crewmates into the frigid night.

'What about guidance?' Murphy said.

'I could help there,' Weaver chipped in, surprising them. 'What? I can't have ideas?'

'No, usually not,' Kohl said deadpan.

'Futa!' Weaver countered.

'Meathead!'

Murphy didn't break it up. They were playing their usual roles, trying to normalise the situation, at least enough for them to get things done. 'What is this idea?'

Weaver jerked his thumb at his ladder. 'The turret is pretty fucked-up. That cannon is more fucked up than a centenarian gangbang, but the targeting system is working, which means we've got telemetry.'

Kohl got it. 'You can tell us where to point the Reggie. How far over the border are we?'

'Two miles, last I checked, but we're drifting farther in. Could be three or four. Need to verify it again,' Weaver said.

Kohl thought it over. 'Should be okay, but the farther away we get the smaller our window of error becomes. We need to move fast.'

'That's what I've been saying,' Weaver said. 'Time to nut up or shut up.'

'You really are a poet.'

'Bet you'd like that, wouldn't you, Kohl?' Weaver said and blew him a kiss.

'How is that even an insult?'

CHAPTER 9

BEHIND THE SNUB turtle head of the Reggie lay the main body of the ship. From the rec and med bay area, two corridors curved around the flanks of the hull. Crew quarters took up the first fifth of the port and starboard sides, four on either side, room for eight in total. As only seven were billeted, the spare room located on the port side was used for storing additional provisions. The remainder of the space was taken up with the larger cargo hold and smaller docking bay at the Reggie's stern. Airlocks and suit rooms were located on either flank at the midpoint, creating a kink in the corridor.

Weaver led the way, his rifle tucked one-handed into his shoulder. Kohl had picked a kitchen knife out of the air and held that out in front of him. It was only then that Murphy thought that was the same knife Ito had used to stab Wu. That did nothing for the thumping inside her ribcage. Ito free and loose; Wu steeling away the statue and pursued by Grover; and they were battered and incapacitated and floating in Algol space, with an Agoul ship, which had done the incapacitating, somewhere nearby.

They waited at the corridor's entrance and Murphy heard the insistent squeal of baby Jack. She was sure it wasn't real, couldn't be, but Weaver tensed at something too. Nothing major. A tightening of his jaw Murphy saw only by the greenish glow of the emergency lights. At the same time, Kohl flashed a guilty look across at them.

'You hear that?' Murphy said.

Both turned to her and looked at each other.

Weaver was surprised. 'You hear it too? I thought . . . '

Kohl appeared to finish what Weaver was thinking. 'I thought it was just me. Bang to the cranium or something.' He put a hand to his forehead, wincing. 'But you can hear the singing too, right?'

'Singing? No, I hear kids laughing and . . . ' Weaver trailed off, tightening his grip on the rifle.

'What about you?' Kohl asked Murphy, more anxious than curious.

'A baby crying.' That was true, though crying didn't quite cover what baby Jack was doing. Murphy wondered if they were all telling some but not all of the truth of what they were hearing. 'Is it . . . ' she paused, wondering if asking this would expose something too private and secret, but she said it anyway. 'Is it something from your past?'

'Yeah,' Weaver said.

'No,' Kohl said. 'Not exactly.'

Weaver hefted his rifle. 'We don't have time for this. The clock is literally ticking. We've all been shaken up. Bangs to the head. The shock and stress of combat.'

'What about the statue?' Kohl said. There was a touch of Kohl's old natural wonder for the universe back in his demeanour. An eagerness trying to find clarity. 'We all saw the way Wu was with it. You've heard the Agoul legends, right? You know, it could be like—'

'What does it matter?' Weaver snapped. 'The mission remains the same, and if we find that freaky fucking statue, I'll happily throw it out of a goddamn airlock. But it's all going to mean shit if the chaos gun spins back up and the defence net incinerates us along with anything else that's in this quadrant.'

Weaver had slipped back into the proficiency of a professional marine, though Murphy could tell it was wavering. Murphy needed him back on point; they all needed him back on point: cold, direct. But she could see the personal battle he was fighting. A thing from deep down, too complicated to get into now or maybe ever. She could see it because it was what she was experiencing too.

She put a hand on his arm. He went rigid. 'Hey, Marine, you're right. Let's keep going. You keep us safe; we'll fix whatever needs fixing. Just like always.'

He pushed the fear down and squared his shoulders. 'Just like always, Baby Girl.' One corner of his mouth twitched up.

They began to pull themselves slowly down the corridor using the waist-high handrail. Murphy thought they must have looked like three floating zombies. Her with her bloody trouser leg in tatters, sweating and grey with fear. Weaver, his eye closing shut, and Kohl worst of all. Blood in his hair, masking half his face and darkening his collar and chest.

Sparks spat overhead from a nest of loose cables. Unable to fall, they crackled in place, biting and spitting at each other, growing angrier. Kohl used his ceramic knife to disperse the sparks before they combusted into something else they'd have to worry about. The scintillas of fire drifted away in all directions, burning themselves out, embers to ash. The cables fizzed on, but they couldn't stop to fix it.

Murphy tried to ignore baby Jack's cries. They felt as though they were attached to the sinews of her gut. An invisible cord tugging at her. What would really be at the end of that cord? Perhaps the truth would be the worst possibility of all. An impossible reality at that, and all the more frightening for it.

They drifted down the corridor and soon came up on the kink, where the port suit room and airlock lay. It was a blind bend. Weaver held up a hand for them to stop. He put a finger to his lips and hand signed for them to wait while he went to check the way ahead. He disappeared around the corner. Glutinous seconds dripped away like a slow leak from a tap. Murphy found herself white knuckling the handrail. She was about to hiss 'Where is he?' to Kohl, when the marine reappeared.

'It's clear. Let's hustle.'

Weaver covered them as they hauled ass through the air and into the suit room.

'What do you reckon?' Murphy said to Kohl.

'You grab your standard kit. I'll get a modulator, a couple of jellies, and a circuit editor,' Kohl said. He was thinking about needing to patch up any electrical circuits with the clear gelatinous pads. About the size of one of his ancient paperbacks, they could pretty much reprogramme them to become anything they wanted.

'Gel gun too,' Murphy asked.

'Totally,' Kohl said stuffing one in his own bag.

Baby Jack's screams filtered in through the open door, snaking past Weaver, who stood at the threshold, gun up, one eye on the corridor, one eye on them.

'What about these?' Murphy had drawn the bolt gun and a tool they called 'the jaws.' It was both a powerful jack and a cutter they used to wrench open metal seams or chew out sections to make room for a clean patch job.

Kohl's eyes had cleared a little and they danced behind his glasses, scanning over the scenarios they might face. 'Good call. We might need to rip and zip.'

Weaver nodded at the bolt gun. 'That thing fire screws or some shit?'

'Bolts,' Kohl corrected.

'Same shit. Does it?'

'Yeah,' Murphy said, looking at the gun in a new light. 'It's loaded with fifty bolts. Don't know what the range would be.'

Weaver gave a shrug, like it didn't matter. 'If they get by me then it'll be close.'

A cold and fetid idea occurred to Murphy. If she fired the bolt gun to defend herself it could be at one of her crewmates: Ito or maybe even Wu. People she'd lived cheek by jowl with for half a year. Eaten with them, cooked them food, and had it made for her by them. She'd played countless games of cards with them, and basketball and football on the tiny court in the corner of the cargo bay. She'd heard Wu break wind over an open comms line on a long walk outside. They all pissed themselves laughing at that one, even stoic Wu cracked up. Turns out the old joke about a fart in a spacesuit isn't true. And she'd cared for Ito, at least as best she could. He'd been her patient. What was she supposed to do, shoot them with a bolt gun? It was a nauseating idea.

The door to the suit room closed, catching them all unawares. Weaver spun back to the door lock and punched it with the pad of his fist. It stayed shut, so he punched it again as a face briefly appeared on the other side of the glass. Drawn and waxy, it was Ito. His eyes darted around the suit room, noting them all, what they were doing, and the door to the outer airlock.

'Ito, open up, man,' Weaver shouted, punching at the lock.

Ito glanced at the marine before he slid from view.

'He's opening an access panel,' Weaver said, craning to see Ito crouched in the corridor.

They'd all stopped.

'What's he doing?' Kohl thought out loud.

'The fuck if I know.' Weaver banged on the door window. 'Hey, Ito, stop pissing around and let us out.'

Both Murphy and Kohl exchanged a look, a joint realisation behind the fear in their eyes. They turned to the airlock doors.

'Suits!' Murphy shouted, already pushing off the deck to float fast to her locker. The action sent a burst of pain through her leg, but adrenaline was already pumping. Kohl was a heartbeat behind her.

Weaver eyed them uncomprehendingly. 'What's the deal with you two?'

'Space suits now,' Murphy said. 'The airlock.'

Weaver's face paled, his gaze drawn to the airlock doors and the cold terror of the vacuum beyond. 'Oh, bollocks!' He pushed off the wall hard and dented a locker with the collision.

Murphy already had her two legs in her suit and was tugging it up over her knees. Kohl had one leg in, but weightlessness was making it a slower job than normal. When the alarm started to sound, and the orange lights began to flash their warning, Weaver was only just yanking his suit from the locker. He swore. They all swore, bluer than Martian miners, as they struggled to get dressed, turning in the air.

Having more walk-time on this tour, Murphy was the quickest. The alarm seemed to be quickening, as she fastened her collar, but she hadn't yet snapped on her boots, gauntlets and helmet. Weaver however had overtaken Kohl.

'Tethers. We'd need to tether,' Murphy shouted, thanking her drill sergeant for putting the fear of God into her about airlock accidents.

She fixed her own, reeling it from her hip to the overhead line with a sound like a mosquito. Weaver and Kohl wouldn't be able to do the same until they'd zipped up their suits. How long did they have? Murphy's stomach rolled. Seconds maybe? And the doors would open. Ito was the best electrical engineer among them. A wizard with neural-gel circuits and wetware interfaces. Maybe he'd depressurise the cabin before they had their suits airtight, and the internal pressure balanced. But if they didn't have helmets and a tether, well then, the tortuous death her drill sergeant foretold would be theirs.

The only merciful part would be they'd have the length of the time it takes for deoxygenated blood to circulate from the lungs to the brain before they passed out. Because in a vacuum the way the gas exchange process works was reversed, that would be approximately fifteen seconds depending on their build. Murphy being the smallest would probably pass out the quickest. That's assuming she remembered in the panic to exhale. But if she didn't and held her breath it would cause her lungs to rupture due to the pressure differential between inside and outside her body. If Ito opened the outer door, and they'd exhaled, then they'd have around a ninety-second survival window for a crewmate to pull them back inside. Take any longer than that and their blood pressure would drop too low and then the fluids in their body would begin to boil. And while they cooked in their own juices on the inside, on the outside they'd crisp up with skin blistering sunburn from unfiltered UV radiation which would cause the water in their muscles to evaporate, swelling dermal tissues and mottling their flesh with bruising. And before the deep freeze of space would harden their bodies to a human shaped slab of ice like Dr Sue-Ann Merryweather in her coffin, the moisture in their mouths, noses and eyeballs would freeze in severe frostbite. Blinded by the dying tissues, their bodies would convulse as the starless veil of death shrouded them.

Their frantic movements were slowing them down. Kohl couldn't get his last arm in and was in a comic mid-air pirouette as he made grabs behind himself for the sleeve. Weaver had managed to get in his suit and was scrambling for his boots but knocked one summersaulting across the room. Floating face down, just below the ceiling, Murphy was putting her last glove on, when the gravity kicked back in.

They all dropped to the deck, Murphy, like a skydiver with no chute, covered her face with her arms as the ground rushed towards her.

The alarm stopped.

The orange warning light turned off. Even the green emergency illumination was replaced by overhead white lights.

They lay there processing the shock of the fall, breathing air and not the vacuum of space.

Kohl was the first to laugh, a contagious chuckle that spread between them, growing until Murphy turned on her back, laughing out loud and holding her stomach. Weaver's shoulders hitched and they let themselves escape into a shared moment of joy amplified by relief.

Staggering to his feet, Kohl said, 'He was fixing the gravity.'

Murphy got up too, the moment of levity waning already. Ito had fixed the gravity, and the lights were back on, so he was able to get into the life support systems. The man was technically brilliant, and they could use that skill. But why lock them in?

Weaver tried the door, and nothing happened. 'Shit!' He punched the release pad again. The door didn't budge.

'Is he still there?' Kohl asked.

Weaver peered through the glass, checking left and right. 'He's at a control panel. Hey, Ito! Let us out.'

Kohl came up on Weaver's shoulder. 'What's he doing?'

'Wiping his spaceball ass? The fuck if I know.' Weaver banged on the glass and then tried the intercom. 'Ito, you prick. Stop fucking around.'

'That'll persuade him,' Kohl said.

Murphy came over. 'Let me try.'

Weaver moved aside with a grunt.

'Ito, it's me, Murphy. We want to help. We're trying to get us moving again.' He didn't respond. The light of a small diagnostic screen was reflected in his face. He was reading, code probably, eyes flicking left and right, up and down, like a furtive animal. Murphy checked the time on her suit's gauntlet and tried again to connect. 'Ito, look at me.' She kept her voice soft, caring. 'We only have ninety minutes left before the chaos gun comes back on-line. We are right in its range. If we can—'

Ito stopped what he was doing and looked up at her. *Yes*, she thought, *yes, that's it. See me.* She willed him out of whatever psychosis he was mired in and smiled like she did when trying to calm him out of his raving.

Ito turned back to the console, tapped the screen a few times, and checked the corridor from for to aft and scampered away towards the stern of the ship.

'No, wait!' Murphy called, but it was too late. He was gone.

'That's just great,' Weaver said. 'Fucking nutjob.'

'At least he didn't blow us out of the airlock,' Kohl said flatly.

'That's your idea of a win? Great, we can sit here and wait to die.'

'Shut up, both of you,' Murphy said. In the panic, baby Jack's crying had stopped, or at least she hadn't heard it over the alarms. However, it was back, Jack's desperately high-pitched wail tugging at her insides. She wasn't about to sit around, listening to that until they were vapourised. 'There's another way. At least, I think there is.'

CHAPTER 10

'I'M NOT SURE about this. Wouldn't it be better to get back inside the ship?' Kohl said. Doubt wrinkled his broad forehead, cracking the dried blood.

'If you think you can out programme Ito?' Murphy said, already fixing her helmet. Her leg throbbed angrily at having to bear her weight.

Kohl countered with, 'How do you know he's not locked the docking bay, or this airlock for that matter?'

'I don't. But if we don't try, we won't know. And if he hasn't, we can walk our way across the fuselage to the docking bay and let ourselves in the back door. We'll end up right where we need to be.' *Along with the corpse of Dr Merryweather in her coffin, and the Fat Boy watching over her like a guardian of the afterlife,* Murphy thought. But in a universe of crap choices, this one stunk the least.

Weaver attached his tether to the overhead line and picked up his helmet. 'I'm with Murphy. Gotta keep moving, and we might not need to worry about the cargo bay.'

'Enlighten us, oh wise one.' Kohl looked and sounded on the edge. He kept rubbing his head. Maybe it was because of a headache, though Murphy didn't want to risk giving him more pain relief as it would dull his senses. The pain in her own leg was keeping her frosty. But maybe it was whatever he was hearing, the singing, he'd said. If it was anything like baby Jack's crying, it would be needling his brain, picking at psychological scar tissue.

Point checking his rifle again, Weaver said, 'While you were asleep, remember, just before we saved your twink-ass, the Reggie took a beating. There's a chance we've a hull breach in one of the sealed aft sections. No need for a door if there is a hole we can drop through. Or is that too dangerous for your pussy-ass?'

'Fuck you, Weaver. It's not about being a pussy,' Kohl said, but Murphy could see the fear. Their brush with the airlock had made him skittish. She couldn't blame him. If he wasn't scared, he would be stupid, and that's one thing Kohl wasn't, even when doped up on pain meds and stimulants.

Weaver smirked. 'And yet you want me to fuck you. Sounds like a pussy to me.'

'Enough.' Murphy raised her voice, using the tone she'd heard Valentine adopt when she was all business. 'Let's go. If we're wrong, we fall back here, and you can go head-to-head with Ito's code. Okay?'

Kohl sighed but nodded agreement.

All three of them lined up at the door. Murphy was about to depressurise the airlock with a code keyed into her gauntlet, when Weaver opened a comms link. 'Not a rookie anymore, hey, Murphy?'

She didn't respond. Her heart was beating against her ribs like a trapped animal trying to escape. Of all the people in the world, Weaver was the one who'd said the right thing for her at the right time. Or rather, it was the *way* he said it. A rhetorical question. He didn't think she was a rookie anymore. He didn't call her 'Baby Girl.' It's not how she felt. But until she did feel different, she'd take Weaver's opinion and use it.

The airlock depressurised and the gravity deactivated. Stomach butterflies fluttered as Murphy lost her sense of proprioception. She opened the airlock door; it silently slid aside. The only sound was her breathing and the faint hiss of her air supply. Weaver went first, pitched out to check their flank, before turning back to indicate they were good to go, but as he did, Murphy pointed over his shoulder.

'Oh no! Oh Bishma, no! Please.' Kohl was panicking behind Murphy. Her own breath halted, frozen by the wave of cold fear washing over her. Her heart rate spiked and turned from green to orange on her visor readout.

The Agoul ship lay off their port side. It was close, so close, and yet the shape was indefinable. Murphy wanted to think of it as a collection of triangular sections, formed together into something hawkish. Then that idea felt wrong; it had no edges, no fixed shape, or not one the human mind could settle on. The current stance taken by the military was that the Agoul used a kind of cloaking technology, which bent light around it. Up close, Murphy wasn't sure she'd put her money on that idea. The ship was both there and not there. Was it a psychic camouflage? Like a predator in the long grass. Murphy certainly felt like prey, frozen to the spot. Belittled. There was a cupboard in her mind she wanted to go and hide in. They were being watched by a thing far more powerful than their frail little bodies wrapped in synthetic materials. Nothing more than foil wrapped field rations ready and waiting to be torn open and devoured.

Then the ship vanished. One second it was there, the next it was gone.

'Everyone okay?' Weaver said. 'Kohl, did you she-wee yourself?'

'No, did you?'

'I think maybe a little, yeah,' Weaver said.

'Good to know. I'm okay, but now can we forget this idea?'

'Ah, nut up buttercup. Die here; die out there. What's the difference?' Weaver swung himself out.

Murphy followed the marine and catching hold of the handhold just outside the door, she turned back to Kohl. 'He's definitely not a poet, but maybe he's a philosopher.'

She swung out and magnetised her feet to the fuselage. The universe dropped away into eternity in all directions. For now, the Agoul ship was nowhere to be seen, but its possibility stalked them from beneath the black cowl of the unknown. Kohl climbed up with the mucilaginous movements of a man negotiating zero gravity in a space suit, and single file, the three of them started their walk to the rear of the Reggie.

CHAPTER 11

THEY WALKED IN time with the sound of their own breathing. Murphy tried to keep her focus on the deck of the Reggie. Her leg was doing better, though it hummed with nebulous pain that spread into her hip and down behind her knee. They had everything they could carry in backpacks and saddle bags strapped to their thighs. One advantage of zero-G was that weight wasn't a problem. Murphy heard Kohl swear and turned to see him down on one knee, a hand gripping the ridge of one of the Reggie's armoured plates.

'I'm okay. Looked up. Lost my footing.' His breathing was ragged. Murphy knew what he must have done. Nervously looking around for the Agoul.

'Eyes on the deck. It's just another day at work.' She smiled thinly. Hazy-eyed, Kohl managed to twitch a smile back at her before getting back up.

'Can you hear that?' Murphy said.

'I don't hear anything?'

'Not even singing?'

Kohl listened, cocking his head as if it would make a difference inside his helmet. 'No, not a thing, apart from my heartbeat.'

'Tell me about it,' Murphy said and carried on walking.

'What does it mean?'

'I think it's the statue, or whatever it is. We're out here. It's in there.'

'Could be, yeah sure. Makes you wonder—'

Weaver cut in over the com. 'Will you two ladies stop flapping your labia and move double time? Unless you want to hang around for that ship to come back, because it will.'

Definitely not a poet, but point taken; they pressed ahead.

The Reggie was battle scarred, her outer shell dented, but these scars carried no burn marks or discoloration. Whatever weapons the Agoul used they weren't like any of Earth's. It was as if the Reggie was a toy marked by the tantrums of an infant. Over the cargo bay, there was a particularly large indentation, but no breach of the fuselage they could drop through. That would have presented its own problems, like having to patch it from the inside, eating up precious time as they welded it shut and repressurised. The time readout on Murphy's visor was a ticking bomb in the corner of her vision. They were closing in on eighty minutes left.

Weaver reached the end of the Reggie first. He paused to scan all around down the barrel of his rifle, before walking over the edge. Murphy and Kohl came down beside him and switched their tethers over to a new anchor. Hanging at the corners of the Reggie's hull, they could see the two aft engines were badly damaged. One barely hung on by a twisted sliver of alloy. The other was crushed like a food wrapper discarded in a waste bin.

Power drill in hand, Kohl moved over to work the lug nuts open on the access panel.

'We could try knocking first,' Weaver said.

'Very funny.' Kohl tested the drill with a practiced pull of the trigger, spinning its head.

'He's got a point.' Murphy was already checking the uplink on her gauntlet. 'Ito brought the lights back up. That might mean we can talk to the Reggie, or at least the docking bay airlock.'

'If he didn't shut us out.'

Murphy didn't answer; she was concentrating. The Reggie had life support back on and some of its subroutines, including the power circuits to doors and hatches. Murphy found the docking bay on her readout, tapped to connect, half expecting it to flash red and deny them entry. Instead, she got the green light, uplinked to her crew ID and *voila*, or maybe it should have been *hey presto*, the two hulking docking bay doors lit up with a halo of floodlights. Murphy depressurised the bay with another tap on her wrist. Open mouthed, Kohl drew back the drill, as the docking alarm bleeped through the comms link and the doors glacially opened.

They pulled themselves inside. The Fat Boy still stood sentry from his docking station, but the coffin had moved in the dogfight and subsequent loss and reestablishment of gravity. Before the chaos, it had been magnetised to the deck. That must have cut out too. It lay tossed to the side of the dock, with its lid ajar.

'What the hell is that?' Kohl said, noticing the fragments around the coffin.

Murphy closed the doors behind them and started the process of repressurising and establishing gravity via her gauntlet.

Weaver magnetised his boots to the deck and clunked closer, rifle at ease across his belly. 'I think that's our breast-feeding doc. Looks like she's gone to pieces.' He turned to them grinning.

'Hilarious!' Kohl looked away.

With the strange sensation of the body's weight materialising from nowhere, gravity kicked in. A few pieces of Dr Merryweather that had been floating slightly off the deck, fell with the dull tinkle of ice cubes. As if woken, baby Jack lamented, his squeals muffled by time or shame or bulkheads. It was impossible to tell which.

'Coffin must have come open in the battle. When the gravity went out, she ended up floating around.' Weaver gestured over their heads with his gun. 'Then Ito did his little reprogramming thing . . . ' He waggled his fingers in the air as if performing a magic trick, 'and the doc must have hit the deck and . . . ' He made a sound like shattering glass.

Murphy felt a sickening burn at the back of her throat. The thousands of fragments had once been a person. Most were unidentifiable, too small. It would be possible to imagine they could have been anything if it wasn't for the clothes, lying limp and empty. That and a few pieces were horribly recognisable. A couple of fingers, one still wearing a gold ring. Her nose with a piece of upper lip attached. Shoes with ankles jutting out, cleanly sheered across, exposing vivid cross-sections of bone, muscle, and skin. And possibly worst of all, one complete breast, bone white but for the darker pink areola and nipple peaked from the bitter cold of space before death.

Kohl was muttering something, under his breath. Murphy couldn't make out the words, although she thought it might be a prayer. She knew Kohl was into old things and that maybe included religion. He'd never spoken about it. Then again, they all had secrets. Whatever the Agoul statue was making them each hear was testament to that.

'You okay, Kohl?' she asked, turning her upper body to see him.

He was eyeballing the doors into the cargo bay as he stopped his muttering. That look on his face, it reminded her of Wu. 'Not a baby,' he'd said when they'd first opened the coffin, as if trying to convince himself. What did Wu see? What did Kohl hear? Kohl's eyes focused on her and managed a watery smile. 'I propose we get the thrusters started, before . . . '

He didn't finish the statement. Murphy wished he had. Before what? The chaos-gun flambéed them alive? Or something else? Whatever it was, he was right and only getting more right as the seconds ticked down.

'Well, pucker up then, sailors,' Weaver said, 'and do your thing. T minus seventy-five minutes.'

Helmets and gauntlets off for easier work, they had to move some of Dr Merryweather aside before they could start. The sound the good doctor's remains made being swept away produced a feeling like cold fingers with ragged nails raking down Murphy's back. Weaver helped move the coffin to access the junctions they needed. Between them, Kohl and Murphy unscrewed the panels and located the circuits controlling the docking bay thrusters. There were six of them, linked into a gelatinous web of telemetry connections, including proximity sensors for coupling ships and the pitch and yaw of the Reggie.

Kohl plunged a couple of nodes into the thick, rubbery gel of a circuit board, and started to run a diagnostic, giving Murphy directions to assist him. Weaver loitered nearby, saying nothing but moving anxiously over to the cargo bay doors to listen, and then backing away again. Was the laughter he heard as grating as the crying Murphy endured? Probably. There was no time to wonder or ask.

The two engineers tested each thruster in turn, Murphy adjusting or double-checking connections as Kohl diagnosed each problem. The seconds and minutes leaked away like coolant in a faulty resonance drive. Finally, they both slumped back. In frustration, Murphy threw her wrench back in her pack.

Elbows on knees, Kohl rubbed his temples, scrunching his eyes closed, as if trying to unsee the conclusion. 'That's it, then.'

'What is it? What's the matter? You fixed it right?' Weaver asked.

'Only three of the thrusters.'

'That's great, right? Fire them up and let's bug the fuck back across the border.'

'Can't' Kohl said, dejected, and he momentarily pressed his palms over his ears.

Baby Jack's screaming had reached a high-pitch squeal that sliced into Murphy's chest and wrenched open her heart; he broke into hitching gasps before finding his breath and squealing once more. Having a task to focus on was all she'd had to block him out. Tears were welling as she looked up at Weaver. 'We can't manoeuvre. The three that work are the thrusters for braking. They're the ones that push us forward.'

'Great,' Weaver said, 'I don't get why you're acting like someone just shat on your cornflakes.'

Murphy wearily shook her head. Her leg hurt badly, and she felt physically drained, emotionally exhausted, and more. They were going to die, sitting here waiting for the galaxy's largest firing squad to wake up. And while they waited, she would have to fight off the memory from the worst part of her life. 'The directional thrusters are offline. We can't turn.'

'And we are facing the wrong way,' Kohl added flatly.

Weaver's face fell. His jaw locked and hands tightened on his rifle until he was gripping it so hard he started to shake. He let out an animal roar through gritted teeth. He was looking for something to hit or kick, eyes flashing around, alighting on Kohl for a fraction of a second, then deciding against it and resting back on his gun. Suddenly he froze. His face softened, and something gleamed in his eyes.

'What is it?' Murphy said, softly, not wanting to rile him further.

'What about the cannon?' he asked.

'What about it?' Kohl said, head hung, eyes closed.

'It still turns.'

'So?' Kohl's voice was lifeless and so unlike him.

'And its telemetry is still working. It's on an independent circuit. The whole turret has its own back-up power system.'

Kohl sighed heavily and shook his head.

'Wait!' Murphy said. 'You think it could turn us?'

'I don't know. It's an idea, is all. If I can turn the gun turret and fire, the energy would push us, right? If we angle the shots to our flanks, we should turn? The telemetry will tell us when we're facing the right way. I'll fire back the other direction, like a brake when we're on target and you guys hit the docking bay thrusters.' He said all this in an uncharacteristic way, laced with doubt, like the dyslexic kid in class asked to stand up and read to everyone.

Murphy and Kohl exchanged a look. Kohl nodded to himself first and then more vigorously to Murphy. 'Yeah,' he said, unable to disguise his surprise. 'That could work.' Then brightening and hauling himself up, 'That could actually frigging work, Weaver.'

'There's one problem,' Weaver said.

Stiff-legged, Murphy pulled herself up too. They had a goal, and if they had that, they had a chance. 'There's always a problem,' she said, testing how much weight her leg could take.

'We'll have to split up, and I've got to get back up to the foredeck.'

CHAPTER 12

THE DOORS BETWEEN the docking and cargo bays weren't a problem. However, they decided to fix helmets and gauntlets, because for one thing it was freezing, and they needed the comms in the suits which could work independently from the ship's system. They also figured it was better to be ready for anything. They didn't need to say what "anything" meant. The image of Valentine and Hendrix's final embrace was a fresh wound in everyone's mind, that might well leave a livid scar for the rest of their lives. If that was going to be longer than the thirty-nine minutes they had left, it was all down to this final plan.

They walked the length of the cargo bay together. It was almost empty after six months in space. They'd used up all the spare parts. In one corner there was a basketball net with a five-a-side football goal painted in white on the wall underneath it. Off duty they'd played many a game together, tussling, sweating, trainers squeaking on the deck. Now the two goals resembled an ancient hieroglyphic of an armless man hanged atop the gallows.

'If the way is clear, should be a straight run up either flank. Two-minutes tops for me to get there and strap in.'

'Assuming you don't meet anyone,' Murphy said. They could have killed each other, but as far as they knew, Ito, Grover, and Wu were out there. None of them seemed of sound mind. Shit! Murphy wasn't sure about her own mind. And there was another *thing* out there, lying at the heart of all this: the Agoul effigy, with its puckered mouth and uneven features and wizened arms. The way the light seemed to slip off it like mercury, and worse, the way it made real things that Murphy kept locked down deep.

'I don't plan on stopping for a chat.' Weaver patted his rifle. 'You guys be ready. Once we get back into Earth space, we can worry about the others.'

'What about the statue?' Murphy said as they reached the far side of the cargo bay. 'Won't the Agoul follow us for it?'

Weaver sniffed thoughtfully. 'You ever gone into a firefight only to remember you forgot to take a shit?'

'Can't say I have.'

'I did once on Titan. Little fucking Neo-Foucauldian dissidents, No-Fos, trying to make everyone equal by blowing up schools. Baggy twats the lot of them.' He released the doors and they rolled apart. 'We were sent in to settle the debate. Got nasty, hand to hand stuff in some of the old disused mineshafts.'

'Lovely story,' Kohl said. 'What's the point?'

The doors clunked to a stop.

Weaver grinned and charged up his rifle. It gave a faint hum. 'Sometimes you got to shit your pants if you want to gut a No-Fo.'

Kohl blinked. 'What does that even mean?'

A scream came from the starboard corridor, and it wasn't baby Jack. It was followed with a cry of pain and the straining grunts of a fight.

'Grover and Wu,' Murphy said. She was torn. They had hardly any time left. Weaver could run up the port side. They could leave Grover and Wu to it. Let them fight over the statue if that's what they wanted. But they were her crewmates, her friends, people she'd come to think of as her family over the long months working on the defence net, where you only had each other to rely on.

It was Kohl who moved first, breaking to the right at a sprint.

'Wait,' Murphy cried and went to go after him, but Weaver caught her by the arm. She tried to pull away from his grip and failed. He was much bigger and stronger than her. 'Let go, we've got to go after him. I can't do the thrusters by myself.'

Weaver frowned in thought. 'Bollocks!' he spat and let Murphy go.

They both broke into a run, their boots clanging on the walkway. Murphy's injured leg exploded to new levels of pain. They'd patched her up, but this level of physical exertion was undoubtedly tearing apart internal stitches and glue, re-rupturing clotted vessels. Rounding the bend to the starboard corridor, Murphy heard the pitiful cries of a man losing a fight and saw Kohl staggering, knocked back against the wall, hands up in surrender.

Weaver swore and put on a turn of speed, racing ahead, carrying his rifle across his chest. She watched as he nocked the gun into the groove of his shoulder, training his eye down the barrel while at full tilt. He eased up as he approached Kohl and the kink in the passageway for the starboard airlock and suit room. Stopped at Kohl's shoulder, Weaver pulled the smaller man behind him and was shouting.

'Stand down, Sailor. Stand down.'

Murphy came up behind Weaver and Kohl. They were both taller than her and she struggled to see through the gap between them. Grover was a bloodied and broken man, slack-limbed against a low set ventilation grille. Red dripped from his nose and one ear. A huge egg sized hematoma bulged from his balding scalp. Something else too. It took Murphy a beat to understand what they were. Bolts protruded from his body. Three inches of grey titanium alloy stuck out from under his collar bone, another from the meat of his thigh, and a third was impaled right through Grover's left hand. A few feet beyond the old engineer, at the entrance to the suit room, was Wu, helmet fixed, bolt gun in one hand, and baby Jack tucked in the crook of his other arm, screaming. His brown skin greyed, mottled with bruises, lips dark with death's kiss, ribs showing through his paper-thin skin. It couldn't be. It wasn't possible. It was a trick of the mind. 'Not a baby,' Wu had said when they'd opened Merryweather's coffin. He had been telling himself what the alien artifact wasn't as it tried to invade his mind. Murphy did the same. She shook the image off, squeezing her eyes shut to wipe away the illusion. When she opened them again, sure enough, Wu was holding the alien artifact. Brown and deformed, the light quicksilvering over its surface. Baby Jack's screams were still there. Those she couldn't escape.

Wu brandished the bolt gun at them, moving to enter the suit room.

Weaver repeated his command. 'Stand down, Sailor. Lower your weapon.'

Kohl was shouting, 'Bishma the One; Bishma the Infant; Bishma the Demanding; Bishma, Lord of the Black, Creator of the Void.'

Grover coughed up blood, muttering something about Wu wanting to go outside. And baby Jack, oh baby Jack was squealing and squealing in agony and fear, calling for her.

Murphy could hardly think. She wanted to cover her ears.

Then everything changed. All went silent as their nightmares came true.

From nowhere, the Agoul ship materialised: not on their starboard flank, but *in* their starboard flank. One second Wu was brandishing a bolt gun at them, the overhead lights reflecting from his helmet visor. The next the indefinable fuselage of the Agoul ship had replaced the airlock, the suit room, and half of Wu. He stiffened. Lips quivering, as if in an uncomfortable kiss with the invading space craft, his right eye blinked once, its pupil blown into an imbecilic black disk. The remaining half of his body from head to groin went slack and slid down, leaving a shimmering wet streak of red. Amid a gush of crimson, his corpse rolled into the middle of the corridor and with a wet slap out fell what was left of his internal organs. The effigy he had been cradling tumbled across the deck to Grover's feet.

Kohl started to shout again. No, not shout, chant. 'Bishma the One; Bishma the Infant; Bishma the Demanding; Bishma, Lord of the Black, Creator of the Void, Devourer of Life . . . '

Murphy didn't know what to do. Her mind couldn't comprehend what was happening. She felt the ghost fingers of her mother's old clothes caressing her shoulders. It would have been so easy to close the wardrobe door in her mind. Hunker down in the blackness and block out the universe.

First to move, Weaver hauled Grover to his feet. The old man scooped up the effigy with his good hand as he stood and slung his injured arm across the marine's shoulders. Murphy heard her name and realised Weaver was shouting it. She snapped back to reality—oh, what a dreadful reality.

Between Kohl, Weaver, and baby Jack's screams, her mind was floundering to stay afloat and grasp onto the here and now. Weaver was back peddling, shouting something about a hull breach if the Agoul ship disappeared. Apparently without being conscious of it, her feet were moving backward. She bumped into Kohl, when a shape materialised—was that the word? Maybe it had been there all along. Either way, it was there, a black form towering above them, stooping to stand in the corridor, its outline pixelating. No, that wasn't right either? Shimmering like fish scales in the sun. No, something more like one of those optical illusions made of lines. At first it looked as though it was one thing, a scene, a still life, a portrait, but stare long enough, learn to un-focus your eyes, and from someplace hidden in plain sight, an altogether different image overlayed the first.

With dumb surprise Murphy realised this was an Agoul. They'd been boarded. She stood, unable to move, that feeling of being prey before a predator pouring solid ice into her limbs. Then she thought of Valentine and Hendrix and all the damage and destruction, and she hated it, this black thing, like a piece of the night sky. Not merely black but flecked with silver and the golden fusion of distant suns.

Weaver raised his gun to fire, but Grover pulled away and stepped in front of the marine. He staggered towards the humanoid shape of the Agoul.

'Here take it,' Grover said, offering the dark brown effigy up to the Agoul with his good hand.

'Move, you old bastard,' Weaver shouted, trying to get a clear shot that wouldn't take Grover's head off.

'Grover, stop!' Murphy cried, and as she did the Agoul moved, or rather one moment it was a solid shadow stood motionless before Grover, the next, its posture had changed. Grover's back arched. His arms flung out to the sides; head craned to the ceiling, in a pose of crucifixion. The statue, no, baby Jack's limp body, jounced from his grip, tossed back towards them, screaming in his descent to the floor.

'No!' Murphy lunged for her brother, but Kohl got there first, catching the statue before it hit the floor. He hugged it close to his chest, and Murphy had to blink to check it wasn't Jack.

Meanwhile, Grover was twitching with the Agoul's arm plunged deep into his chest. Like its ship, it hadn't seemed to punch through as much as simply materialise there. The Agoul tilted its head, maybe observing the human creature mawing for air as blood grouted from its mouth. Just as its limb wasn't and then was inside Grover's chest, it was out again without apparent movement.

The strings stitching Grover's lifeforce together were severed and he crumpled to the ground. His heart, lungs, and digestive tract hung in mid-air, dripping with gore, at the end of the Agoul's arm. That's when Weaver opened fire. Compression rounds exploded, thunderclaps in the enclosed space. The first shot was on target, but the Agoul wasn't there to take it. Like its ship, it instantaneously jumped from one place to the next.

Weaver pushed Murphy back, yelling at her to run as he pumped off another two shots. She staggered back, half-turning to go, half thinking she should stay. Weaver's shots missed, and from nowhere, the Agoul was in front of him.

Murphy heard baby Jack scream and from the corner of her eye saw Kohl running away with him.

In his last moments, Weaver's eyes locked onto hers. The Agoul had him by the throat, lifting him from the ground, choking, face red, spittle flying. 'Run,' he mouthed, and brought the rifle to bear under the Agoul's head. Before he could fire, his arm was torn from its socket. His scream was awful. Murphy was back pedalling, trying to turn away from the horror as the Agoul's massive hand, with its unspecified outline, twisted Weaver's neck like the lid on a jar of pickles and yanked straight up. The marine's head separated from his body with a sickening snap. The Agoul pulled the dripping red eel of his spinal column from Weaver's twitching body.

Gorge rising, Murphy finally tore herself away, sprinting after Kohl. Baby Jack's anguish echoed down the corridor, because just like in the past, the monster had arrived.

CHAPTER 13

MIND REELING IN a flat spin, Murphy's boots clanged off the corridor grates. She was sure the Agoul was coming. It could materialise in front of her to rip her limb from limb. Its ship could jump away leaving a breach in their hull, sucking her back down the corridor and into space. She had her suit and helmet on but no tether to stop her drifting into the infinite beyond, her lifespan measured in air-supply. But she didn't care. Baby Jack was screaming for her, and Kohl had him. Had *her* baby boy. Not her brother. *Her* baby. It wasn't true, this illusion. She knew it couldn't be, but her thunderous heart said otherwise, longed for it to be real. She felt the savage wound deep inside that had never healed. A different heart, a cartoon red facsimile flashed in the corner of her visor, next to it 189bpm counting her terror.

She slammed into the wall at the turn in the corridor to see Kohl's heels disappear through the cargo bay's doors. The warning light above blinked orange as the doors started to close.

Murphy grunted, pushing off the wall and kicking hard. Many years ago, a child herself, she never made it. She'd hidden too long, frightened by the monster in her home. She knew while baby Jack screamed there was a chance. He was alive. When he stopped, she would have to face the end of the world. Push open the cupboard door, brave the monster. Too late. Always too late. And now, here in her new home, the claxon was blaring; the doors were closing again.

Muscles on fire, forcing her heavy legs forward, she covered the distance, expecting to never make it. When she reached the frame of the cargo bay doors, the gap between them was narrowing. She could be crushed between them if the sensors, like everything else, had been damaged in the battle. Murphy reached for the closing gap, grabbed an edge and pulled herself through.

The door did sense her presence and halted its slow progression. Her helmet casing and chest plate cracked against the second door, and she fell through the gap.

On her knees, tears misting her vision, Murphy panted. Behind, the doors closed with a heavy shunt. The flashing warning light and alarm stilled. Cavernous, the cargo bay's scale made Murphy feel like a child again. She looked up, feeling the pressure of time, not the countdown of the chaos-gun, but the final turn of the clock from her childhood. Eleven years old, her world was a shitty apartment on the 53rd floor of the sink estate of Gallows Court, in the East End of London. Black mould on the walls. Brown water stains on the ceilings. A rank stench in the empty fridge. Sweet, sour, and earthy smells of drugs mixed with body odour, damp, and faeces. A gnawing hunger that ate her young body, dried out her milk for baby Jack, sucked the skin between her ribs and nobbled her knees, made skeletal her face.

Baby Jack is calling for her, calling for his Mummy to come and save him from his daddy . . . her Mum's not-so-new boyfriend.

On the Reggie, Murphy staggered to her feet. She wasn't eleven anymore. She had a voice.

'Kohl, where are you?' Her pained voice reverberated around the cargo bay. 'I need to see him.'

She floundered forward, footfalls irregular on the metal deck. Her feet were as heavy as her soul.

Off to the right, there was the crash of falling storage cases. Murphy veered that way. A little down from their basketball-court-cum-football pitch the last remaining pallets of spare parts and tools were stacked in an eight foot high block, with a narrow path down the middle of them.

Part of her knew her baby wasn't real. Not anymore. Still, what she wouldn't give to believe a lie that looked and sounded like the truth. It wasn't as if she wasn't used to it. She lived a lie dressed up as the truth. That she was okay. That she was just a young woman from a rough background drawn to the adventure of space. Like the slogan said, *Explore, Protect, Serve.* Playing hero, when she was anything but. She'd been running away, ever since that banging came at their apartment door. So yeah, Murphy was okay with some epic self-deceiving bullshit. She needed this lie.

'Kohl, come out. I only want to see him.'

She rounded a corner into the container alley, only to catch a glimpse of Kohl, naked, exiting the other end. Murphy ran down the narrow passage to the tangled mound of Kohl's discarded spacesuit and clothes. A case lay fallen on its side, disturbed in Kohl's haste. Murphy rushed ahead.

Coming out the other side of the containers, her heart leapt. There, lying squirming on the ground in front of the airlock doors, was baby Jack. He was flailing his skinny little legs and arms. Eyes scrunched shut, mouth wide in a perfect O, wailing his lungs out. Unthinking, uncaring, she ran to see him once more. The clock impossibly turned back. Just one look and then she could give up the lie.

She was about to pass from behind the storage containers when she was blindsided. Something crashed into the side of her helmet. It whipped her head to the side as if she'd been shot. An alarm went off in her helmet. Red words flashed their warning: "Breach. Pressure and air compromised."

She fell against the wall and down to her hands and knees. Before she could get her bearings, a second blow smashed into the rear of her helmet, slamming her visor into the deck. That's when she noticed the titanium bolt punched through the side of her clear polymer face screen. Before her thoughts could catch up, she was flipped onto her back. A weight landed on her chest, pinning her arms. A second bolt wedged into the casing behind her head, preventing it from lying flat.

Kohl sat astride her completely naked, pointing the bolt gun at the base of her neck, where the helmet attached to her suit. At point blank, the bolt would fire straight through into her throat. His eyes were aflame, lit from beneath by a manic smile that twisted his boyish features. 'Bishma is here. We are blessed, Murphy. We can serve him. Take off your helmet.'

She didn't move.

'Now!' Kohl shouted and pressed the gun into her neckplate.

Murphy unclipped and pulled the helmet up. Kohl grabbed it and flung it aside and pointed the gun at her face. He clambered from her chest saying, 'Undress.' More than once she'd thought she and Kohl would hook up. Not on this tour. Maybe during R-n-R at Caliban Station. It was a bad joke, darker than any Weaver ever told, that he was telling her to undress now in this way. What had happened to them?

Answering her own question, she cast a glance over to baby Jack, his caterwauling screech clawing at her, calling her.

Kohl noticed and leered. 'Hurry he said. He is impatient. He is Hungry. *Move*.' Kohl brandished the gun at her.

Murphy stood and began to strip off her spacesuit. Without the helmet, it was useless anyway.

Kohl was unable to contain his newfound fanaticism. 'What do you see, when you look upon him?'

'A baby,' Murphy muttered, pulling off her gauntlets.

'A baby? Yes.' In excitement, Kohl clapped his free hand against the side of his weapon. 'Bishma the Infant; Bishma the Demanding.'

The words hit Murphy like a sobering slap of cold water. Things that had been impossible to place in the maelstrom and distracted by her own delusion now began to make sense. Bishma! She had heard that word before.

'Bishma: why do I know that word?'

'Not a word,' Kohl snarled and stepped to her, pushing the bolt gun at her head, making her flinch back. His breath was hot on her face. 'Bishma is the name of God, Lord of Blackness, Creator of the Infinite Void, Devourer of Light.'

Finally, she thought she understood. Kohl and his old things. There was something there. His own secret he had been hiding. He was searching for something.

'You're a Demon-Star cultist,' she said.

Kohl took it as a grand question. He stood back, bolt gun trained on her belly and looked down his nose with zealous madness. 'A cult? What's in the Algol system is millions of years older than humanity. Our religions are nothing but stories to help children sleep at night. Life after death? Elephant gods and men with stone tablets? We made gods in our own image. What arrogance; what narcissism.

'The Algol system is a holy site. The communiques and videos that made it back from the Palatine, the Erebus, the Abergavenny, the Stormharvest, Conquista and Confucius Expeditions. They brought us back so much. It was suppressed, of course. But others have been and told their stories. Those on the periphery, the air scrubbers and third-gen low-G workers from the Kuiper Belt when their mines ran dry, and Earth abandoned them. The privateers too. The Red Woman fable. Off-the-books econ-war fought with off-the-books ships. The wisdom they brought back!' Kohl shook his head in admiration. 'I had to come, had to get as close as I could to it, and Bishma heard my prayers. He came to me.'

Baby Jack's keening was easier to block out now. From the periphery of her vision, the deformed statue squatted on the ground, watching them. 'It was a coincidence. You can't believe we found that coffin on purpose?'

Kohl laughed. 'You can try to rationalise it any way you want. Without faith, you'll never see. Bishma has shown you a baby. He has plans for you. Now, strip the rest. We must meet the universe as we were born. The Devourer of Light demands it.'

Murphy tugged her suit over her knees and shook off her boots to stand shivering in shorts and vest, one leg stained with smears of blood. Breath pluming, she hugged her arms across her chest, feeling exposed.

'And the rest of it. Bishma is waiting, can you hear him?' Kohl seemed to be listening to music, a sublime tune that caused his head to sway and eyelids to droop.

This was the moment. He was distracted, but as Murphy readied herself to make a break for it, the Reggie shook violently. As an alarm shredded the air Murphy lunged away over the unsteady deck and fell as Kohl's finger slipped on the trigger. A thick bolt punched into the wall behind where she had been standing.

The Agoul ship, Murphy thought, *it's decoupled*. She'd have a matter of seconds as the air vented and the pressure equalised in the forward sections of the ship. They'd be safe enough behind the sealed cargo bay doors. Although with Kohl out of his mind, perhaps safety was more like one of Weaver's sick jokes. There was no route back to the foredeck and gun turret, not in the time left.

Kohl fired another bolt. It thwacked into the wall behind Murphy, as she lurched over unsteady ground for the cover of the storage cases, dragging her leg. Nearing the narrow passage down the middle of the cases, the stupidity of her idea almost crushed her. A case fell from above. Sensing the descending cube of brushed chrome hurtling down on top of her, she dived to the side. Her roll overshot the passage, and she came up on her knees.

The Reggie's shaking wasn't stopping. Instead, it was getting worse. Murphy looked up to see more cases jostling under the weak spot in the cargo netting from where the other case must have fallen. With the resulting slack, all the other cases could come tumbling down.

Behind, Kohl levelled the gun. The lights blacked out, and she ducked. A bolt whipped above her head. When the lights came back on, Kohl was distracted, as if something was calling him. He glanced back at the alien statue, toppled on its side. He lowered the gun, horror riven into his face. He ran to the statue and scooped it up in his arms.

Murphy remained crouched, ready to leap away if a case fell or Kohl shot in her direction. Then the gravity failed, and she knew the Reggie was doomed. The damage sustained was too much, and finally their faithful little ship's structural integrity was collapsing.

Murphy's mind raced. This was how it would end. A quick titanium bolt to the head would be a better way to go. She pushed off and propelled herself forward through the stuttering light.

Kohl floated in front of the docking bay's control pad, working to gain access if he could. He was stabbing his fingers into the pad unable to get it to do his bidding in the panic. Murphy was closing in on his flank, when Ito flew at speed from behind and caught Kohl around the waist, smashing them both into the docking bay doors.

Murphy arrested her flight and held onto the wall. Between the flashes of darkness, she saw them struggling. Teeth bared. A tangle of limbs whirling weightlessly. There was a glint of something polished, and then the sickening compression, hiss, and thunk of the bolt gun. Grunts and cries of pain; splashes of red. Droplets floated like so many crimson bubbles. It ended with a final cry of effort and a sound like an airless squeak, weak and pathetic.

In a moment of light, two limp bodies drifted apart. The field medic in Murphy came out. They were injured. She was conflicted, but staying put meant dying alone, and hadn't she just been willing to let Kohl end it quickly for her? So, weary and fearful, Murphy pushed off.

She got to Kohl first. A kitchen knife was buried into his chest up to the hilt. Eyes blank and fixed, his lips were parted as if in mid-gasp. The bolt-gun hung loosely in his slack grip. Her friend was dead, changed in his final moments of life into something she told herself wasn't the real him.

There was a cough from behind. Ito was alive, and so she let her best friend go. When she got to him, Ito was coughing up blood. Bolts stuck out of his stomach, his thigh and worst of all, his neck. He tried to swallow and grimaced in agony. Murphy cradled him in her arms.

'I'm here, Ito,' she said, pressing at the wound in his neck, unable to stop the flow of blood as much as her tears. In the strobing light, his blood coiled up and away like satin ribbons in the breeze. His eyes were misting over. 'Ito, stay with me. It's Murphy.'

His gaze cleared a little and focused on her. With difficulty he spoke. 'Murphy?' He gave an uncertain smile. 'I think I'm seeing things. Don't think my mind is right.'

'Shush, don't speak.'

Ito shook his head. 'Please tell me. Is any of this real? I thought something attacked us. Broke the Reggie. I tried to fix it. But I . . . ' Fat tears leaked from his eyes and drifted away with his blood. 'I saw monsters. I heard things, terrible things. Please.'

While the Reggie tore itself apart around them, Murphy hushed him in her arms. 'It's all a bad dream. That's all. You just need to rest. You're so tired. None of it is real. Everything is okay.'

Ito calmed and turned his gaze unseeing to the guttering lights above. 'I knew it,' he said in the whisper of his final breath.

CHAPTER 14

LETTING ITO FLOAT AWAY, Murphy wept. How could she have thought he ever had Astraecy? Even in his madness he retained his humanity to the end. While the Reggie was in the throes of its own violent death, he looked almost serene drifting on thin air. Murphy was numb. All her friends were dead, and she was the last surviving member of the crew. But for how long?

The sadness was such a heavy burden, she was about to conclude that it didn't matter, when she caught sight of the small, hunched form adrift in front of the docking bay, its malformed body turning slowly. Her rage flared. A pure bright thing as hot as chaos-gun fire. A sharp taloned idea clawed its way to the front of her mind; maybe there was a monster hidden deep inside each one of us.

Her spacesuit was where she left it. Snatching up a gauntlet, she checked the time. Just under eleven minutes. It didn't seem like enough to get back over the border, but that wasn't what she had in mind. Murphy moved fast, pulling her suit back on, eating up precious minutes. The helmet was of no use, but Kohl's was intact. She clipped it on, magnetised her boots to the deck, and walked over to the alien statue. Before her eyes it turned into baby Jack, writhing and screaming for her. She took him into her arms and opened the docking bay.

CHAPTER 15

DR MERRYWEATHER WAS a loose nebula clouding one side of the room. Some pieces were as tiny as grains of sand, others were hideous reminders of who she once was. Her coffin, the albatross Grover had warned them about from the start, was suspended three feet from the deck, standing up on its end, lid half open. Murphy ignored it and headed straight for the only way off the Reggie.

With eight minutes left, Murphy had one chance to end things her way.

All their plans had been about saving all of them. That meant focusing on the ship itself. The Fat Boy only had room for one and he had jet propulsion. He was waiting for her, resting in his usual place. The Reggie shook violently, and a deep lamenting moan reverberated through the bones of the ship. Murphy demagnetised her boots and leapt the nine feet up to the Fat Boy's domed cockpit. She slipped inside, nestling the squirming baby Jack in the space between her chest plate and the Fat Boy's internal dashboard. She tapped the controls on the dash, bringing up the Fat Boy's right hand, palm up. Baby Jack howled so shrilly, his bottom lip quivering like it used to when he was so cold and hungry and afraid, that Murphy couldn't help but shed a tear. It felt like her heart was breaking all over again, placing him in the Fat Boy's giant hand, and programming it to curl his fingers around the screaming little lie.

Six minutes left. Murphy closed the Fat Boy's dome and pushed her arms into the control sleeves. She uncoupled from the docking station and marched him over to the airlock. Sparks flew from power junctions. The deck quivered beneath the Fat Boy's feet. There was no time for a decompression, so when she opened the airlock, the coffin and what was left of Dr Merryweather flew past her. The pieces of corpse sounded like rain smattering against a window. The coffin smashed against her shoulder and spun into the void, but the Fat Boy didn't move.

Detaching from the deck and thrusters firing, the Fat Boy gracefully flew away from the Reggie. A hundred yards free, Murphy took her bearings and turned them around to face the defence net. It looked like a regular pattern of dull grey dots stretching a permeable wall across space. The ID codes for the last gun placement were the most recent entry in the Fat Boy's mission log. Though the defence net wouldn't recognise the Fat Boy as friendly—that worked for ships not equipment—she could use the access code call as a beacon to lock onto.

Four minutes and two miles to cover. She could stay still. The guns would fry her good and crispy right where she was, but she wanted to make sure. Thrusters at full, the Fat Boy's head tilted forward, and she began to race for the defence net.

Below the Reggie was a crumpled mess. An explosion bloomed from its starboard side. Another followed and another. They were silent in the vacuum of space, but Murphy thought she could hear them. Bang, bang, bang: like fists clamouring at the apartment door. With under two minutes left, the Reggie didn't go out with one final massive explosion. Instead, all its lights went dark, and it seemed to hang in the black abyss, a dead thing that had once been so full of life. For Murphy, it was like looking down into a crib from her bad dreams in which the past survived into the present.

It was hard to ignore the sight of her baby struggling in the Fat Boy's grip. But he was a gentle giant that would not hurt him.

The grey dots of the defence net grew to fist sized squares; one second passed reluctantly to the next. Murphy looked around, searching the black void.

'Where are you?'

As if she'd summoned the devil, the Agoul ship materialised in front of her. Gold and silver flecks burned shimmeringly from its angular body. Under the monster's hunting gaze, Murphy's skin tightened, and her body didn't feel like her own. The adrenaline, the concussion, her injured leg with the painkillers, the fatigue and fear and the haunting from her past, all of it left her feeling like a husk. Just a hunk of dead meat ready for the monster's jaws. All she had to do was give in. Let it have her.

Just.

Let.

Go.

She flexed open her hand; the Fat Boy mimicked her gesture and released the alien statue.

'Bye, bye Baby Jack,' Murphy breathed. 'Mummy's sorry, my love.'

The squalling infant drifted away, its emaciated and bruised limbs flailing, screams sounding impossibly in Murphy's head.

She veered away, expecting the Agoul ship to destroy her. Not caring if it did. Correcting course and forging ahead at full power, she waited and waited for a death blow that never came. The chaos guns had grown to be as large as the Fat Boy and were getting bigger by the second. Too big, too fast. She hadn't expected to get this far before the end and was coming up on gun placement K32,171 at full speed.

Murphy hit the reverse thrusters a little too late. The hull of the gun placement came rushing towards her as the eternal night sky turned a blinding orange. She closed her eyes, slamming shut the gold welding shield, and smashed into the fuselage of the chaos-gun, as its two cannons joined all the other proximal guns incinerating that sector of Algol space.

The Fat Boy bounced once and sent Murphy into a spin head over heels, alarms flashing. When she brought the Fat Boy under control and turned around, it was like floating before the fiery oceans of a Red Giant star. She stared in awe at the vast conflagration, ignoring the heat sensor's warning.

Then the guns quieted. The wall of chaos-fire ebbed to nothing but ageless stars glinting in a forbidden corner of the galaxy.

Gently this time, Murphy hit the thrusters and glided back to gun placement K32,171. She touched down and walked to the edge of the deck. There was a time she'd lost another family. It wasn't so long ago.

Eleven years old, she'd climbed out of a wardrobe, because just like now the screaming had stopped. Someone was banging on their apartment door, but Murphy wasn't allowed to answer it. Not ever.

She'd crept carefully, quietly, through their apartment. In the living room, her mother sat motionless and blue lipped, staring at nothing. When Murphy shook her arm to rouse her, she was cold. Cold as space. Cold as death.

Shadows at the windows. Shouts through the door, and more hammering to get in.

Through another door, one with a fist sized hole on one side, was a room as cold and damp as the rest of the place, with nothing but a crib, a mattress for Murphy next to it, and her mother's boyfriend unconscious from a heavy dose of booze and crystal-nova. There were long pauses between his breaths, his head lolled on his chest, lank hair plastering his face.

Ever so slowly, ever so afraid, Murphy tiptoed closer. Don't wake the sleeping giant.

The banging on the apartment door was no longer fists. It was boots. The apartment door crashed in and hit the wall.

Murphy looked down into the crib.

There was Baby Jack, her beautiful son, looking so peaceful and still, too still and too quiet, and too mottled with bruises. A final touch on his cheek. There was still some warmth but no life there.

The shouts outside had moved inside, coming closer until arms swept her up and carried her away.

Too late.

Too late.

Far, far too late for her and for baby Jack.

Murphy sat the Fat Boy down on the edge of the chaos-gun, like she'd seen Grover do so many times. *The grumpy old bastard*, she thought warmly. There was no sign of the Reggie, or the Agoul ship, or that malignant statue. Maybe the chaos-guns had done their work?

She had air in her suit and more in the Fat Boy's tanks. It might be enough to wait it out until the Reggie's rendezvous ship turned up, or whatever military detail was sent to see why the defence net had fired twice, when it had never fired before. Maybe enough. If not, she might as well sit here awhile. After all, there was nowhere else to run when you're sitting at the edge of a graveyard of stars.

THE END?

Not if you want to dive into more of the Dark Tide series.

Check out our amazing website and online store
or download our latest catalog here.
https://geni.us/CLPCatalog

We always have great new projects and content on the website to dive into, as well as a newsletter, behind the scenes options, social media platforms, our own dark fiction shared-world series and our very own webstore. Our webstore even has categories specifically for KU books, non-fiction, anthologies, and of course more novels and novellas.

ABOUT THE AUTHORS

Joseph Sale is the critically acclaimed Amazon best-selling author of more than 30 books, including The Book of Thrice Dead, Virtue's End, Dark Hilarity, and The Claw of Craving. Bram Stoker Award Finalist Ross Jeffery described Joseph Sale as "a gothic master".

He has been published by Blood Bound Books, Crystal Lake, The Writing Collective, Nonbinary Review, Dark Hall Press, and Storgy Magazine, and his work has appeared in anthologies such as Tales From The Shadow Booth, Exit Earth, Burnt Fur, and Blood Bank alongside writers such as Richard Thomas and Neil Gaiman. In 2017 he was nominated for The Guardian's Not The Booker prize.

Despite growing up in the Lovecraftian seaside town of Bournemouth, he now lives in Winchester (in the UK) with his wonderful family, where he obsesses over table-top RPGs, trading card games, book bindery, esoteric Christianity, and anime.

To read a free prequel novella in the critically acclaimed series The Book of Thrice Dead, visit Joseph Sale's website: themindflayer.com

You can find him on:

Twitter / X @josephwordsmith

Lee Mountford is a horror author from the North-East of England. His first book, Horror in the Woods, was published in May 2017 to fantastic reviews, and his follow-up book, The Demonic, achieved Best Seller status in both Occult Horror and British Horror categories on Amazon.

He is a lifelong horror fan, much to the dismay of his amazing wife, Michelle, and his work is available in ebook, print and audiobook formats.

In August 2017 he and his wife welcomed their first daughter, Ella, into the world. In May 2019, their second daughter, Sophie, came along. Michelle is hoping the girls don't inherit their father's love of horror, but Lee has other ideas . . .

You can find him on:
Twitter / X @leemountford1
Website Leemountford.com
Instagram @leemountford1

Once **Dan Soule** was an academic, but the sentences proved too long and the words too obscure. Northern Ireland is where he now lives. But he was born in England and raised in Byron's hometown, which the bard hated but Dan does not. They named every other road after Byron. As yet no roads are named after Dan but several children are. He tries to write the kind of stories he wants to read. His short fiction has featured in *theGhostsSory.com*, *Disturbed Digest*, *Devolution Z* and now *Sanitarium Magazine* among other. Five novels have spawned from his pen, including *Neolithica*, *Witchopper*, *The Ash*, *Savage*, and *The Jam*.

You can find him on:
Twitter / X @writerdansoule
Website Dansoule.com
Instagram @writerdansoule

Readers . . .

Thank you for reading *A Graveyard of Stars*. We hope you enjoyed this 15th book in our Dark Tide series.

If you have a moment, please review *A Graveyard of Stars* at the store where you bought it.

Help other readers by telling them why you enjoyed this book. No need to write an in-depth discussion. Even a single sentence will be greatly appreciated. Reviews go a long way to helping a book sell, and is great for an author's career. It'll also help us to continue publishing quality books.

Thank you again for taking the time to journey with Crystal Lake Publishing.

Visit our Linktree page for a list of our social media platforms. https://linktr.ee/CrystalLakePublishing

Follow us on Amazon:

MISSION STATEMENT:

Since its founding in August 2012, Crystal Lake Publishing has quickly become one of the world's leading publishers of Dark Fiction and Horror books. In 2023, Crystal Lake Publishing formed a part of Crystal Lake Entertainment, joining several other divisions, including Torrid Waters, Crystal Lake Comics, Crystal Lake Kids, and many more.

While we strive to present only the highest quality fiction and entertainment, we also endeavour to support authors along their writing journey. We offer our time and experience in non-fiction projects, as well as author mentoring and services, at competitive prices.

With several Bram Stoker Award wins and many other wins and nominations (including the HWA's Specialty Press Award), Crystal Lake Publishing puts integrity, honor, and respect at the forefront of our publishing operations.

We strive for each book and outreach program we spearhead to not only entertain and touch or comment on issues that affect our readers, but also to strengthen and support the Dark Fiction field and its authors.

Not only do we find and publish authors we believe are destined for greatness, but we strive to work with men and women who endeavour to be decent human beings who care more for others than themselves, while still being hard working, driven, and passionate artists and storytellers.

Crystal Lake Publishing is and will always be a beacon of what passion and dedication, combined with overwhelming teamwork and respect, can accomplish. We endeavour to know each and every one of our readers, while building personal relationships with our authors, reviewers, bloggers, podcasters, bookstores, and libraries.

We will be as trustworthy, forthright, and transparent as any business can be, while also keeping most of the headaches away from our authors, since it's our job to solve the problems so they can stay in a creative mind. Which of course also means paying our authors.

We do not just publish books, we present to you worlds within your world, doors within your mind, from talented authors who sacrifice so much for a moment of your time.

There are some amazing small presses out there, and through collaboration and open forums we will continue to support other presses in the goal of helping authors and showing the world what quality small presses are capable of accomplishing. No one wins when a small press goes down, so we will always be there to support hardworking, legitimate presses and their authors. We don't see Crystal Lake as the best press out there, but we will always strive to be the best, strive to be the most interactive and grateful, and even blessed press around. No matter what happens over time, we will also take our mission very seriously while appreciating where we are and enjoying the journey.

What do we offer our authors that they can't do for themselves through self-publishing?

We are big supporters of self-publishing (especially hybrid publishing), if done with care, patience, and planning. However, not every author has the time or inclination to do market research, advertise, and set up book launch strategies. Although a lot of authors are successful in doing it all, strong small presses will always be there for the authors who just want to do what they do best: write.

What we offer is experience, industry knowledge, contacts and trust built up over years. And due to our strong brand and trusting fanbase, every Crystal Lake Publishing book comes with weight of respect. In time our fans begin to trust our judgment and will try a new author purely based on our support of said author.

With each launch we strive to fine-tune our approach, learn from our mistakes, and increase our reach. We continue to assure our authors that we're here for them and that we'll carry the weight of the launch and dealing with third parties while they focus on their strengths—be it writing, interviews, blogs, signings, etc.

We also offer several mentoring packages to authors that include knowledge and skills they can use in both traditional and self-publishing endeavours.

We look forward to launching many new careers.

This is what we believe in. What we stand for. This will be our legacy.

Welcome to Crystal Lake Publishing—
Tales from the Darkest Depths.

Printed in Great Britain
by Amazon

39917971R00145